A Scarlet Fever

Bloodborne Pathogens, Volume 1

C. René Astle

Published by C. René Astle, 2017.

This is a work of fiction. Similarities to real people, places, or events are entirely coincidental.

A SCARLET FEVER

First edition. October 8, 2017.

Copyright © 2017 C. René Astle.

ISBN: 978-1775159100

Written by C. René Astle.

To my parents, who gave me a curiosity about the world and a love of story. To George, Mary, Amanda, Mark and Susan - the Other Writing Group - who gave me caring critiques and constant encouragement. To Amy, Alana and Jeannette, who gave me their eyes and ears.

CHAPTER ONE

MINA'S DARK EYES SCANNED the faces in the crowded club, seeking the eyes that flickered red in the pulsing light. She found them watching her. Her mouth opened as if to speak, even though the owner of the eyes was too far away to hear her in the cacophony of the club. Instead, her lips twitched into a sly smile as she turned to Cam, who'd just returned with another round of beers. Despite being perennially broke, Cam always managed to score free drinks, the good stuff too. If asked, Cam would wink and say it was her winning smile; Mina expected it had more to do with her roommate's cascading locks and bedroom eyes.

Mina took the beer Cam offered her, giving up on keeping a tally, then leaned towards her. "What do you think of him?" she shouted over the music, indicating the location of her watcher with her chin, forcing herself not to look in his direction. She took a swig of the beer, and her lips tingled and her ears buzzed: the good stuff was stronger than the swamp water she was used to.

"Him who?" Cam shouted back, looking in the direction she'd indicated. Mina looked over her shoulder. Amber Eyes had disappeared again.

"Hmm, he was just there," she said as her gaze trawled the crowd. She took another mouthful of beer. "And I'd just started to have high hopes for the night."

"Doesn't matter what I think of him anyway. What do you think of this mystery man?"

Mina allowed herself a smile. "Hot. Sweltering."

Cam grinned back, draping her arm around Mina's shoulder. "Now aren't you glad I dragged you out? Made you shave your legs and clean the paint from under your fingernails?" Cam turned her pearly smile on the hulk of a man who was checking her out before returning her attention to Mina. "All work and no play makes Mina a dull, tense girl."

Part of her hated to admit it but Cam was right: she was enjoying herself. She didn't know how Cam had managed to convince her to come out. Mina needed to go to school at frickin early o'clock in the morning to spend some time in the studio before her other classes, banging her head against the major art project she'd been struggling to complete so she didn't fall even further behind. Then there was work in the afternoon since the rent wasn't going to pay itself.

And she had an appointment with the executor of her mother's estate tomorrow, in between school and work. She groaned. But maybe that was how Cam had managed it – she knew when Mina needed to cut loose. It always started with the reasoning that Mina needed to come to keep Cam out of trouble. But, more often than not, it ended up with Mina getting into trouble right along with her.

But some guys are worth the trouble, Mina thought as she scanned the club again.

The next song started, the bass pounding in her blood. Cam gave Mina a hug before going off to dance with the football player sidling up to her: her roommate had a soft spot for the beefcakes that Mina didn't understand.

Still not finding the wolfish grin in the dark club, Mina sighed and downed the dregs of her beer, then jostled her way around the crammed dance floor to the bathrooms. She found the rear door ajar and went outside to cool off, making sure to replace the brick that had been left there to keep the door propped open. Despite the cool weather, the club had been close and sticky. She took a deep breath and looked up at the sliver of sky visible between the buildings. Part of the full moon was visible in the clear sky, but the ring around it presaged rain, or so her grandpa, smelling of salt, seaweed and cigarettes, had told her years ago when they went to visit him in his small house by the sea. She lit the cigarette she'd bummed from a woman in the bathroom. She felt buzzed but she usually only smoked when she was hammered. She could almost hear her mother's disapproving voice.

"You shouldn't do that, you know – it'll kill you," a deep voice said, definitely not her mother's.

Mina felt a twitch in her gut. Her blood pounded a little quicker in her ears. She looked over her shoulder at the speaker. The amber eyes and puckish grin met her gaze. His skin was a warm caramel, even in the blue light of the night, and he had an accent she couldn't quite place. Not Spanish, not French, but something Romantic.

She smiled and looked at him out of the corner of her eye. Long lashes framed the rich red-brown eyes and he had full lips ripe for kissing.

Throwing the cigarette butt to join the others that littered the ground, she crushed it with the heel of her boot.

"Yeah, there's always something though, don't you think?" she said, turning away and looking up at the sliver of moon again.

"Yes, there is always something." He eased up behind her and placed his hands on her hips. "So we should make the most of each day. And each night."

Mina's breath tripped and her skin flushed. "Wanna dance?" she asked over her shoulder, trying to reassert her good sense. But that good sense got jumbled when she felt his breath whisper over the hairs on the back of her neck as he leaned into her. She could have sworn he was sniffing her, even though she had no perfume to smell.

"Not really." He shifted a little closer. "But I will if you let me buy you a drink."

She felt his lips move by her ear when he spoke. She weighed the effects of another drink on her good sense versus continuing their conversation here. She didn't like the odds either way.

"Deal," she said, resigned to getting into trouble again. She grabbed the hand that was moving her short skirt further up her thigh, threatening to expose the moth tattooed on her hip, and led him back into the packed club. After a couple of clinging, grinding turns on the dance floor, all good sense had left the building, and one of them decided it was time to head back to her place.

She scanned the club for Cam, or the football player she'd been dancing with, but couldn't see either of them. Mina had a suspicion about where they'd gotten to. She pulled out her phone to let Cam know what she was up to but saw that Cam had beaten her to it: GONE 2 PLAY WITH A BALLER CU 2MORO.

Some wing man.

JACK SCOWLED DOWN AT the dance floor from the upper level of the club, ignoring the buxom brunette slithering up to him, trying to get his attention. Normally, he might have let her distract him for a while. However, tonight he was here to tail Luca, not a new assignment, and not one he enjoyed. So he scowled as he watched.

Luca was unmistakable even in the mass of bodies. There were shades of his father in the lean, hungry look on his chiseled face, and Jack was more familiar with both father and son than he'd like to be. Luca was off to the side, at the edge of the strobe lights, nodding his head out of time with the music, as if he were listening to someone, though Jack couldn't see who. What was clear to see was that Luca had a woman in his sights. Following Luca's gaze, Jack caught glimpses of her: short skirt, lithe legs and high heeled boots, and black hair that kept obscuring her face, only allowing Jack glimpses of red lips and dark eyes. And the intricate compass rose tattooed on her bare shoulder. When she headed out back, Luca followed. Jack waited, tapping his fingers on the rail, not keeping time to a song he didn't hear.

"God, you're a pill tonight," Bee said, coming to stand beside him. Jack glanced her way. Judging from her ruddy cheeks and the smell of her breath when she spoke, she'd had something to drink. He didn't respond; instead he stepped away from the railing – and the brunette who hadn't been dissuaded by Bee's appearance.

"Where are you going?" Bee asked.

"To see what he's up to."

"What do you think he's up to?" she said, her eyes rolling.

"Who knows what he could be doing right now. Our instructions are...."

"To watch. Not to interfere."

Jack looked back at the door Luca and the woman had gone out of. He was about to go in search of his prey when they came back, together now, and started dancing, though he was pretty sure her mom would not approve of those moves. Judging from her tattoos, he guessed she didn't care what mom thought.

When Luca and the woman made to leave, Jack started to follow, ignoring Bee's loud sigh, but he found his path blocked by a leather-clad woman with long, blond hair tied in a severe ponytail.

"Emily." She sneered at him: she hated 'Emily'. Em, one of his failures. Despite his best efforts, she hadn't wanted to be rescued – she'd found a happy home in Matteo's circle.

"Jack, is that the welcome I get after all we've been through?" She ran her red fingernails over his chest, up his neck and into his carefully tousled hair. She regarded the brunette with icy blue eyes then growled at her; the brunette, smarter than she seemed, backed away.

"I don't have time for a reunion." He picked Em up and moved her out of his way. She grabbed his arm, her grip strong, and dug her nails in.

"If you don't leave Luca alone, you'll have Matteo after you," she said, flashing him a wicked smile of perfectly formed teeth, and ran a red fingernail along her cleavage. "I just say this because I have a soft spot for you. We're supposed to be getting along now."

"If Matteo doesn't want me bothering Luca then he should keep him on a shorter leash." Jack disengaged himself but by the time he and Bee got down to the main floor, Luca and the woman were gone.

CHAPTER TWO

HE OPENED HIS EYES onto darkness. Sniffing the air, he found traces of metal and mould, tainted by a whiff of rotten eggs. His palms touched dampness, and where he lay was rough and hard, grating against raw flesh. The cold prickled skin stretched tight over taut muscles. Water dripped, and a low hum pulsed in his ears. His stomach ached and his body shook with the hunger.

He blinked, forcing his eyelids to open and close over gritty eyeballs. As he peered into the darkness, he started to pick out some tinges of gray amongst the black. Metal and concrete. He pulled his hulking frame off the moist floor, pushing himself up with knobbly knuckles. Sore muscles slid over aching bones as he moved stiff joints. He stood, hunched, and rubbed both hands over his almost hairless head. Picking at a festering wound on his neck, his teeth flashed in a grimace and a gurgle rose in his throat as a shadow slithered through his mind, carrying memories of freezing fire and burning ice. His hands were clammy and the skin was gray in the near dark. He looked at the oozing scab he'd picked off with a large, blackened fingernail. He stuck his finger in his mouth and sucked it clean.

An itch gnawed at his back, below his shoulder blades. He tried to scratch it with a grimy fingernail, but he couldn't reach, no matter how he twisted or turned. He rubbed the spot against the rough surface behind him, but the itch niggled deep beneath the skin.

His ears twitched at a far off scratching, distracting him from his quest. He looked in the direction of the sound and thought he saw a lighter shade of black. Instinct took over. He shuffled his way down a corridor, searching for the moonlight, thinking of nothing beyond his gnawing hunger and burning thirst.

CHAPTER THREE

MINA'S HEAD THROBBED and her mouth was dry. The unnatural sun shone cheerily through a kink in the blinds, piercing into her brain like a hot needle.

Sun? That's not right. Why isn't that right? Mina threw her arm over her eyes. "Because I have to be at school by 8:00," she said to herself, her voice whiskey rough and smoke haggard.

That meant getting up before the sun did.

"Fuck." Mina turned a stiff neck to look at the alarm clock. It wasn't where it was supposed to be. She lifted her head and blinked to clear her bleary vision, the lids scraping like sandpaper over her eyeballs. Through narrowed lids, she saw that a lot of things weren't where they were supposed to be. The usual state of organized chaos in her room had descended into just plain chaos.

Fighting a bone-deep lethargy, she sent a sore arm searching for the clock and eventually found it just under the edge of her bed. Setting it back on the bedside table, she looked at the time: 9:00.

"Damn." Mina was about to draw her arm back and crawl out of bed when she noticed the mottled purple and blue. Bruises that hadn't been there yesterday. She became aware of her phone ringing but it seemed very far away at the moment. As her gaze slid along her forearm, flashes of the night before played in her head. She noticed the crusted red under her fingernails. It wasn't paint: Cam had made her clean them before going out. In her fuzzy memory, she felt them raking flesh. Then she saw the streak of dried blood on her other arm.

A metallic taste filled her mouth as bile rose into her throat from her unsettled stomach. Her mind was jumbled. Her last clear memory was inviting the man into her apartment; after that it was mostly shadowy gaps with a few jagged jigsaw images in between. Her cheeks burned as those fleeting images played in her mind. She'd never been much of one for the anonymous rough-and-tumble, hot-up-against-the-wall, on-the-pull sex, but she'd apparently been into it last night. Maybe it was the drink, or maybe the stress. Or maybe it was the amber eyes.

Her phone started ringing again, somewhere nearby, and she sent a hand searching for it. Finally, she found it beside the nightstand, on the floor under her bra, just as it stopped ringing. Seeing the name, she groaned and dropped the phone on her jacket.

Mina lay back down. Her head pulsed and her stomach clenched. Tumbling out of bed, she stumbled to the bathroom, reaching it just as her stomach twisted again. Draping herself over the toilet, she retched. Mostly it was dry heaving but when she looked down, she saw flecks of blood in the water. When the heaving passed, she stood up on shaky legs and looked in the mirror. Her eyes narrowed at the bruises on her shoulder and the faint trail of blood across her chest. And a massive hickey on her neck.

Great. She hadn't had one of those since high school. *Good thing I like scarves.* She went down on her hands and knees as her stomach heaved again, but this time nothing came up. She must have drunk more than she realized, though she could usually hold her alcohol. A disturbing thought crept into her brain.

Unless he drugged me. But she hadn't let her drink out of her sight – she was too smart for that. She lay down on the tile floor, letting the cold numb her throbbing head. *Maybe I'm getting sick.*

"I can't afford to get sick," she said to the tiles. The tiles didn't respond. Remembering that she was late for school, and hearing her mother's voice tell her that a hangover was no excuse for skipping, she dragged herself up and into the shower, letting the hot water wash over her stiff, aching body. She felt better by the time the water started to go cold.

Wrapping herself up in a towel, she headed back to her bedroom and surveyed the mess in front of her. The items from her bedside table were strewn across the floor, and the pile of books beside her desk had been toppled. She thought about not going to school, about going back to bed instead. This time she heard her mother's voice telling her to do just that, if she was really sick, but Mina didn't listen. Instead she shut her eyes against an untethered memory of her mother rubbing her back, saying she'd make her some kimchi jjigae.

Mina sighed and opened her eyes again. Her clothes from last night were scattered across the room. She picked these up and checked that everything that should be there was, not that she had anything worth stealing except her art supplies. The rest of the mess would have to wait. She tugged on a pair of dark jeans and a T-shirt that both passed the sniff test, then pulled on a pair of boots, high-heeled black leather that hugged her calves – she needed to feel a bit more bad-ass today.

She put on her necklace, as she did every day, wearing it everywhere except running and clubbing: a silver square, the Korean letter M, that her father had given her for her 13th birthday.

The year before he passed. She turned it over, straightening out the chain.

Assessing herself in the mirror over the dresser, she took a few precious seconds to rub some lip stain into her pale cheeks and lips, and smudge on some eyeliner. She brushed on some mascara, somehow managing not to make a mess of it despite her shaky hands. She looked like a tarted up zombie, but it would have to do. She tousled her hair with the towel until it was barely damp, dry enough not to drip on her leather jacket.

Mina scratched at her neck as she packed up her bag, then grabbed a glass of water from the kitchen to wash down a couple of aspirin. Her stomach protested but didn't revolt. She was starting to feel human again.

She rubbed her neck. The spot under the M pendant was itching, and the scratching made it worse. She checked out the spot in the mirror – a red patch had bloomed where it touched her skin. Mina frowned, then took off the necklace and placed it on her dresser. The itching subsided but the spot was still a petulant pink. Looking at the clock, she grabbed her jacket and messenger bag, collecting the few things she needed from the floor, including a scarf to cover the hickey, and headed to school.

There was still no sign of Cam.

CHAPTER FOUR

MINA HAD MADE IT TO a bathroom before throwing up the coffee and half a bagel she'd wolfed down on the way to school, thinking they were bland, that they'd settle her stomach. But almost as soon as she finished them they'd threatened to come back up, sending stabbing pains through her abdomen every time the subway lurched or jostled.

In the end, she was ten minutes late for her second class, the first one being a complete write-off. She groaned when she thought about all the school work she had to catch up on just to keep her head above water; in between shifts at work, it would consume her weekends and evenings, maybe even the holidays.

That's the last time I listen to Cam, Mina thought as she tried to ease open the heavy door to the lecture hall and sneak in the back. The door creaked loudly and a number of heads turned as she entered, including the professor's. She slunk into the back row and slouched into the seat as far as she could.

She rubbed her temples to ease the pounding, without success. *Yup, the last time I listen to Cam.*

Luckily Astronomy 101 was one of her elective non-Arts courses, and her parents had given her the mind of a scientist, something her mother had repeatedly reminded her about when she hadn't followed the family footsteps into medicine.

The person to her left smelled like they hadn't bathed this semester, while the one on her right smelled like they'd dunked themselves in cologne. The flickering lights of the lecture hall shot sparks across her vision. Mina traced the lines of the words on the bleary board at the front, tracking the professor's hand, seeing what he'd write before he wrote it.

She would have skipped the class entirely, just shown up for the test, if it weren't for the professor and his voice. She usually sat at the front so she could drink him up. She let her eyes slide over him then close for a minute, just a second to ease the stabbing.

She jerked awake thirty-five minutes later, sensing something beside her. She lashed out her hand, grasping the wrist by her head, stopping herself when she realized it was the cute prof shaking her shoulder. She raised her head with an embarrassed smile and let go.

"Sorry," she said. Her pulse quickened when he smiled at her. Maybe the twitter in her stomach was something besides a hangover.

"My class was that riveting?" he asked with a sumptuous drawl, like warm molasses taffy.

Mina cringed. "Sorry, really. I probably shouldn't have come at all. I might have caught that flu that's going around." She pressed her hand to her forehead, which did feel a little warm against her palm.

"Ah. The flu. I've had that flu before." His smile was delicious. "Well, you should get yourself off to bed then."

Mina took a quick breath. "Yes, sounds like a good idea." She watched every step as the professor climbed the last few stairs to the rear door.

"What the fuck is wrong with me? Hungover, sure, maybe sick, but still mooning like a horny teenager?" she said to the empty seats as she tilted her head back. The pin-prick sparks that caused in her vision made her sit up again. "Maybe I should call in sick." The thought of working that afternoon made her head hurt all over again.

Mina picked up her bag, dug out her sunglasses and decided to head home rather than to the studio. Her project would have to wait. If only she could blow off the meeting with the lawyer.

MINA DRAGGED HERSELF up the stairs and fought with the door, stabbing the key at the lock repeatedly before it found its way in. Her hands shook and her brain was loopy: it felt like her blood sugar was dropping through the floor, but when she looked in the fridge for something to eat, her stomach did a belly flop, remembering the coffee and bagel that morning. Looking around, there was no sign of Cam but the dishes in the dish rack told her that her roommate had at least stopped in to eat.

There was still an hour before she had to leave for the lawyer's office, and the best way to kill that time was with a nap. Her bedroom was warm with rare winter sunshine, though today she would have preferred its usual chill. Mina sighed at the mess. She wished she could remember more of last night, not just flashes of sherry eyes, warm lips and white teeth in a lascivious grin. It had been a long time since she'd been so careless, and so care-free.

Mina lay down and gave up the fight against bone-deep lethargy. With her last ounce of energy, she remembered to set her alarm before passing out, fully clothed, boots and all.

In the end, she didn't need her alarm. Her phone rang instead, five minutes before she'd set it to go off.

Dale.

Big brother checking up on her. She looked at the display and saw she'd already missed one call from him. *Damn.* Knowing her brother, he wasn't going to give up despite the fact that she'd see him in a half hour.

"Yoboseyo." *Hello.* There was always an echo of mom's disappointment in his voice if she didn't at least try to speak Korean, even though he knew she wasn't as fluent as he was, and 'yeah' was never a good way start to the conversation. Ten minutes later, Mina was out of bed and trying to find a polite way to hang up. She hadn't developed that skill yet, in all her 21 years.

"Ne." *Yes.*

She ran her fingers through her hair.

"Kureyo?" *Really?*

She dabbed some pressed powder on her face.

"Umhum." *Umhum.*

She lightly brushed more mascara onto the tips of her eyelashes.

"Mina?" Dale said, his voice sharp. She could hear his frown. "Are you even listening?"

"Hmm? Of course." She reapplied stain to her lips and cheeks. "Look, I've got to go if I'm going to get to the lawyer's on time." Mina hung up before he could say another word.

She paused in front of the mirror. The nap had left her groggy but seemed to have done some good. Maybe she'd go to work after all, when she and Dale were done at the lawyer's.

She slung her bag over her shoulder and headed out the door, locking both locks after her.

A SCARLET FEVER

IT WAS A RARE SUNNY day, a change from the seasonal norm of damp and chilly. The air could even be called warm on the sunny side of the street. But the incongruous pair strode down the sidewalk in the shadows thrown by the tall buildings: a mountain of a man in metal and black leather, looking every inch like a bouncer for a biker bar, walked next to a blond woman in a tight V-neck sweater and pleated skirt, looking every inch like a cheerleader from some teenage boy's fantasy. Ivan and Em. Or Em and Ivan, depending on one's point of view.

"The fucking princeling," Ivan said, the tattoos on his neck flexing as he crossed his arms over his chest. "He makes a mess and expects us to deal with it. Everyone else has to clean up after themselves. Why not him?"

"Really?" Em said, her long ponytail flipping as she turned sharply to look at him. "You just asked that? You know why...he's not everyone, is he? He's Matteo's son, blood *and* bone. So don't let him hear you complain. You don't want him to run to daddy."

Ivan stayed silent as he scanned the street, keeping to himself the thought that it might be good to get Matteo involved. No one seemed to be paying them any attention, not the drug dealer leaning against his fancy ride, not the kids he was selling to, not the bum with the cat in his lap. He laid a hand on Em's shoulder, stopping her in her tracks. She scowled at him.

"Is this it?" he asked, pointing to the building across from them. It was very much the worse for wear. Paint peeled off the concrete, graffiti tags covered the first eight feet of wall. A few windows were boarded up while others were covered with tinfoil.

The only shops at street level were a dilapidated donair place and a small corner store whose open sign flickered sporadically.

"No?" Em shook her head and checked her phone, then looked up at the building. "Yeah, it's the right number."

"Our prince was slumming it a bit, eh?" Ivan said. "I didn't realize that he liked to rough it."

Faster than he could duck, Em lashed her arm out, stretching to smack him on the back of the head. "I swear, I am not working with you anymore if you can't mind your tongue. You'll bring us both down." Em readjusted her sleeves. "Apartment 403, he says."

They didn't have to waste any time forcing the lock on the exterior door, since its lock was now purely decorative, if it had ever functioned. They waited for a minute for an elevator that never moved from the fifth floor, then ran up the stairs. The hallway on the fourth floor was in a perpetual dusty twilight, lit only by the last two surviving lights and a dirty window at the end of the hallway. The dimness almost hid the grime and the worn carpet. As they entered the hallway, a woman came out of a door halfway down.

"Mmm, Italian, my favorite," Ivan whispered into Em's ear as she pretended to be absorbed by a message on her phone. She sent an elbow into his stomach this time. His grunt almost sounded like a laugh.

"Behave," Em said to her phone. "We're here to do a job, remember?"

"Yes sir," he said.

After the woman passed then headed down the stairs, they continued down the hall. To the door that the woman had come out of.

"403," Em said, looking down the hall towards the stairs.

"Who was she?" Ivan asked, following Em's gaze.

She shrugged. "Roommate?"

"Who didn't call the police?"

"She didn't look upset," Em said as she dug around in her shoulder bag for a small case. She pulled out a couple of slender tools and made quick work of the locks as Ivan watched the hall.

"Ladies first," Ivan said as Em opened the door. She answered with a smirk, and entered the apartment. "I don't see anything," he said as he closed the door behind them.

"I think we need to go beyond the doorway."

He stepped into the apartment and sniffed the air. "I don't smell anything either."

"I smell a lot," Em said.

"You know what I mean."

Em didn't answer. Instead she began her tour of the apartment. The kitchen-living room combo contained a worn couch and a small, old TV. The fridge held little in the way of real food – soy milk, pickles, cheese, a jar of kimchi, a bag of rice and a couple of cans of cheap beer. The cupboards held cans of beans and tuna, and a few packages of instant noodles.

"Who puts rice in the fridge?" Em said, in a tone that didn't expect an answer.

"People who don't want the critters to get at it, my privileged one." Ivan smiled that he could provide an answer she couldn't. He went down the hall and checked out the bathroom and the nearest bedroom. Nothing.

"In here," Em called from the end of the hall. Ivan followed her voice to a sunlit room. The room was in disarray. Clothes were strewn across the floor and cascaded from open dresser drawers. The small closet was bursting, disgorging boots, shoes and bags onto the floor. A desk against the wall had an old laptop perched precariously on one corner. A few books lined the shelf above it, some more had toppled from a wobbly pile on the floor. But most of the desk held sheaves of paper and sketchbooks, and pencils and markers neatly arranged by type and hue. The picture on the top of the jumble was in the same style as the prints that hung on the wall: bright colours and bold lines.

"She's not here," Em said.

"I can smell the blood though. You don't suppose it was the tasty Italian dish we passed?"

Em shook her head. "Luca was specific. Asian, chin-length hair. And dead."

"I smell blood, not death." Ivan's jaw clenched.

Em nodded.

"Do we call him?" Ivan asked, not wanting to be the one to give the answer.

"I don't know." She looked from her phone to the room, biting her fingernail before coming to a decision. "Better him than have Matteo find out we failed."

"Will he be awake?"

Em looked at the window, and the light streaking through the bent blinds. "Maybe I'll just text him." She entered the message: She's not here. She hit send and slid her phone into her bag, but had to fish it out a few seconds later when it started to play a dirge.

Luca. He wasn't asleep after all. Em looked at Ivan and put Luca on speaker.

"What do you mean, she's not there?" Luca said. "I left the body there. In the bed. Are you sure you're in the right place?"

"We followed your directions," Em said. "Apartment 403. We've searched the whole place. There's a faint aroma of blood but no taint of death."

There was silence on the other end. After a long minute, Em hazarded to speak again. "I don't think she's dead."

"Thanks for the obvious. Find her." The call was cut off.

Em dropped the phone into her bag, then clenched her hand, knuckles white. Her cheeks flushed. She took a deep breath in through her nose. "Look around for anything that might tell us where she is."

CHAPTER FIVE

JACK SIGHED AND OPENED his eyes. Last night kept replaying in his mind's eye.

Luca slipping his watch. But, much as he hated to admit it, that had happened before.

Jack released his hands from *vayu mudra*.

Emily and her pit bull sidetracking him. Although it was stagnant water under a decrepit bridge, it still rankled that she'd chosen what Matteo had to offer rather than him.

He clenched his hands into fists, then released them.

Dark hair and red lips flashing at the edge of his vision. And glimpses of a compass rose tattoo.

He sighed, got up from half-lotus, and headed upstairs, where he started practicing his own personal kata instead: meditation through motion. After bowing to the four directions, he focused on the first few movements, one flowing into the next, his mind yielding to the memory imprinted in his muscles, his body taking over from his brain.

Which left his mind free to once again drift back to the previous night. His ears filled with the throbbing bass.

His left hand travelled up, wrist first, stirring up eddies of dust in an early morning sunbeam. But what he saw was Luca across the club, in flashes of a strobe light, talking to someone in the shadows.

Stepping his right foot forward and punching with the palm of that hand, Jack exhaled sharply, trying to block out distracting thoughts. He paused, arms down at his sides, and breathed in deeply, out slowly, in an attempt to let go of his frustration. Instead he smelled the heady mix of perfume, beer and sweat.

He brought his right knee up and paused. In flashes of coloured light, he saw Luca looking at him, giving Jack a small smile and nod of his head while Emily distracted him.

Jack kicked out to the side, dislodging Emily from his thoughts. For a second. Then he felt the imprint of her hand on his chest, heard her voice trawling through the murky waters of memory. He scanned the dance floor with his mind's eye, trying to uncover the source of his unease. It was just another night, another patrol, another babysitting assignment.

He should have stopped Luca as soon as he'd seen him. But Dar had given explicit instructions: watch from a distance, don't interfere until he causes trouble.

Jack's toe traced an arc through the air before coming to rest on the cold marble tile. His left arm went down, forcing out of his mind the flashing lights and the sight of Luca tracking a path through the crowd, following the silhouette of a woman. Luca had certainly looked like he was heading for trouble.

Jack swept through the next few movements, honing his focus. The music of the club faded.

He gazed over his left shoulder, focusing on a pinpoint on the wall, preparing to spin and kick. Rather than the spot on the wall, he saw black hair and red lips. Then the vision faded away.

Instead of kicking, he flowed into half-lotus, closing his eyes, hands in *vayu mudra*: thumb pressing index finger, index finger into the venus mons. Trying to pursue the ever elusive calm.

Then Jack opened his eyes, realizing what he needed to pursue: Luca and the woman with the compass rose tattoo.

CHAPTER SIX

WHITAKER, WHITAKER and Lee.

Mina stood in the dim light of the office building hallway and stared at the gleaming brass plaque, its shine muted by her sunglasses.

The office was close enough to her apartment that normally she'd have walked, an easy twenty minutes, but not today. Today she had spared the change for the bus. Even now standing still, her legs were leaden despite the nap, her eyes burned despite the sunglasses and her head threatened to start throbbing again.

The ding of the elevator door opening behind her stabbed into her temple, propelling her forward. She took a deep breath and pushed the silent door open into the hushed reception. She could hear the susurration of activity somewhere in the hidden recesses of the office, but the reception enforced the image of assured calm.

Kind of like the funeral home. Right down to the receptionist who looked at her expectantly.

"May I help you?" she asked Mina in an even tone. Her hair was pulled back into a chignon, not too tight, but each hair knew its place. The woman's manicured nails were a neutral colour, and her makeup was carefully applied to look natural. Under a dark blue jacket, her shirt was buttoned up to the top. Mina didn't doubt that her shoes were polished and had moderate heels. Mina shifted in her scuffed boots and mostly clean jeans.

"I'm here to see Mr. Whitaker," she said, her quiet voice swallowed by the hush. "I have an appointment. My brother should be here soon."

The receptionist looked at her computer screen. "Ms. Sun?"

Mina nodded. The receptionist gave her a small, close-lipped smile. Definitely like the funeral home.

"Please have a seat. I'll let Mr. Whitaker know you're here. Can I get you anything while you wait? Coffee? Tea? Water?"

Mina was about to accept the tea, but then remembered her reaction to the coffee and bagel earlier that morning. "No thanks."

She sunk into one of the lush arm chairs that still smelled of leather, and picked up a magazine, which she flipped through, not stopping on anything in particular.

"Ms. Sun." Mina looked up, lifting her sunglasses onto her head. Mr. Whitaker had been her mother's lawyer at least since her father died, and he always looked the same the few times she'd seen him. Her head spun and her ears buzzed as she rose with a slight wobble to her knees and shook the hand he offered, as the other landed gently on her shoulder. A whisper of pine wafted from behind her: Dale.

"And Mr. Sun," Mr. Whitaker said, looking over her shoulder.

Mina watched as Dale shook Mr. Whitaker's hand. She hadn't actually seen him in person since the funeral. He was always her big brother, watching out for her, but they didn't share many interests. And she always felt that he shared some of her mother's disappointment at her choices in life, though he tried to hide it. She returned Dale's brief hug then they both followed Mr. Whitaker, the executor of their mother's estate, into his office.

An hour later, the meeting was over. There hadn't really been any major surprises, other than that the bulk of the estate would be split evenly between favoured son and prodigal daughter, after minor bequests to other relatives and a few charities.

In the elevator, Dale kept glancing at her. Maybe he was disappointed that he hadn't gotten more, being the good son. She stopped herself in that uncharitable thought. It was one of those days, a permanent snark.

"How's Hana?" she asked at the same time her brother spoke. "You look like shit."

"Thanks." Mina half smiled, half grimaced.

"That came out wrong," he said. "You look tired."

"Mmm. Some late nights trying to catch up on course work."

"You should come over. Let Hana make you some kimchi jjigae. Not as good as....It'll set you right."

Mina knew what he had started to say: not as good as mom's. She let it slide. "You're a doctor, Dale," she said instead, as her stomach clenched. "You know kimchi doesn't fix everything."

"But it's a good start. And family helps. Besides Hana worries about you. She sounds like Mom sometimes. 'She needs to stop getting tattoos, find a real job, meet a nice Korean boy to settle down with.'" He smiled. "Sorry. She won't say it to your face at least."

"Unlike Mom?" Mina smiled at her brother's warped reflection in the chrome elevator door. Sometimes the brother she knew growing up shone through.

"By the way, how's that nice non-Korean boy you're seeing? Maybe you could bring him over."

Mina fidgeted. "Not around anymore."

"Another one bites the dust?" He looked like he had more to say, but she was saved by the elevator door opening. "Come over," he said as he held the door open for her.

"Maybe next weekend. I'll call. Right now, I have to get to my unreal job." She dropped her sunglasses back in place. She gave him another hug, longer this time. "Saranghae, Oppa." *I love you, big brother.*

"Love you too. Take care little sister."

BY THE TIME MINA GOT to the shop, she'd returned to her senses: work was out – who wanted to get tattooed by someone with a killer migraine, shaking hands and a possible contagion?

"Hi Sam," she said to her impeccably turned out boss. Today's vest was gray with purple pinstripes, matching the purple in his paisley tie and his perfectly pleated gray dress pants. The cuffs of his white shirt were rolled up to his elbows, and his tattoos crept like vines down his arms and up his neck, twining around the faded, half-hidden tattoo shaped like an ouroboros – if the ouroboros were packed into a square Mayan glyph – before straining towards his punctured ears.

"Hey." He looked up at her. "You look like hell. Let me guess: the whirlwind named Cam struck again?"

"Mina, my anime biker babe," Paul's voice said from the back.

"I'm not your anything," Mina said. "When are you going to get rid of that creep?" she added, not caring if Paul heard.

"When I get another one of you," Sam said.

"About that...." Mina grimaced. She hated to let Sam down, after all he'd done when her mother was sick.

"Don't tell me."

"I might look like hell but I feel worse."

Sam held up a hand. "I said don't tell me."

"I think I might have the flu. My head hurts and I'm shaking all over. I thought I could work but...can you call my two o'clock and cancel?" Mina gave Sam a sad look. "I'm sorry."

He sighed. "Go home. Go to the doctor. Go eat that soup that fixes everything. Do whatever it takes to get better ASAP."

"Whoa, looking hot," Paul said as he emerged from the back. "Sweaty chic. I like it."

Mina looked from Paul to Sam. "I'm going to take a boot to his head one of these days." She took a deep breath, her aversion to Paul amplified by her queasy stomach. "As soon as I can lift my foot higher than my ankle."

"Anything you do can only improve that face," Sam said.

"Hey. This face is a piece of art," Paul said, pulling a face. "You know, if you're hurt, I could kiss it better."

"I'm sick, not wounded. That would just make me vomit."

"Get better soon, please," Sam said. "Go."

Mina sighed and did as she was told, slinking out of the shop. She stood on the sidewalk, debating what to do next. The back of her neck was damp despite the brisk wind, and her palms were clammy. She felt like throwing up even though her stomach was empty. She hated going to the doctor for the flu, when she knew fluids and rest were usually the best medicine. She contemplated taking a cab the few blocks home, irrespective of her constant cash crisis. Which, she had to remind herself, would be eased soon.

She walked to the corner, undecided.

"Beware," a voice said from the shadow of the building. Mina looked to see Mike, a fixture of the streets in the area. He was ragged and rough around the edges but otherwise seemed like someone's lost grandpa. "Beware. The night comes on desiccated wings, and creatures of earth stalk the darkness. Repent your wicked ways or the devil will take you."

"That's a new one, Mike," Mina said as she reached into her bag for some change. "Do you think that's the right marketing approach in this area?" She always tried to give him something, even though he rarely asked directly, just sat with his hat and his cat. Everyone said she shouldn't; it would only encourage him. But he seemed relatively harmless, like a homeless Santa. Until his mumblings got louder and more persistent. She wondered again if she should call someone, but she still had no idea who. He didn't seem a danger to himself or others, and he seemed happy where he was, him and his cat.

"The Angel of Death whispers in the wind." His voice dropped and he grabbed her hand as she dropped the coins into his hat. "Night comes."

She pulled away. *Maybe I shouldn't give him money anymore.* His cat rubbed against him and looked at her with its orange eyes. Mike's hand left her wrist to stroke the cat.

"The night comes every day, Mike."

"Not this night."

"Okay, if you say so. Gotta go. Have a nice day."

Mina looked at the intersection. The doctor, she decided as her stomach clenched again, and turned left towards the walk-in clinic just around the block. She didn't want to leave Sam in the lurch any longer than necessary.

A SCARLET FEVER

AROUND THE BLOCK HAD never seemed so far. Mina begrudged going to the clinic; she never got sick. She shivered despite the warm winter sun that stabbed into that space between her nose and eyebrow. By the time she got to the clinic, her head was spinning.

Sitting in the waiting room, there was no way to escape the invasive smell of sick people with its overtones of blood, urine and disinfectant. Luckily the wait was mercifully quick and Mina got in to see the doctor before hitting the tipping point into nausea. In the treatment room, away from the throbbing humanity, she quickly started to feel better as she waited for the doctor to arrive. When he did, she saw that he was one she hadn't seen before. He was rocking the 'surfer in a lab coat' look, with unkempt hair and a chiseled face that seemed carefully not clean-shaven.

She felt weak and her heart fluttered into her throat as she described her symptoms as delicately as possible, watching his hands as he wrote in her file. She examined the sharp planes of his face when he looked at her, and noted his elfin ears when he didn't. Her stomach still made a sound between a gurgle and a growl but she was definitely feeling better. She tilted her head back slightly when his warm, confident fingers probed the lymph nodes on her neck.

"It sounds like it's just a bad case of the flu," he said. His voice was deep and smooth, like chocolate porter. "There's not much you can do other than time, rest and lots of fluids."

Mina opened her mouth to say that she vomited up everything she ingested, but then checked herself. That was not a pretty picture to leave in his very attractive head.

"You could try the Chinese pharmacy around the corner," he said, his voice deepening a shade. "If you're into that."

Mina stopped herself from asking what he was into. Instead she breathed deeply, her nostrils flaring, and looked into his blue eyes, flashing a small smile. "Thanks. Maybe I'll try that."

He ushered her out the door, and she could almost feel his hand on her lower back. Almost. Damn professional ethics. She sighed and left the treatment room.

She stepped out onto the sidewalk, into the early fall of a winter night and a drizzle that had snuck up while she was inside. She raised a shaking hand to hail a cab: she was feeling better but around the corner was just too far. And she didn't have to count pennies anymore.

In the ten minutes it took the cab, reeking of pastrami and aftershave, to navigate the rush hour roads and one-way streets to her building, Mina had started to shiver and sweat again.

"You okay?" the cabbie asked, peering in the rearview, while she rummaged in her bag for some bills, struggling against double vision. He sounded more suspicious than concerned.

"Yeah, fine," she said, her voice quiet and far away. She shoved the money into his hand and got out. She groaned as her eyes traveled up her building. Most days she had no problem living on the fourth floor of a building where the elevator was permanently out of order. But today was not most days. She took a deep breath of cool air and pushed open the door.

By the time she reached her apartment, stabbing pains shot through her stomach and her pulse raced. Even her gums ached.

There was still no sign of Cam. She dropped her bag at the door and struggled to kick off her boots, stumbling to the bathroom to douse her face. She dared to glance in the mirror. The skin under her eyes looked bruised and her cheeks were hollow. Reaching for a washcloth to use as a compress on her forehead, she knocked over the toothpaste which dominoed into the hand soap which sent the moisturizer onto the tile floor.

Mina stared at the splatter of white against the not-so-white tiles. Treacherous tears started to slide down her cheeks. She sunk to the floor and cried.

"Mom?" she said to a ghost. "What do I do? I'm never sick like this." Slowly the silent tears turned into gulping sobs, which faded into snuffles, until eventually she had no more tears left. She dragged herself up, and blew her nose, noticing the bloody tissue she tossed in the garbage. She washed her face again and plodded to her room with the compress and a roll of toilet paper.

She lay down and placed the washcloth on her forehead, blocking out the neon that seeped through her window. The thought that she might have some tears left after all crept into a corner of her mind. But she passed out before the thought got very far.

CHAPTER SEVEN

IVAN WALKED A FEW PACES behind Em. Frustration seeped out of her pores and caused her hands to clench and flex. It was not an emotion she was used to and she tended to lash out when she didn't get her way, and Ivan didn't want to be the nearest thing at hand for her to vent on. His ears were still bloody from her last harangue at having to play errand girl. Besides, it gave him a chance to catch the people she jostled and elbowed as she plowed towards the subway.

The only hint they'd been able to glean as to the woman's whereabouts were some textbooks from the University library and a schedule stuck to the desk: Astro 101 @ 10:00. Em had a stubborn streak though, and that was before she'd laid eyes on the man who now found himself the subject of her razor-sharp focus. Ivan didn't understand her attraction; from what he knew of Em's life pre-bite, this was the kind of person she'd tormented: skinny, spectacled, and smart. Though she did have a tendency of working out her frustrations by going on the prowl. But this Professor MacMillan was having none of her, despite her laying on the glamour.

"You know professor, I have a particular fascination with the night sky," Em said, nudging closer. "Maybe we could get together sometime and I can make you see stars."

Ivan almost groaned out loud, but he'd learnt the hard way to have a dreg of self control in his afterlife.

"Who'd you say you were looking for?" the professor asked, edging away from Em, looking at Ivan.

"Mina," Ivan said. "Asian. 5'8"-ish. Short hair. She's in your Astronomy 101 class."

The professor's eyebrow raised. "I have almost 100 students in that class. I don't know that I can help. Why are you looking for her?"

"Her brother's been in an accident. Motorbike." Ivan crossed his arms over his chest, muscles straining against leather, and watched the professor step back as Em ran her fingers through her long, blond hair, and leaned ever so slightly closer on the pretense of looking in her purse. With his sharp eyes and keen ears, he knew she was smelling the man. Ivan placed a hand on Em's waist, trying to pull her back from the ledge. He could feel her ire, or her pent-up desire, in her tense muscles. "He's okay but in hospital."

"Mina? Mina...Sun. Right. Sick, she was sick today."

Ivan's hand tightened on Em's waist, as she placed her hand casually on the arm of the professor's wool jacket in feigned concern.

"Sorry I can't help much." The professor shrugged, dislodging Em's hand. "But she's a Fine Arts student, you could try their office. They might have an emergency contact."

"Sure, we'll try that. Thanks anyway." Ivan grabbed Em's arm. "Come on," he said then quietly added, "Let's leave the nice man alone." If looks could kill...well, it wouldn't have been the first time Ivan died.

"I swear I'm going to sink my teeth into that man's throat and suck him dry," Em growled as she flashed a last vicious, vivacious smile over her shoulder at the professor. Ivan almost laughed out loud at her frustration, but turned it into a cough, remembering that hard-won self control.

"Keep your teeth to yourself. We have a job to do."

They had no better luck with the woman manning the desk at the Fine Arts office, even though she was more susceptible to Em's flirtations than the professor had been. Still she repeated the standard line about not being able to release students' personal information, in between giggles and small smiles.

Finally, the student in line behind them chimed in. "You're looking for Mina Sun?"

"Yeah." Ivan glanced at the lanky kid in tight hipster jeans who was tapping out a rapid percussion on a ratty notebook with a felt pen that Ivan wanted to grab and shove up the kid's nose. But he was getting a lot of practice in restraint today.

"She works at a tattoo shop downtown, near Beacon Street somewhere." The kid looked him over, seemingly unimpressed by his bulk or Em's allure. "You could try there."

"Thanks," Ivan said, glancing at the pen before hauling Em away.

DESPITE THE RUNAROUND at the university, the sun was just starting to set when they left, sending sharp rays slanting into their eyes, which didn't put either of them in a better mood. Ivan donned his mirrored sunglasses, while Em hailed a cab to take them downtown.

There were a surprising number of tattoo shops 'near Beacon Street'. When they did finally track down the right tattoo shop, they were quickly shut down by another skinny, spectacled and smartly-dressed man. Ivan used the same story he'd concocted for the professor – her brother's motorbike accident.

The man behind the counter laughed harshly. "Mina's brother wouldn't be caught dead on a bike. Who are you really? And what do you want with our Mina?"

Em started to lay on the allure, but Ivan stopped her. He wasn't as dumb as people thought, and realized right away that the man wouldn't be interested in her particular charms. He was about to try himself when the chime on the door rang, announcing the entrance of a couple of skater punks. Em's fists unclenched, and, even though she'd forced her face into a waxen mask of disinterest, Ivan felt her frustration like a wave of flame: the uptick in her pulse, the tension of her lips, the coiling of tendons ready to pounce. Ivan cast his gaze over the photos of people displaying their ink, considering their options.

The man behind the counter continued to glare at them as he settled in to conversation with the two young men, flipping through samples in a book. Ivan recognized that they were out of options at the moment.

"He's lean and he thinks too much," Ivan grumbled as they left the shop. He didn't relish returning to Luca empty-handed any more than Em did.

"What?" Em said.

"Nothing," Ivan said, looking back through the shop window at the man, who stared back at him.

THE SHOP WAS QUIET: the two young men had left along with their long boards, having been persuaded to abandon their ill-conceived ink; the two who'd been looking for Mina hadn't returned; and Paul had gone for a break that Sam was sure would last until his shift tomorrow. And with holiday season consumerism and revelry the current priority of the masses, Sam didn't expect anyone else tonight.

He'd loosened his tie and absentmindedly stroked his neck, his index finger running back and forth over the tattoo on the right side, hidden amongst the others. The pen in his other hand moved across a piece of paper, in between peering out the window into the gloaming. His phone buzzed, vibrating on the counter. He looked down at it then turned to the sketch he'd been drawing without conscious design: the two strangers and Mina looking not quite herself.

He picked up his phone and dialed Mina's number. No answer. He waited for voicemail to kick in. "Hope you're feeling better, and it's nothing worse than the flu." He looked at the drawing again. "Call me."

His eyebrows drawn together, Sam looked up at the street outside, as a gaggle of club-goers walked by. His fingers rubbed the Celtic cross tattoo on his forearm. He fidgeted with his phone, his thumb scrolling through screens, then stopped and walked to the door. Turning the sign to 'closed', he dialed another number.

FATHER PIETRO STOOD up in the confessional, his joints protesting at having sat for so long. They didn't like being still, they didn't like moving. And they definitely didn't like the damp. He slid the door open and entered into the hushed church. Although the lights were dim, they were still bright compared to the shadows that haunted the confessional. He walked around the inside perimeter of the church, lubricating rusty joints and loosening stiff muscles. As he walked his measured paces, he listened to the staccato of rain pelting against stained glass.

No, the rain didn't do much for his joints. And it always put him in mind of Italy, with its sunlight on warm red stone and soft caramel skin. He sighed. That was a lifetime ago but still he tortured himself with memories, atoning for things he no longer considered sins. He lit a candle, as he did every night, for one ghost or another.

When he reached the front of the church, he knelt to pray, unsure of what exactly he was praying for. Certainly not something to ease the knot in his stomach, his constant companion lately, his barometer of bad moons rising, even though he couldn't pinpoint the cause this time. Just rumors, whispers on the wind of wicked things haunting the night and heralding dark times ahead. But that wasn't any different from normal.

He crossed himself absentmindedly and rose. He could have gotten Father Marc to take confession on nights like this. But Father Marc was young and righteous, still seeing the world in black and white, rather than imbued with gray.

As if sensing his uneasy mood, an alarm sounded, jostling him out of his reverie. It took Pietro a few moments to realize where the sound came from. When he did, his heart slowed and his cheeks flushed – realizing he'd forgotten to turn the infernal thing off again, he pulled out his cell phone.

CHAPTER EIGHT

THE WINTER SUN HAD set hours ago but light from the street still oozed in around the edges of the heavy curtains, turning an angry crimson around the edges of the burgundy velvet.

Ivan stood back and stayed silent, and for once Em followed his lead. They'd just told him they hadn't found Mina Sun, and with Matteo still asleep, Luca was playing up his power.

He leaned against the mantel, poking a fire that sputtered under his mindless ministrations and cast an aura around his silhouette. He was outfitted for a night of prowling the clubs. In black matte leather with carefully tousled curls, he channeled that dead rocker Ivan had met once, Jim Morrison. Despite his rough and ready rock star looks, Em had never tried to make a move on Luca. Ivan shuddered at the thought.

At the moment, a vein ticked under the smooth olive skin of Luca's temple. His amber eyes were fierce when he finally deigned to look at them.

"What do you mean, you haven't found her?" he said, his voice measured, as he stepped away from the fire still holding the fire poker. "She's sick, she's tired, she's confused. She can't be that hard to find."

"We searched her apartment," Em said, rocking back. Luca stayed silent, his jaw clenched, his hand tensing around the handle of the poker. "We followed her trail from school to work." Em paused, looking sideways at Ivan.

"That's when we got stone-walled," Ivan said. "We trawled the club district again, just in case."

"Do you really think she'd go out partying at a time like this?" Luca said, pinning his gaze on Ivan. "You know very well the state she's in. We all do."

Ivan stayed silent.

"We just wanted to cover all the possibilities, before we reported to you," Em said.

"Have you tried her apartment again?"

Em looked at Ivan and he knew she was also kicking herself for not thinking of that delay tactic.

"Check her apartment," Luca said. "Home. She has no where else to turn yet. Unless the others have found her." He stabbed the poker at the fire again. "We shouldn't have to worry about them, shouldn't have to skulk, like rats in the sewer."

With nothing more from Luca, Ivan assumed they were dismissed and started towards the door. Em turned to follow him.

Luca grasped Em's wrist in his free hand as she passed, fidgeting with the poker in the other. She looked at Ivan as Luca raised her hand, turning the palm up. Ivan bristled, his muscles tensing to match hers. But Luca brought his lips to her palm rather than the poker.

Em didn't relax. Luca kissed her hand, then nipped her wrist gently, his fangs caressing the surface without breaking the skin. Then he bent her hand back until it was at an unnatural angle. Em looked him in the eyes.

"Don't fail me." Luca released her hand.

Em strode out ahead of Ivan, back straight, eyes ahead, skin a paler shade of white.

Ivan paused then followed her without a word.

EM'S MOUTH WAS SET in a hard line and her usually coiffed hair was hidden under a damp hoodie. Nonetheless Jack knew it was her. He would have known even if Ivan weren't following her dressed in his usual denim and black leather, seemingly impervious to the drizzle. Jack and Emily had known each other a long time.

He stepped out in front of them, forcing Em to stop. Her eyes narrowed, but she didn't bare her teeth at him. Clearly, she was preoccupied.

"Emily. Darling." She tried to step around him. He moved with her. "Long time, no see."

"I don't have time for this, Jack."

"No time for an old friend? The other day you couldn't get enough of me." Jack's tone changed, the false front sliding away. "Why is that? What's up?"

"Nothing," she said, her gaze steady. "I just have better things to do than stand around talking to an errand boy," she continued. "What's Dar got you doing today, since you're not harassing Luca? Fetching his dry cleaning? Ivan, a little help." She stepped sideways and flicked a finger at Ivan, who stepped towards Jack.

"Are you going to take that, having her set you on me like a dog?" Jack asked. "You should at least make her ask nicely." Jack swore he heard a growl as Ivan reached out to take him by the shoulders, ignoring the throngs of people flowing around them. Jack threw his arms up. "All right, I'm going."

He stepped out of their way and walked in the opposite direction, far enough that he no longer felt their eyes on him. He then did an about-face and headed in the direction they had gone. He'd been a hunter for a lot longer than either of them had been hunted. He tailed them out of the square, down a side street and out onto a main road. Once there, he slowed, weighed down by the bad feeling that settled into the pit of his stomach, gnawing at it like a snaggle-toothed rat. His ears started itching, filling with static. A familiar sensation, but one he hadn't felt in a long time. He scanned the busy street, stepping under an overhang, and continued to watch Emily and Ivan, who were now arguing.

Jack pulled out his phone and made a call.

"We've got a problem," he said to the person on the other end, keeping his voice low while keeping the other two in his sights.

"LIGHTS." LUCA TRIED to speak but his throat was ragged, his mouth parched. A sheen of sweat covered his torso and the pain pulsed in waves across his chest. He turned onto his side and tried again. "Lights."

His whisper wasn't loud enough to be picked up. His room stayed shrouded in darkness, except for the low fire and the candlelight. He flicked a finger and the flames swelled. A wan smile flickered across his face – he wouldn't have been able to do that three months ago. The smile was wiped away by a searing pain.

The inkless tattoo etched into his flesh throbbed warmly, as if his skin were bleeding, a large sinister stigmata. He rolled over onto his hands, making sure his chest didn't touch the cool concrete floor. Crawling up to his knees, he glanced down. The new mark was red and raw, but not bleeding.

A blood sacrifice was needful, the voice said, its evenness not quite masking its displeasure.

"Matteo is a fitting sacrifice."

Your father is hard to kill. We're not picky.

"He keeps us subservient."

Luca was wracked by a bolt of icy anger, throwing him into rigor. Just as suddenly, the energy abated and he tried to crawl out of the shadows into the halo of light cast by the fire. But then another shock spasmed through him.

I don't care. You could have used the girl.

Luca wanted to stay where he lay, letting the cool concrete numb the pain but instead he forced himself upright and turned to face the shadows. "I tried."

Not hard enough. There's a new vampire instead of a dead sacrifice. Why?

Luca knew anything but the truth would just lead to more pain. "She bit me."

The wolf cub got bitten? A sound like metal on metal filled Luca's brain. Luca bristled: the voice was laughing at him. The sound stopped and the voice that lurked in the dark corners went silent.

Luca started to get chilled, and dared to step a toe over the line that separated light from shadow, while wondering if he'd been abandoned, which left his mind waffling between elation and abjection.

A shock coursed through him, sending him to his knees again.

Find her. Bring her to me.

MATTEO LAY MOTIONLESS, eyes still closed, sending out sensory tentacles to his flock as his body woke. He heard a pair practicing with blades in the great hall, perhaps waiting for the day when the ceasefire was broken. Judging from the lopsided gait of the one and the over-eagerness of the other, it was Timothy and Lily. Lily was still young; she would learn or she would die.

He discarded the sound and continued his probing. Jin and Alex were at it again, getting ready for the night with a different form of physical exertion.

He moved on, sifting and sorting the muted sounds. Finally, underneath the pile of grunts, sighs and clangs, he heard a different sound – a too fast, irregular pitter pat.

Matteo opened his eyes. Luca was definitely up to something. He breathed in deeply, letting it out slowly, measuredly. In and out, in a technique he had learned in the Far East, when he was young and impetuous and thought himself impervious to the control of others. He'd learned some lessons the hard way.

He couldn't sense Em or Ivan. His lips tightened; his son had dragged them into whatever scheme he was plotting. His own fault in a way: he had assigned them to watch Luca. Matteo sighed. He needed to place a firmer hand on his flock. And around Luca's neck.

Matteo pressed his hands against the silky cotton sheets and rose. He strode over to the window and smoothed a hand over the heavy blue silk of the drapes. He pulled these aside, just as the metal blind behind them started to rise in response to a light sensor, revealing the starry lights of the nighttime city flicking on before him now that the sun had set. Fat, thick pellets of rain hit the window and slithered down the glass.

He pulled on a finely woven silk shirt and twilled cotton pants. Soft against his sensitive skin but able to pass the requirements of social norms; and he was a master of blending in despite his pale skin and odd angles. He had trained himself to ignore the incessant itch, but every once in a while, when he was distracted, it would sneak up on him and he would want to tear his skin off. Instead he'd take it out on whoever was nearest.

He looked out over the city again, the dark deepening to black. It was beautiful. But something niggled at his mind, a worm of a memory, a sound, a scent, a sensation buried deep in the whorls of his gray matter. He placed a hand on the cool glass. He sensed some disturbance, some eddy in the ebb and flow, that went beyond Luca's plotting. He needed to go out, prowl the streets, investigate it himself. Maybe have a bite while he was at it.

Matteo sighed. He had work to do: numbers to crunch, allies to appease, and Luca to deal with. He turned away and went in search of the guilty pitter pat heartbeat.

CHAPTER NINE

WHEN MINA FINALLY WOKE up, night had fallen. Her alarm clock told her it was almost 9:00. She tried rolling over and going back to sleep.

9:07. Her limbs ached and her head hurt.

9:18. She tossed and fidgeted.

9:25. She threw the covers off. Sleep remained elusive, no matter how hard she pursued it. Finally, a burning thirst drove her from her bed to the kitchen. She grabbed the orange juice and drank it in big gulps straight from the carton. A few gulps in, she knew it was a mistake, and made a beeline for the bathroom.

That's where Cam, her roommate, found her some time later, dry heaving. Cam knelt beside her, her chestnut curls cascading onto Mina's shoulder, tickling her skin.

"What's wrong, sweetie?" she asked as she rubbed Mina's back. Mina's stomach lurched.

"Flu," she said in between deep breaths, inhaling Cam's unique scent of lavender and Castile soap. Though she wasn't convinced it was the flu – it might still have been something from last night – she didn't want Cam to feel guilty about leading her astray then abandoning her. Mina forced herself to breathe even and slow in an attempt to calm her roiling stomach. She tried to stand, forcing her weak knees to work. Cam helped her up with a hand on her elbow and one on her back.

"Come on, we're getting you to bed. I'll bring the bucket."

Mina smiled weakly and shook her head. "I don't need a bucket." Despite the cold night, Cam radiated heat, dressed only in the tiny boy briefs and tank top that she always wore lounging around the apartment. The warmth of another human being made Mina feel a titch better.

"Thanks, but I can't sleep. All I do is toss and turn."

Cam frowned at her. Mina followed the flick of her roommate's thick eyelashes.

"Fine, the couch then," Cam said, guiding her to what they called the living room – the part of the main room where they put the couch and TV. Mina sat on the couch while Cam went into the kitchen. Mina heard her rummaging around before she came back with the bucket, which she set down on the floor beside the couch. "Just in case," Cam said as she sat down beside Mina. "I'd rather clean it out of there than off the floor." Cam made Mina lie down and lay Mina's head down in her lap. Cam then grabbed the afghan her Nonna had made off the back of the couch and arranged it over Mina before turning on the TV.

"When did it start?" Cam asked as she rubbed Mina's back rhythmically. Hypnotically.

"This morning," Mina answered, her jaw moving against the smooth skin of Cam's inner thigh. Her voice was quiet even to her. "I thought I was just hungover."

"Did you go to the doctor?"

"Mmm. The clinic near work. Flu. Rest. Fluids." Mina started to relax as Cam's hand moved up and down her back. She breathed deeply, slowly in and out. She hadn't realized how much she liked the scent of lavender. She sighed, and turned her face towards Cam's thigh. She breathed deeply and wondered if Cam tasted like lavender too.

Mina's eyes flew open and she clamped her lips together. She ran her tongue along her itchy palate and gums while she racked her brain. Her stomach rumbled in the silence. Whatever the hell was wrong with her, she needed to get Cam away from her.

"Don't you have a test tomorrow?" Mina asked. "Organic chemistry or some such?" Cam was the daughter Mina was sure her mother had wished she'd had – pretty, popular, Pre-med. Of course, her mom had never seen the Cam of last night. "Shouldn't you be studying?"

"Nah, I'll ace it. Organic chem is in my blood."

"Still, you should get some sleep." Mina lifted her head off Cam's thigh. "I may look like death warmed over but I'll be okay."

"You sure?"

Mina swallowed, as Cam's stomach moved against the back of her head. "I'm sure."

"Well, if you're sure you're sure, sleep couldn't hurt." Cam extricated herself from under Mina's head. She leaned over to rearrange the blanket around Mina. "If you need anything, just holler."

Not trusting herself to open her mouth again, Mina nodded, aware of the void of warmth left under her cheek with her roommate's departure. Cam sauntered back to her room, and Mina breathed deeply, laying her heavy head on the sofa.

Eventually, she managed to doze off, only to be woken up some time later by a woman shouting. She raised her head and blinked to clear her gritty eyes. Random shouts and sirens were almost white noise in the neighbourhood. When she managed to orient herself, she realized that it was the TV. Some schlock, shock talk show. The screen was piercingly bright in the twilight of the shuttered room. Eyes half closed, she groped around for the remote. Finding it on the floor beside the bucket, she turned the TV off then closed her eyes again and did a quick mental assessment.

Better. She was feeling better. But her mouth was dry and pasty, and her gums hurt.

Water. The world spun as she sat up, and her brain felt seasick. She placed her hands on her knees and waited for the spinning to subside. Slowly, with the help of the couch, she stood up. With the help of the table, she made it to the fridge. Booze and the dregs of the carton of sketchy orange juice. She looked at the tap suspiciously. Usually she didn't trust the pipes in the old building. But the filter jug sat empty on the counter. She ran her tongue over her dry lips and gritty teeth.

She tried the tap water. She didn't get sick right away, so she drank a bit more. That's when the pain stabbed through her abdomen, sending her to the bathroom again. The stabbing subsided, and gave way to blood-flecked watery vomit which gave way to the shakes and the cool tile floor. As she lay on the tiles, she admitted that she was sick, really sick. She was not hungover, and this was not an everyday flu.

The hospital was around the corner and down the block. Manageable, if she could just get off the floor. She dragged herself off the tiles. Her eyelids itched, her head throbbed and every muscle ached. She pulled on a pair of skinny jeans and her boots, then grabbed her bag and leather jacket.

She wrote a note to Cam: Gone to ER. Cam would be upset that she hadn't woken her, but she stuck the note to the fridge anyway and headed out the door.

The brisk air outside brought her back to life a little. As she walked by the convenience store, she saw that Mike was in his usual nighttime haunt just outside, stroking the tabby cat in his lap. He also saw her. Mina sighed.

"Death stalks you," he said. "And statues lurk in the shadows."

"Nice to see you too."

"Watch out for the night."

"It is night."

Mike made a dismissive noise and flicked his hand, then returned to petting his cat.

"Gotta go, Mike," Mina said, walking quickly away. "Stay warm."

MINA HADN'T SEEN THE shadows peel themselves off the wall opposite her apartment building when she'd left.

But they had seen her.

"That's her?" Ivan said, half statement, half question, though he knew in his bones that they'd found their target.

"Definitely her," Em said, running her nails over the arms of her jacket. "I feel it in my blood."

"So we take her," Ivan said, stepping into the desolate street, populated only by the denizens of the dark.

"No," Em replied, looking around. "We follow."

"Why?" Ivan bristled. "I can have her in one of these alleys before anyone noticed."

"No. You're not as quick as you think you are. Besides, Luca wants to see her now. Alive." Em drew her shoulders back and down. "We bide our time. We follow. And we don't harm."

They didn't have to wait long to see where their prey was headed. The convergence of sirens would have told them if the big glowing sign and thrum of humanity had not.

"Shit," Em said as she pulled out her phone. "I hate hospitals."

CHAPTER TEN

HE SLUNK DOWN DARK passageways towards his hovel. A thick rain, threatening to turn to snow, pelted his ashen skin. He paid it little mind, running a hand over his nearly bald head, sweeping away some of the droplets. His hand wandered down to his mouth, and he picked away a bit of something from between his teeth. He looked at the fingernail, smelled it, then sucked it clean. His fingers fell to his bulging belly, sign of his temporarily sated hunger.

He came upon a patch of light on the dark asphalt. He sniffed, and looked both ways before crossing the gap. He continued down the corridor of shadows. His bare feet squelched through an icy puddle, and something skittered then stilled. A rat, frozen in fear. Its black eyes peered into his. Lucky rat. Tonight he'd found a better meal.

He crept quickly from this alley to another, narrower one, and clung to the wall on his left, shying away from the imposing stone building on the right. The blessed places hurt his eyes: the crescent, the cross and the star, and a number of other obscene shapes. So he looked away, down at the dark puddles and the building's shattered reflection. Still it loomed large in his mind, as droning chants oozed from its bowels, drilling into his skull and muddling his mind.

Once he was past its hulking presence, his thoughts cleared. He stopped and breathed deeply, sniffing the air, canting his head.

He felt them out there. Though they didn't seem to know he was there, just one of the unnoticed, invisible things that go bump in the night. He hunched over, the tenacious rain dripping over his heavy brow onto his nose.

He shuffled down another dark corridor. Wet all over, the chill had just started to ooze through his skin into his bones when he reached his destination. He crawled into the cave-like basement that he had made his home.

He took a deep breath in between his teeth, tasting the air over his tongue, then let it out through his nostrils. It was dark and musty, smelling of rusty metal and festering rot. He sighed – he'd have to move soon. The air was moist but the floor was mostly dry except where the overhead pipes leaked onto the dirty floor. But he could avoid those patches, and there were pipes that didn't leak, that radiated warmth.

He curled up in his corner, pulling his pile of rags around him, and scratched his full belly. He fell asleep listening to the knocks and pings of his hovel, backed up by rain on glass and the constant hum of the city.

CHAPTER ELEVEN

MINA SLUMPED IN THE hard plastic chair, waiting for her name to be called. The hospital waiting room was excessively bright. The flickering fluorescent lights cast the people in the room in a ghastly green. Lights from the ambulances flashed through the windows like lasers slashing into her brain. Babies cried in an off-kilter chorus, accompanied by the low rhythm of coughs and the high timbre of sneezes.

She opened her bag and dug around, pulling out her phone and ear buds. The soothing sounds of classic thrash metal – too bad she had to take the earphones out to listen for her name every time the nurse came out.

It was also unfortunate that, with the sound blocked out, her other senses dialed up and she focused on the people instead of their noises. On the far side of the bench opposite her, a couple of punk kids, both so pierced it was amazing that they could unlink themselves, were making out. The girl stuck her tongue down the guy's throat as she pressed a once-white T-shirt to the wound on the back of his head. Fresh blood trickled bright red onto the girl's hand as the guy leaned in to bite her lip. Mina licked her lips, and breathed in through her mouth, out through her nose as her stomach gurgled.

An old man sat down beside her and smiled at her. He had an oozing wound on his arm. A mixture of blood and pus seeped into the gauze that he kept lifting so he could peek underneath. Mina's stomach flipped. He started speaking to her in Korean, asking questions. She smiled a little but shook her head, shrugged her shoulders. She couldn't imagine opening her mouth to speak. Her head started throbbing again – maybe thrash metal wasn't the best choice after all.

Mina had to sit up straight as a woman and her boy sat down across from her. The woman held a baby in her arms, rocking it as she admonished the boy to hold a towel to his bleeding mouth. The boy stared at Mina. She stared back. But she was the first to blink when he treated her to a gaping, red smile. She looked at the boy's mother, as the woman pulled up her shirt and pulled out a breast, shoving it into the baby's smacking lips. Mina didn't realize it had started crying. The baby started to suck voraciously when the nipple was placed in its mouth.

Mina's head pounded and her stomach twitched. She sat for a minute longer, trying to find somewhere to focus her eyes, before she stood up. The world listed as she walked over to the desk.

"Where's the bathroom?" she asked, breathing deeply. The attendant pointed down a hallway, where the lights dimmed and the only people were those lying on stretchers.

She felt better as soon as she started to walk away from the noise and pestilence of the waiting room. At the end of the corridor, she saw the sign for the bathroom pointing down the hall to her right. An exit sign pointed left.

Mina looked down the right hall as far as she could, then turned left. Once outside, she took deep breaths of fresh, cool air, tilting her head back. The rain had stopped for the moment and a lone star twinkled in a small break in the clouds. After a few more breaths, she felt able to face the waiting room again, but the door that had let her out wouldn't let her back in, so she walked around to the front of the hospital.

With every step, every breath, she felt a little bit better. So instead of going back in, she turned right and walked down the street, heading towards St. Frank's square and the shortcut through the square back to her place. She continued to improve the further she got from the hospital, the rain having petered out and the crisp air reviving her, cooling her sweaty forehead.

She forgot that to get to the shortcut, she had to survive passage through the night market and its gauntlet of stalls selling random street meat. In that press of people, crammed with even more intimacy and immediacy because of the upcoming holiday, she found her recovery fleeting. She alternated between waves of feverish heat and shivering cold as she wove through the crowd. The one constant was the searing thirst.

Despite this wooziness, she found herself checking out the men – and women – decked out for a night at the clubs. Her gaze traveled over the tight pants, short skirts and casual smiles. Her eyes lingered on the flashes of exposed skin, and her ears filled with a throbbing that almost drowned out the voices. Her cheeks flushed. The world spun and her head reeled – nausea warred with an unexpected and unwelcome sexual hunger.

Nausea won out. Her stomach gurgled, even though there was no solid food left in it, while her shaky hands told her she needed some sustenance. Water at least.

But right this second, she needed to stop. Stop and sit. The mossy steps leading up to the library had never looked so inviting, even though they were already in use. A homeless man, bundled in a grimy parka two sizes too large, sat stroking a cat.

Mike.

Mina paused, not up for conversation, especially with the tenor of Mike's ravings lately. But she needed to sit. Just for a minute. She plopped down on the steps, as far away from him as she could manage while avoiding the slimy corners, and lay her head on her crossed forearms.

She closed her eyes against the stabbing shards of light that reflected off the wet asphalt. For a second that helped, stopping the spinning. But then a carousel of images began playing in her mind: her professor's sandy hair and ten o'clock shadow; Cam's dark curls and toned thighs; amber eyes, soft lips and...something she couldn't remember.

She opened her eyes but kept her head on her arms, pondering the grimy concrete steps.

Her forehead was hot, her skin buzzed and a hundred heartbeats pulsed in her ears. Her throat burned. She ran her tongue over her dry lips, snagging it on a sharp edge, drawing blood. She swallowed over the lump in her throat and swore. She'd bit her own tongue.

What the fuck's wrong with me? She hadn't realized she'd spoken aloud but Mike responded.

"The dead stalk you." He continued to stroke the cat. "But then they stalk us all."

Mina turned her head towards him, her cheek on her arm. "Yeah, I guess we can't get away from our ghosts." She thought of her mother – her high expectations and ferocious love. She tried to call up an image of her father, but all she saw was the face in the photos. But she still heard his voice sometimes when she read. Looking at Mike, she wondered what his ghosts were, that had chased an avuncular and, until recently, articulate man to a life on the streets.

"You're the ghost," he said, watching the passersby, while his cat looked at her. It lifted its chin as he scritched underneath it, nodding his head. "They're the dead. The messenger comes, and only god can help you now."

Mina sighed: back to good old new Mike and his senseless rambles. She lifted her head, looking left then right down the narrow side street. The rain had started again. She tilted her head up, letting the soft drops coat her face, settle on her eyelashes. Across the way, a red swastika shone against the charcoal sky: a Buddhist temple.

Maybe religion wasn't such a bad idea, or at least the serenity of the space. Mina dug into the pocket of her jacket and pulled out some change.

"Mina?" he said, as she dropped it into the container in front of him. "Long time no see." He touched his hand to his toque then went back to stroking his cat, which continued to look at her with its golden eyes.

Mina hadn't been in a temple for years: it was her father's religion. Surprisingly it was open, the door giving way to a dim interior, where a handful of people knelt. She remembered her father's temple being quiet, peaceful and tended by kind monks. What she had forgotten was the redolence of incense; she fled the temple as the smell sent pain stabbing into that spot between nose and eyebrow. Further down the street, kitty corner across the square, she saw a cross. The lights inside were still on. But it had been almost as long since she'd been in a church.

Except for her mother's funeral.

IVAN HAD ONLY NEEDED to look at the woman across the crowded waiting room to know that she was their quarry. He had only to glance at Em to know that she saw it too. Em had called Luca but he kept asking questions, looking for answers Em didn't have. She'd just hung up on him when the woman got up and headed down a hallway.

A gaggle of girls, flocking around a limping friend, gabbing in a language he didn't understand, came pouring through the door and blocked the path of pursuit. Em tried throwing elbows but it was pointless against the cluelessness of the young. By the time she and Ivan made their way through, their prey was gone. They followed her trail as far as they could, Ivan sniffing the air, trying to catch the thread of her scent amongst all the others, without success. They made their way back to the waiting room just as Luca made his entrance, followed by his posse of hangers on, who hoped to benefit if Luca made a power play.

The sounds of the hospital fell away into the background. In Ivan's experience, it was the shit that rolled down hill, so he was happy to take a step back.

"Where is she?" Luca asked, scanning the room.

"We lost her," Em said, a vein ticking in her throat.

"Again?"

"We didn't lose her before," Em said. Ivan wanted to kick her; he was the one who was supposed to say stupid things. But Em continued, "We just couldn't find her, since she wasn't where you'd left her for dead." Ivan tensed, the leather of his jacket straining over taut muscles.

Luca's amber eyes fixed on Em. He leaned in as she gazed over his shoulder. "What happened?"

Ivan saw Em shiver. Even from where he stood, he could smell the metallic tang of Luca's breath as he spoke.

"She was sitting over there," Em said. "She got up. We tried to follow but...." Em paused, her nose wrinkling as she indicated the mass of humanity in the waiting room. "People got in the way."

"You understand that I need her found and dealt with?"

"Before Matteo finds out that you've been a bad boy?" Ivan swiveled his head to look at her. From the look on her face – mouth open, eyes round – it seemed like she hadn't intended to voice the thought out loud. But there was no time to take it back, with Luca's hand closing around her throat. No matter how pissed off Em was at being blamed for Luca's fuck up, she needed to be in better control.

Luca's fingernails, black nail polish chipping, dug into the pale skin of Em's neck.

"Hey!"

They all looked at the security guard as he spoke into his radio. Luca slowly released his grip on Em's throat, and strode out the door, into the street, followed by his posse, with Em and Ivan bringing up the rear.

"Sorry," Em said, coughing. "I'm just tired. Hungry."

"We'll talk later about how you can make it up to me," he said, his hand on her throat again, caressing it. Luca turned to the rest of his group. "But right now we need to go. Spread out. Find her. She won't have gone far."

JACK STOPPED IN THE middle of the square. The pooled water on the asphalt reflected the street lights and neon signs in a kaleidoscope of colour. As night had fallen, the downpour of the afternoon had turned into a cold mist that clung to the skin and left little means of escape. Still, the space in front of the church was full of people crossing well-worn paths. Drunk office workers heading home after an extended happy hour, shoppers laden with bags full of Christmas paraphernalia, revelers heading from restaurant to club.

He closed his eyes and let the crowd flow around him. He had a fondness for large, anonymous cities, despite being a country boy by birth. Though sometimes, worn down by the tenacious drizzle, he longed for the crisp, clear winter skies of his childhood.

He'd followed the trail to the edge of this mass of people. He'd lost it briefly outside the hospital; the tendrils of humanity got jumbled as he kept outside of Emily and Ivan's periphery. So far, he didn't think they realized they had been followed. Despite being predators, they had never been hunters. He briefly tipped his head down, chin to chest, and felt the pulse of humanity. The sounds of laughing and fighting, breathing and beating. The smells of smoke and coffee, sweat and fear. He opened his eyes and looked around again.

He was here to find someone but he couldn't find his prey by feel in this crowd. He couldn't hear the slightly slowed trip-hop beat. He couldn't smell the copper tang. So he scanned the crowd.

An elderly woman who sat on a bench feeding pigeons looked at him every few seconds with pursed lips. Three women, one holding a shivering rat dog, walked by. One of them looked him over, throwing him a smile over her shoulder with a flash of dark hair and red lips, as his gaze followed her by. He tore his eyes from her toned legs and back to the square. A group of boys on long skateboards tore past him and clattered across the stones of the square. Jack quickly disregarded these and the multitude of other visual stimuli in the light-streaked darkness. He looked for the tell-tale signs that would mark his quarry: a cast to the skin, a tightness of the lips, a glaze in the eyes. He looked inward, to his gut, to see what it had to say. Nothing. His lips turned down, while he turned right, heading back into the night market.

It was jammed with people, pushing, shoving, haggling. Bargaining shoppers shouted over musicians strumming for a few coins. The odor of knock-off perfume swirled with that of dried squid. He shut down some of his senses in order to focus on the ones that might still help him. He searched the dark corners at the edge of the throng. He scanned the faces around him, looking for the dazed, the confused, the hungry. He began to lose hope of picking up the trail again. Then his phone rang.

"Yeah?" He knew the question at the other end before it was asked.

"Not yet." He paused, only half listening as he continued to his scan. "I had the trail, but I lost it. You know I'll find it again." Jack kept working his way through the crowd from the cover of an awning.

"Yes, I have done this before, Dar. I know the stakes. And I'm the best you've got." That's when he saw her, on the other side of the pedestrian mall, on the far side of the river of humanity. There was no doubt: he knew too well the look of the lost, the confused, the hungry.

"Gotta go, Dar." He didn't wait for a response before hanging up. She was heading in the direction he'd just come from, back into the square. He swiped a quick message into his phone. Then he turned around and followed, fighting his way through the crowd, which fought back with seasonal vigor.

CHAPTER TWELVE

A FINE MIST OF RAINDROPS fell on Mina's face, forming droplets in her eyelashes, as she stood, neck craned, staring up at the church. She could barely make out the soft edges of the eroded carvings high up the facade of weather stone, beyond the scaffolding that surrounded them.

Gargoyles. They looked funny now, blobs of melted stone, but had terrified her as a child, when she hid behind her mother's legs. She could still feel the hand her mother had kept on her back, maybe realizing her fear that they were going to swoop down and take her away.

Weak light filtered through slender panes of stained glass from inside, though the large front doors were shut against the dark night. Despite the dimly lit sign hinting that it was still open at this late hour, it looked resolutely closed. Which was probably just as well. The chills were catching up to her again, as she exposed herself to the weather. Halfway up the steps, she decided to turn around and go home when a man came out.

He was older, the neatly clipped hair on his head and face streaked with abundant silver and blazing white at the temples. He was dressed in the modern priestly uniform of black pants, black shirt and white clerical collar. Mina stilled. Maybe if she didn't move he would think she was just passing by.

"What are you looking for?" he said. Mina hesitated. He had a faint accent that snagged at some thread of memory. "Maybe I can help," he continued.

"Oh, no, it's nothing," Mina said, caught between the church and the square, not facing either. She smiled a sort-of smile. "Just a few minutes of peace and quiet."

He returned her smile with a broad, avuncular one, his eyes crinkling. "You've come to the right place. Father Pietro." He held out his hand, surprisingly calloused, more like a mason's than a priest's, but his grasp was gentle.

"Mina."

"Come in. I can give you quiet at least, you'll have the place to yourself, and I'll let you be. The peace, however, is in someone else's hands." He shrugged his shoulders and glanced upwards.

Mina followed him into the church where, true to his word, he left her alone in the heavy hush of the sanctuary. She lit a candle, more out of memory than conscious thought, then walked up the aisle, the staccato of her heels echoing off the marble and ricocheting around the stone columns before being swallowed by the cavernous space above. She sat down in a pew halfway to the front, placed her arms on the back of the one in front of her and laid her pounding head down. To an observer, it might look like she was praying, but she hadn't done that since childhood. She didn't think she remembered how. Instead she thought: about the last twenty-four hours since bringing that guy home with her, about how she was slipping at school, about her mother's death. She tried to pull a coherent thread from the jumble behind her aching eyes, without much success. Her mind raced but her limbs were leaden. Her nerves twitched and her blood tingled.

"So the temple didn't do it for you?"

Mina started, her head shooting up, sending small sparks across her vision. A man was standing in the centre aisle at the end of her pew. He was tall, broad shouldered, with high cheekbones and a flat nose that flared at the end. His tousled hair and casual stubble had the look of being carefully styled to be careless. His black eyes bored into her.

How does he know about the temple? Unless he's been following me. She shivered as a chill passed through her.

"Sorry?" she said.

"You know, the Buddhist temple you stopped at before you turned to the church, the one down by the market."

"It was closed." Mina started to inch towards the far end of the pew, as the man sat down. She looked sideways at her stalker. Obviously Asian, not Korean but otherwise she couldn't place where. She was sure her mom could have, right down to country, province and village. Mina could only guess his age as somewhere between thirty and forty.

"You know, I really can't blame you, being born a Buddhist myself. The monks may well be on their way to enlightenment, but they don't always have solid answers to the problems of this world, I find. Especially not problems like us."

Mina reached the end of the pew. "I am not a problem." She got up and walked quickly down the outside aisle towards the door.

Before she could complete a cycle of breath, in and out, the man was standing in front of her with her arm in a vise-like grip. The smile was gone from his face.

"I think most in the Holy Catholic Church would disagree," he said, his voice low and rough. His teeth flashed white when he spoke. A wolf in wolf's clothing. She ran her tongue across her aching gums. She struggled to pull away. His pupils dilated in the dim light.

"Frightening the parishioners again, Jack?"

Mina turned her head to see that the priest had returned. She breathed deeply and relaxed her muscles.

"Ah, Mina. I thought so, you had that look about you," Father Pietro said, then turned to the man. "I'm glad you found her."

"Mina, is it?" Jack said, looking at her before turning to the priest. "Yeah, thanks for calling. She's already cagey, with a nascent sense of unconscious evasion. I was surprised to see the others exit the hospital without her. I couldn't believe they'd lost her."

"Others?" Mina said, ignored. Her narrowed eyes flitted from Jack to the priest.

"You lost her too," the priest said. "The hallmark of a great hunter, losing his prey to the night?" Father Pietro continued when Jack didn't respond to his jibe. "Lucky for you some of the lost sheep still seek the Shepherd."

"Lucky for you, I don't like the taste of mutton." Jack's lips twitched. "They'll pick up her trail soon enough, just like I did." His nostrils flared as he looked towards the door. Mina tugged away from him again, but he didn't budge. Her arm was getting sore where his fingers dug deeper each time she fought. His free hand rubbed the side of his neck as he crooked it and cracked his jaw.

"Sense her, can you?" the priest said.

Jack nodded. "If I can feel her pulse beat in my veins, hear her buzz in my ears, the others can too. Her maker obviously left her untrained."

Mina's mouth made like a fish, opening and closing without a sound, then she found her voice in her indignation. "You're a priest," she said. "You should be protecting me."

Father Pietro looked at her, and his face softened. "I am, dear," he said. "You don't know yet, but I am. Take care of her, Jack. She seems impulsive, maybe a bit head-strong."

"So I should take care of me?" Jack said.

"That too. I've left the side door open. You may want to get going. Father Marc is lurking around somewhere." The priest smiled at them as Jack tried to lead Mina down the aisle towards the altar. She dug her heels in.

He turned to her for a second, his head cocked, before speaking. "You've gone to the doctor who says you have the flu. It makes you tired, not jazzed, and doesn't stoke your libido to the point where you want to jump every person you meet despite wanting to pass out. And it certainly doesn't do that to your teeth. Fluid and rest won't help what ails you. So now you try religion. But this is not something you can repent. No amount of Hail Marys will fix this."

"How do you know?" Mina tried to sound like she was rebuffing him but, to her ears, it came off as petulant. He dragged her a little further, and she resisted a little harder.

He eased his pulling but didn't let go. Mina almost fell, held up by the fingers still around her arm. He stood fast, dark eyes focused on hers. "Because I know what's in your blood. I know it should have killed you, yet here you are."

"How do you know what I have? *I don't* even know what I have, and I don't peg you as a doctor."

"You don't need a doctor," he said, his voice lowering as he stepped close. Her pulse quickened as his breath traveled over her cheek. "Your blood itches," he continued. "You look at people and feel a hunger, a thirst, a lust, you can't explain."

Mina started to shake her head in denial.

"You've never been into women before but now you see them in a whole new light."

Her head stopped shaking as she glanced sidelong at him before looking away.

"You can't eat," he continued, as she ran her tongue over her teeth. "Anything you consume causes pain until you throw up. At night you toss and turn, but during the day you suffer from headaches and a deep-seated lethargy. How's that for a list of symptoms?"

She responded by resolutely staring over his shoulder at the statue of the Madonna.

"At first you thought it was a really bad hangover, or maybe something he slipped you."

Mina looked back at him sharply.

His eyebrow raised. "But you remember the night too well, whether you want to or not."

"How do you know what happened?" Mina was curious enough to stop pulling.

"Because I know what you are," he said.

"You're talking in circles."

"Come with me and I'll explain."

"Fuck off."

"Come," he said, a keen edge on his voice.

"No." Mina dug her heels in again. His grip on her elbow tightened and she felt his fingernails bite into her flesh. She used the pain to steel her resolve.

"Yes." His resolve was steelier than hers. She could move or be dragged, so she started walking, buying time to think and watch for an opportunity to get away. But instead of leading her out the front door, onto the busy square, he led her out a side door into a dark, deserted alleyway that stank of stale urine and fetid garbage, despite being slick with rain. A dying emergency exit sign cast a flickering red light into the night.

At the doorway, he stopped and peered into the darkness of the overshadowed passage. He sniffled, or sniffed, she couldn't tell. Eventually, he passed over the threshold, taking her with him, and turned towards the street.

Good. Crowds are better. At least there she could scream bloody murder, if it came to that. *Not that anyone would help, but it might cause enough of a distraction to break away.*

But they never made it to the street.

Instead, a behemoth of a man dropped down in front of them. Mina looked up at the canyon of gray walls that hemmed them in, squinting against the icy drizzle. She couldn't see where he could have come from, without breaking a leg, since the closest fire escape was halfway down the alley, the ladder still drawn up.

"Ivan," Jack said. His grip on her elbow tightened briefly before he let go and dropped his hand to his side. A woman sidled up out of the shadows. "And where there's tweedledee, there's tweedle...Em. What brings the foul out on a fair night like tonight?"

"You know what brings us here," Em said, her gaze sliding over Mina. "Her. I want her."

Mina's eyes narrowed as the hair on the back of her neck stood on end, raised by the goose pimples on her flesh.

"*You* want her? Somehow I don't think that's entirely true." Jack looked around, up and down the slick walls. "I'm sorry you crawled out of your hole for nothing. Run back to Luca. Tell him that *you* can't have her."

"We can if we can take her." Em's nostrils flared as she turned all her attention to Mina and smiled broadly, her white teeth shining in the night.

"You and what army?" Jack asked. "I've taken on both of you before."

Ivan's muscles tensed, straining against his jacket, but he stayed silent.

"Oh, they'll be here directly," Em said, her voice low and slow, like warm molasses, a tinge of the Deep South bubbling to the surface. She took a step closer to Mina. "Besides, maybe she wants to come with me." She tilted her head and ran a finger along her lower lip. "Do you want to come with me, sweet thing? Or are you going to make me take you by force?" Her blue eyes glinted, reflecting the relish in her voice. "Either way, I'm good."

Mina stood stock still, lips pressed tight together. She was stunned, not only by the woman's words, laced with violence and sexuality, but also by her own reaction to them: a part of her wanted to say yes. But just a small part.

"Fuck off, all of you. You can't have me," she said to the woman, forcing her voice to stay level. She turned to Jack. "And neither can you. I don't know why you all want me but you can't have me." She turned to walk away only to find the behemoth Ivan blocking her way. She spun around to where he had been standing just a moment before.

"You mean she doesn't know yet?" Em said, her eyes shining, a sliver of a smile on her lips. Mina discovered a deeper pit of fear at the delight in Em's tone. The air changed and something she didn't understand swirled around her in the garbage-strewn alleyway. She went very still, a fine wire of tension running through her body.

"Know what?" Mina said, her voice flat. Just then, in a whisper of movement, Jack drew a pair of short swords from somewhere. Mina stepped back and let a squawk escape. It was enough to bring the priest to the side door.

"Jack?"

"Reinforcements," Jack said over his shoulder, without looking. The priest disappeared back into the church. Ivan ran after him but was thrown back as he touched the threshold. "Holy ground, remember? And you're definitely not invited."

Jack advanced on Em, who had also pulled blades from somewhere, shorter and more slender than Jack's, though Mina couldn't see where she'd had them stashed in her skintight black PVC getup. Jack and Em circled each other, before advancing. Then, all Mina saw were flashes of metal and blurred limbs, unable to follow their fast, fluid movements despite having studied kumdo, the way of the sword. It was one of the martial arts she'd studied as a child at the behest of her father: a girl needed to know how to take care of herself, he said.

After he got to his feet, head shaking, Ivan joined the fray. Listening to metal strike metal, Mina was sure the ruckus would attract the notice of someone in the square. Watching them, she took a step back, towards the square. She took another step then another, not yet daring to turn her back on the group, even to see where she was going. The noise of the square grew louder, vying with the fight for primacy, as she continued to creep backwards. She could sense the end of the alley approaching; just a few more steps. Her stomach fluttered, like a bird's wings. The rush of her heart sounded like hollow woodwinds in her ears.

She backed into something solid. Her stomach sank, the bird's wing became stone as she slowly turned around. She cocked her head as she looked into one of the most beautiful faces she'd ever seen. Golden skin gleamed in the weak light. Dark eyes rimmed with eyeliner peered at her through long, lush eyelashes. The face was framed by a flopped-over mohawk of dark wavy hair, the short hair on either side shaved to the scalp with abstract whorls.

"Hello Mina," the man said, his soft words evenly paced. "I'm glad to finally meet you." A gentle but persistent hand on her arm turned her back around to face the alleyway and prodded her forward. More people had appeared at the other end.

"It looks like my army arrived before yours," Jack said, lowering his blades as his attackers took a step back.

Em and Ivan lowered their own weapons and looked around, coming to stand back to back in the closing noose, before sheathing their weapons and scaling the slick walls like spiders.

Mina gasped. *Something is very wrong.*

"Jack, you're losing your touch," the man beside her said, a pierced eyebrow arching. "You couldn't even collect one girl."

"Excuse me!" Mina said, losing a touch of her fear in her indignation.

"I had her in hand, Dar," Jack said, sheathing his own blades. "But they want her. Or should I say, Luca wants her, if he sent Em and Ivan. Matteo's assigned them as Luca's watch dogs."

"I wonder why he's so interested in her," Dar said, looking Mina over without a hint of sexuality.

"I don't know but if Luca wants her, we should watch her carefully."

"Hello? Right here." Mina tried to pull her arm out of Dar's hand, but had as much success as she'd had with Jack, despite the man's slight frame.

"So you are," Dar said, loosing his grip slightly. "And here is not a good place for you to be right now." He motioned to the rest of those in the narrow passage. They surrounded her and herded her away from the street, into the deepest darkest warrens of downtown.

Weaving through the hemmed-in alleys, the frisson came back to Mina's stomach. She saw pursuers everywhere: a glint of metal here, a skitter there, a shadow darker than the rest. She scanned their route opportunities for escape, either from imagined pursuers or from her present captors. But none presented itself, and soon they were out in the open again, crossing the street to an old building she'd passed numerous times before but never really noticed.

She had no idea what it was. Neo-classical in design, it looked like a giant mausoleum. Or a cryptic government office from a dystopian future, harbouring the nefarious goings-on of some secret service. Beyond the chest-high wrought-iron fence, the lawns were neatly trimmed and the hedges clipped, the grounds dimly lit by lights she couldn't see. The front facade consisted of four massive columns sunk into a limestone wall, two wooden doors in the center. Above the doors, a stained glass window with an image of a tree had letters she hadn't noticed before: IOKI.

She was about to ask what IOKI was, curiosity overruling her desire to stay taciturn with her captors, when one of the group opened the gate and ushered her through. Her vision narrowed and filled with stars. She started to fall.

"Wait, it's okay," a disembodied voice said. "You're invited."

These were the last words she heard before everything went black.

LUCA SEETHED IN DARKNESS, the one hand fidgeting with the blade it held while the other was clenched in a fist so tight his fingernails dug into his palm. His throat was tight, choking down the anger and frustration that had grown as he watched the scene below play out in the alley beside the church.

The inconstant wind had not been enough to drown out his shadow though. Its sibilant whisper hissed in his skull, like an coiled adder, waiting to strike. At first, it had murmured encouragement, as he'd lurked on the rooftop in the web of air conditioning units and antennae, glaring down at Em, Ivan, Jack and the girl. He'd tried in vain to block the voice in his ear as he strained to hear the snatches of conversation that had drifted up from the ground below, as Em and Ivan parried words with Jack over the woman. Luca hadn't liked what he heard. His shadow, like a drill in his skull, had prodded him to act, to leap down and take the woman, face down Jack and Darius. But Luca had remained hidden, despite the needling.

Now, hidden amongst the ramshackle rubble of another rooftop, its words were harsher, as its rusty voice lashed out like a cat o' nine tails.

You fucked up.

Luca flinched but didn't respond. Instead, he tracked his prey as she was escorted towards the security of Darius' lair, skulking like a rat. This was not the outcome he'd been promised when he'd listened to the faceless voice, nor what he'd expected when he'd indulged his hunger with some random pickup at a bar, something he'd done countless times before.

Vampires were horrible gossips. It was bad enough that Emily and Ivan knew that he was the woman's progenitor; he certainly didn't want that sanctimonious Persian or his pet pit bull Jack to know it. And definitely not his own father. He needed this indiscretion, this woman, to go away. A chill wind, frigid enough to raise goosebumps on his inhuman flesh, blew in from the north and drove icy shards of rain into his eyes.

You made a mistake.

"It's not my fault," Luca said, his whisper whipped away by the wind.

You need to fix this or I will clean up the mess you've made.

Luca ground his teeth but remained taciturn. Silently, he cursed the meddling priest. If the man had insisted on disbelief, like the rest of the flock of crows, Jack would have been left alone in the alleyway, and Luca could have taken him down, after Em and Ivan failed. He could have dealt with not only the woman, but Jack as well: something his father hadn't managed yet. Unfortunately, that priest was not only sanctified but saintly, doubly insulated. He hadn't yet corrupted his vows, at least not enough to allow a crack that Luca could exploit.

"I can fix this," Luca finally said, his voice catching on the lump in his throat. "She's nothing, just a slip of the teeth."

A slip that might ruin everything, the voice said, rustling around his brain.

Luca snarled, baring his teeth. If it hadn't been for his shadow, he wouldn't be in this mess in the first place. She wasn't his type; he wouldn't even have pursued her without its prodding, its goading to exercise the power it had given him.

You were a coward back at the church.

Standing with his shoulders hunched against the cold, Luca ignored the Shade. This resulted in the void of its presence pressing even more heavily into the back of his skull. He slowly closed and opened his eyes, wishing away the small speck of blurred vision. He felt its presence all the time now, along with a constant tension that lurked in his mind while he waited for its voice to start up again, a rusty blade against a whetstone.

Don't you trust me to protect you? I've taken nothing and given everything.

Luca shuddered as a drop of rain found the spot of tension before slithering under his collar and down his back.

He frowned. Why had the shadow goaded him into pursuing this one, draining her, over all the other meals he'd enjoyed since its arrival? And why hadn't she stayed in his thrall?

He watched her fall as they led her through the gate. He felt the thrum of her heartbeat fade as the doors closed behind her. A pang stabbed through his gut.

He had fucked up. He knew it, but couldn't quite place where. He rubbed his left arm, feeling the itch even though the marks she'd left had already healed. She'd been willing. Until he'd bared his fangs. At that point, she wasn't supposed to notice the teeth, if she'd been subdued by his heady pheromones and the rhythm of his voice, like the others. But she wasn't, and used the only weapons at her disposal to fight him like an animal: her claws had raked his flesh as she fought.

Luca had been able to subdue her easily enough, and relished draining her dry, savouring her spicy undertones as she struggled. He ran his tongue over his fangs; he could still taste her.

Then her teeth had sunk into his flesh. Focused as he was on teaching her a lesson, he hadn't realized it at the time and had left her for dead.

But she hadn't died. And one drop was all it took for the vampiric strain to spread.

CHAPTER THIRTEEN

MINA AWOKE TO FIND herself in a small, twilight-gray room. A small window high up the wall told her she was in a basement and that it was daytime outside. Other than the bed she lay on, the room held a small desk and chair, an empty shelf, a lamp and a narrow wardrobe. No signs of a current or previous occupant.

Her head was heavy and throbbed when she sat up. A constant thrum filled her ears, in between the pulsing beat of her heart. Breathing deeply, she pushed herself up, grabbing the back of the chair when her wobbly legs threatened to give out. She picked her bag up from where it sat beside the desk and checked its contents. The jumble all seemed there. She tested the doorknob with light fingers: it turned. She inched the door open a crack and peered through the sliver into a dark, deserted hallway. She opened the door wider. Still no sign of any jailers. Cursing the clunky boots she'd donned last night, she walked on tiptoes to the end of the hall, stopping at the bottom of a flight of stairs. She hesitated. The top of the stairs was lost in shadow.

Up is out.

She swore silently when the first stair creaked under her weight. Holding her breath for a couple of heartbeats, she listened for sounds of pursuit. Hearing nothing, she crept up the rest of the stairs.

The shadows lightened as she climbed, step by achingly slow step, but, reaching the top, she forgot to sneak. Instead she stared up into the cavernous space. It was daylight now, and sun filtered through the stained glass dome that covered the space, sending down a cascade of watery light. The scene was a dark blue skyscape strewn with multi-coloured stars of varying sizes. Other than the stars, all of the glass, both in the dome and in the windows along the walls, was stained midnight blue. She guessed she was on the main floor of the building she'd been brought to the night before. Except for the colour scheme, it reminded her of a church. There was a large nave-like space under the domed ceiling, and arcades ran down either side of the vaulted space. Marble floors, their shine softened by a thousand footsteps, spanned breadth and width. As she entered the space, she passed a raised dais on her left, where the pulpit would have been if it were a church.

But the nave was empty, no pews, no chairs, no altar. The arcades, on the other hand, were full of wooden cupboards and metal chests, and, incongruously, video games and overstuffed chairs.

Mina forced her attention back to the task at hand. She headed for the doors at the far end, and passed into what would have been the entry in a church. Sunlight poured through the open doors, displaying an unusually clear winter's day. The rays pierced her eyes, stabbing into her retina. She didn't let that stop her as she strode into the entryway.

A tattooed chest stepped in front of her. The black ink was intricate, a stylized raven with wings spread. The artist had even captured the wily glint in the bird's obsidian eyes. Heat radiated off the bare chest that blocked her way, the warmth penetrating the chill of the drafty space.

"You're not allowed to leave," the chest said, in a voice that was deep and rich and a little rough, like peaty whiskey, with a purr of a long ago brogue.

She looked up into a freckled face topped with brown hair flecked with gold by the sun.

"Really?" Mina said, reaching into her bag without looking down.

"Dar wants to speak to you," he said.

"It's illegal to keep me confined here."

"What are you going to do, call the cops?"

"Maybe," she said, shrugging her left shoulder.

"Huh, try it."

"I spoke to Dar last night," she said, continuing to surreptitiously root around in her bag. Her hand landed on the object of her quest. "We didn't have a whole lot to say to each other."

She pulled out the pepper spray, but his hand was around her throat before she had a chance to use it. Her back pressed against the wall.

"Drop it." His voice rumbled through his chest. "It won't hurt me but it'll sure piss me off." The canister clattered across the tile floor.

"Let her go, Simon." Dar approached out of the dark edges of the entryway, canister in hand. "She promises not to spray you. Don't you?" He trained his warm brown eyes on her. She nodded, and Simon let go, slowly.

"You and I need to talk." Dar handed the canister back and she slipped it into her purse. "Jack, I think you should join us," he said, tilting his head over his shoulder while he kept his eyes on her. A familiar shadow slunk out of the darkness.

Despite Dar's slender build, Mina realized that resistance was futile when he wrapped his strong fingers around her arm, still sore from last night's dragging, and led her back into the nave. Simon stayed to guard the entryway.

"Do you realize what you are now?" Dar asked, letting go of her arm. "Have you guessed for yourself or do I need to elucidate?"

"There's nothing to guess," Mina said, her jaw tight, as she rubbed her arm where his hand had been. "I'm Mina Sun, artist, student, slacker sister...." She stopped, about to say disappointing daughter. "Orphan."

"You forgot to mention willfully ignorant or bloody stubborn," he said, his voice soft and even. "I said what, not who. What are you?"

Mina stayed resolutely silent and Dar turned to Jack to answer for her.

"You are a vampire once bitten, newly made," Jack said, his voice quiet, so close she could feel the breath of his words whisper over the hairs on her neck. "A dhamphir."

"A damn...what?" Mina said, shaking her head as she glanced between them. When she continued, she kept her voice even, as if she were addressing a nervous dog. "You're crazy." She edged a step away. "And if you don't let me go, I'm going to scream."

"Then scream," Dar said, just as calmly. "Even if someone hears you, it won't change your new reality. You know, in your blood, that we're telling the truth. Your blood itches, yearning for something, but you don't know what for. You can't eat without throwing up. You can't sleep at night, you just toss and turn."

Mina glanced at Jack; she'd heard this before. "I slept last night."

"You passed out," Jack said. "There's a difference."

"Okay." Mina tried a different tack. "Riddle me this: if you're all vampires, how come you're up when the sun's up?"

"The same way you're able to walk in the sunlight, despite the pulsating headache and leaden limbs. The Hierarchy: Dhamphiri, Draculus, Nosferata. The orders and rules of vampire-kind. It's not like the movies."

Mina shook her head, as much to get rid of a lingering dizziness as to show a lack of understanding, but Jack continued nonetheless.

"You've only been bitten once, by a dracul or a nosferat, and haven't been infected long enough to become dracul by age. As a dhamphir, you're weaker than other orders but also less prone to the vampiric banes. Dar and I are dracul, twice-bitten: stronger, faster, less human."

"Amen to that," Mina said.

Jack ignored her. "But we can be killed by the three banes - ashwood, silver and sunlight - if applied in the right dosage to the right body part. As a dhamphir, they usually just make you sick unless you're pierced in the head or the heart. Then there's the nosferata — thrice-bitten or ancient of days: they have demonic strength and speed, and invariably a demon's creed. But the banes are lethal to them. If you can catch them."

"A demon's creed?" Mina said, her voice weak, as an emptiness throbbed in the base of her skull. "You're talking in riddles."

"All nosferat are Necrophagos, the wicked undead, devourers of life, the devil's own," Dar said.

"But you just said three orders? Dracul, nosferat and damn...whatever. Now you're saying there are these Necro...thingies."

Dar nodded. "Three orders. Two classes, two choices: Athanatos and Necrophagos."

Jack took up the lecture. "Those who fight the wickedness that lurks within and those who are consumed by it. But it becomes impossible to resist when you become a nosferat."

Mina stared at him for a second, wondering if he really thought that clarified things. "So how does one become one of these nosferat?" Realizing she wasn't getting anywhere with disbelief, she listened to the little cat of curiosity that nibbled at her ear.

"Nosferata, one nosferat, many nosferata," Dar said.

"Seriously? Undead grammar lessons?"

Dar ignored her question, continuing from where she'd interrupted. "One tries not to become one, unless one thrives on evil. But they're formed the same as the draculus, by the strain that lives within us being amplified or distilled: being re-infected, bitten again, or by it becoming stronger with age." Dar ran a fine-boned hand through his flopped over mohawk. "We're always on watch for signs that one of us draculus has moved into nosferat territory, either sudden or slow. Then...."

"That thread of evil that runs through all of us grows to bind a nosferat," Jack added, glancing at Dar. "Regardless of what they were before or how hard they fight. Eventually the siren song of hunger flowing through the blood becomes irresistible, a tune you must dance to."

"So this is the demon's creed?" Mina arched an eyebrow. "And what are you, God's chosen ones?"

"What are *we*, Mina," Dar said. "You're one of us now, like it or not, and you will have to choose a side. Athanatos, undead fighter of death, or Necrophagos, consumer of life."

"And what if I don't? What if I choose to say piss off and leave me alone?"

"Then you'll become one of the wild ones, a revenant forced to fend for yourself in a demon-haunted world. I'd suggest choosing a side."

"Not this side," Mina said, her head drowning in a world she hadn't imagined. Her eyelids felt very heavy, and she mustered her energy to force them open, focusing on the stars that floated in her vision. She tried to marshal the random words that swam in her brain into a coherent thought. "Stalkers...kidnappers."

"If not...," Dar started to say.

"Dar!" Jack said as Mina's dizziness finally got the better of her. She felt a set of strong arms around her as she slid towards the floor.

"Get her something to drink." The arms stayed around her and her head lolled against a broad chest. She smelled cedar and sun-warmed earth.

Soon a glass was pressed to her lips. She drank in big gulps, half-dazed, until there was nothing left but the dregs. Only after the contents started to take effect did she realize what the glass had held: blood. It was thinner than she thought. She looked into the bottom of the empty cup, swallowing hard, licking her lips. Her hand started to shake.

"It tasted good, didn't it?" Jack said, his lips moving against her hair behind her ear.

Mina shook her head, afraid if she opened her mouth that it would be to either throw up or to lap up the dregs. It had tasted like peaches and bourbon with a hint of some warm spice, underlaid with a metallic tang. Not like her blood had tasted when she'd nicked a finger.

"You feel that shaking?" Jack continued, his arms still around her. "That's your body craving more. It knows what it needs even if you don't want to admit it."

Mina wanted to throw up. Instead she placed the cup on the floor beside her and stood up, albeit a little woozily.

"I need to go," she said, her words slurred.

CHAPTER FOURTEEN

HE PEERED OUT AT THE street from his cloak of shadows. The bright lights shattered into shards by the wet pavement and hurt his eyes. He closed them and listened to the rain, which snaked from his forehead, down his nose and off his chin. He opened his eyes again.

Too many people. He didn't like so many people, the...the...he picked his brain for the word but couldn't dredge it up from the mire of memory. Even though he barely felt the cold, he felt the wet and hated it. It washed away all the smells, made them faint, hard to trace. It played tricks with the light and muddled sounds.

He scratched his neck, where a scar had faded against his pasty, damp skin. He sniffed the air, trying to catch a scent, something worth pursuing. He hadn't liked the smell of any of the creatures who'd entered the shadows. Dirt, piss and shit – not tasty.

His stomach growled. He ground his teeth. He would have to venture out of the deep shadows soon and into the twilit border between soft dark and harsh light.

Then he heard a sound behind him in the empty alleyway – maybe not so empty any more. He sank further into the shadows, pressing against the wall, its rough brick rubbing his skin. He sniffed again.

This smelled promising. Like meat. His unblinking black eyes searched the deep dark. As it got closer, it looked like meat.

He stilled and reined in his excitement as it inched nearer, slowly, like it sensed him. Then he lunged out, grabbing its throat with a large, strong hand. His prey snarled, jabbing an elbow into his side and a boot into his foot. It threw its head forward and bared its own fangs, raking them across the flesh of his arm. He grabbed its throat, his sharp fingernails digging into flesh as he choked the air out of it. Then he took his own teeth to the windpipe and bit into it. He started gnashing, gnawing away at the flesh.

He stopped. This one didn't taste like his usual prey. It tasted sweet, savoury. He ran his tongue along the top of his mouth and sucked at his sharp teeth. Definitely not the same – better. He breathed in through tight lips; it tasted like that other one, the one he caught a few moons ago. The one with the teeth and the blades.

He sighed. He needed to find more of these.

"THERE'S A WHAT?" MATTEO said, his voice low and even. Veins in his prominent temples pulsed, betraying his tone. His long fingers grasped the arms of his chair a little harder, the knuckles going a deeper shade of white.

Luca was down on one knee before his father, natural and unnatural. The latest scars, gifts from his shadowy benefactor, throbbed under his crisp white shirt. The voice in the shadows wanted the girl, and Luca needed Matteo to find her. Though when Luca glanced at his father, he still believed that Matteo would make a better sacrifice. So he kept his eyes trained on Matteo's chair, his throne, studying the delicate carvings, even though he'd seen it a thousand times before, even sat in it a few times when Matteo was asleep. The off-white chair was one of many unique pieces his father had collected after setting himself up in the city and quickly taking over as leader of the local Necrophagos in a bloody coup, eradicating the previous conclave in order to build one in his own image: wealthy, wanton, weak. Beautiful at first glance, its ornate carvings danced in the firelight; it was only when you looked closely, carefully, that you realized that the figures weren't cavorting in ecstasy but were contorted in agony. Few would know, just looking at it, that the broken and dismembered corpses depicted were carved not into ivory but into human bones.

Speak.

Luca did as he was told and broke the silence. "There's a new vampire. And the others have her."

"The others?" A muscle ticked in Matteo's jaw as he spoke. Luca turned back to the chair to study a man being torn apart by hounds.

"The Athanatos," he said. He watched Matteo unclench his fist, finger by finger. He knew his father bristled at the fact that the others had laid claim to 'immortal' while he was stuck with Necrophagos, eater of the dead.

"How did this creature come to be?" Matteo asked, standing and walking towards Luca with measured, calculated steps. Luca stayed silent. Matteo grasped Luca's chin, his long fingernails biting into his son's skin. Luca was forced to look at his father. "How do you know about her?"

"I...," Luca stumbled.

Look.

He looked into his father's dark eyes, which shone like pools of oil in his pale face. A shadow passed across the corner of his field of vision, and a twinge of pain shot from his chin down his chest, steeling his resolve. "I made her," Luca said, his voice quiet but strong.

"You made her. And yet she's not here." Matteo's fingernails dug deeper.

Stand.

"No."

"She's with the Persian. How do you explain that?"

For a fleeting second, he thought about lying. But he didn't want the delving for the little lie to lead to the bigger secret. So he told the truth. "I didn't intend to make her."

Before he had time to brace himself, Luca was slammed into a wall. He managed to catch himself before he collapsed into a complete heap. Fists clenched, Luca stood up and looked at his spectral father, who brushed his hands on his black jacket. Veins mapped routes under Matteo's ghostly skin. The rims of his eyes were white and his black pupils huge. His thin lips were crimson, his sharpened teeth bared as his upper lip pulled back in a snarl. Luca smiled inside, thinking how his father would look in death.

"Of course you didn't intend to make her." Matteo's voice was even again. "That would have defied my direct orders. And yet she's made. How?"

Even though Luca knew Matteo would smell a lie, he was nonetheless reluctant to tell the truth. "I drained her."

"And? That's not enough to make a vampire."

"She fought while I drained her."

"Irrelevant."

"She scratched me."

"Enough. What did you do to create her?"

"She bit me. Hard. Still barely a drop. It shouldn't have been enough."

"Yet it was," Matteo said. Luca stepped back, shoulder blades against the wall, and flexed his fingers, reaching for the small silver blade sheathed at his hip, as his father strode towards him.

Leave it.

"So there is a new vampire you didn't even intend to make. If you were not my son, you would be dead," Matteo whispered, his stale breath on Luca's cheek. "Unfortunately, you remind me of your mother. One day that may not be enough." Matteo turned his back on Luca.

"I'll take care of her. I made her – I can unmake her."

Matteo paused. Without looking at Luca, he said, "No, bring her to me. I'll decide her fate."

CHAPTER FIFTEEN

"NO," DAR SAID.

Mina looked at him, her hands on her hips. "I need clean clothes, books. Stuff." She ran her tongue over her teeth. Her first infusion of blood had left her wanting more, a ball of yearning deep in her abdomen. She refused to listen to the hunger. Instead she stubbornly insisted on going back to her apartment.

"You need to stay here."

"No, I need to get out of here." Dar opened his mouth to respond but she forestalled him. "For a bit. To get some fresh air, maybe tell my roommate that I won't be around for a while."

"Forever," Dar said, his face softening. "You need to sever ties."

"What?"

"You need to die," Jack said. "Let go of the people from your day life. Let them move on."

Mina looked down at the tile. "I need to go."

"You need to stay," Dar repeated. "For your own protection. We need to figure you out."

"What's there to figure out – I'm an open book."

"Blunt doesn't equal open," Dar said. He sighed. "You shouldn't exist."

"Tell me something I don't know."

"There's a truce, a sort of ceasefire between us and the Necrophagos. A time to lick our wounds. Bury our dead. No hunting each other, no killing people, and definitely no turning."

"So we need to figure out who turned you," Jack said. "And why they broke the truce."

Mina cocked her head, her cheeks flushed. "I don't care. Right now, I just want to not smell like street meat and hospital."

Dar looked her up and down. "Jack, take her to her apartment. Then bring her straight back."

AT HER PLACE, SHE SOMEHOW knew that Cam wasn't there before even opening the door: she could sense the gap, hear the void. As Jack waited by the door, she threw a few changes of clothes, some personal items, her M necklace even though she still couldn't wear it without itching, into a duffel bag. She almost added some school books before deciding that was probably pointless given the events of the last 24 hours.

Instead she threw a sketchpad, pencils and markers in. She left a note on the blackboard for Cam, saying she was still feeling like crap and was going to stay with her brother and Hana, his wife, for a few days. She hoped that was enough to appease Cam, for now, until she could figure out what to tell her. Somehow she thought 'Hey, I'm a vampire' would result in Cam deciding she'd lost it and calling Dale.

Leaving the apartment, she and Jack walked back towards headquarters. The day was overcast but the oppressive rain and glowering clouds of the past few days had lightened up. Mina watched the world through dark sunglasses. She had to admit they did help with the headaches. Though maybe the easing tension was also helped by the blood she'd drunk earlier. She swallowed hard but it didn't remove the lump in her throat. Whatever the reason, she was feeling better...physically at least.

She watched the office workers disgorge from their towers and move to the cafes and restaurants for a brief respite from their workaday lives. She caught snatches of conversations over the thrum in her ears. Break ups, make ups, tyrannical bosses and lackadaisical staff. Not a word about vampires, sucking blood, or treacherous priests. For them, today was the same as yesterday and the day before that. As she watched, her anger at these vampires and her anonymous maker grew, a burning in her gut.

As she and Jack neared the museum, a gaggle of tourists tumbled from a bus under the watch of a haggard tour guide, trying to make herself heard as she waved a closed umbrella. Mina looked at Jack. He was checking out at a tall brunette in a figure-skimming business suit, who was flipping her exceedingly curly hair at him. Mina stopped. Her minder kept walking, watching the brunette, who was giving him a small smile, looking sidelong at him.

Mina incorporated herself into the tour group and made her way into the museum. The museum and art gallery were her churches – maybe she could find a quiet corner to think. Or an escape route. Once inside, she untangled herself from the clutch of people, waved at the docent and made a beeline for the nearest exit that didn't require a ticket. She had almost reached the gift shop before the hand clasped her arm.

"Come on, dear," Jack said, his voice low and even. "We don't have time for sightseeing."

"How did you find me?"

"I didn't have to find you." His black eyes bored into her. "I knew the moment you left my side. I just had to follow."

The docent, an army vet Mina had gotten to know on her many trips to sketch the museum's collection, was staring at them. Jack leaned in, a smile on his face, his breath in her hair. "I'd suggest not doing that again. All you achieve is trying my patience. Now it's time to go home."

"It's not my home." Mina's cheeks blazed.

"It's the best place for you, the only home you have now." His grip tightened slightly, not enough to cause pain but enough to let her know she was caught. "You can come quietly or not, but you will come." Jack started to walk. The docent stepped towards her. The image of him with the life sucked out of him flashed before her. She smiled at him, and followed Jack.

"And what makes you better than the others, those...what do you call them?" she asked as she started moving alongside Jack. He let go of her arm when it was clear she was following.

"The Necrophagos – for one, we won't kill people to drive you to us. We won't kill your family and friends to take away any safety net from your former life. Though the sooner you're dead to them, the better."

They walked in silence after that. As they neared the gates to the headquarters, Mina slowed. She looked at the building that Jack called her new home. It somehow balanced unassuming and imposing, the lawns neatly manicured, the flower beds weeded, the trees properly pruned into order.

"What's ioki?" she asked, coming to a full stop as she looked up at the stained glass over the door. "It sounds like some anime character."

"It's not ioki. It's I-O-K-I. The Independent Order of the Knights of the Iscariot." Jack undid the latch on the gate, then continued in answer to her arched eyebrow. "A secretive fraternal order that became very rich very quickly then just as quickly disappeared."

"The Iscariot." The name snagged at some long-buried memory from childhood catechism. "You mean Judas?"

"Yes."

"The betrayer of Jesus?"

Jack shrugged. "One man's betrayer is another's enabler."

"Right." Mina changed tacks. "What do you call this place?"

"Home." Jack arched an eyebrow at her. "All right, we call it Sanctuary."

"Seriously?" Mina's eyebrow arched. She continued when she got no response. "Why are you all here? Why this place? Together?"

"Why not? We need some place to live. Over the years, individuals come and go. As for this building, it was bought cheap a couple of centuries ago. And it came pre-blessed. Besides being IOKI headquarters, it was also their church. Hallowed ground."

"So?"

"So, as you learned the hard way last night, vampires and most of the pantheon of Nether creatures can't enter without invitation, not even the grass outside – the graves might not be marked but they're there. That's why you passed out; you crossed the threshold before we could invite you in."

"Am I invited now?" Mina looked askance at the gate.

"Yes, you're invited," Jack said, as he held the gate open for her. Mina stepped through, ignoring the flutter in her stomach. Once inside the building, he led her into the basement.

"Welcome home," Dar said, as he emerged out of the dark hallway, beside the room where she'd woken up that morning.

"You can have the room." He tilted his head. "Or one of the other ones more recently vacated."

Mina settled on the room she knew. "So where's the coffin?" she asked off-hand, the question reflecting her view of the grim interior more than her knowledge of vampire lore.

"Only the nosferata sleep fully ensconced," Dar said. "They're the only ones who sunlight can kill before they have a chance to hide. Sometimes all it takes is a sliver for them to blister horribly and die. Some draculus do it as an affectation, sleeping in boxes like their masters, but it's unnecessary. We go out in the day, though it makes us slower and weaker. For us, it's a long-term poison, not an acute killer. Some of the oldest, old world nosferata even shun the moonlight, claiming it causes them pain."

"Right, sure, makes total sense," Mina said.

"Feel free to do with the room as you please," Dar said. "Ask Jack if you need anything. He's just down the hall." Dar indicated a door in the shadows at the far end of the narrow hallway. "Sorry, if it feels a bit like a prison cell at the moment. The last occupant was a monk in his prior life."

Mina nodded in agreement, as she tossed her duffel down in front of the wardrobe. She considered asking about what happened to the monk, but decided she didn't want to know given their talk of battles and ceasefires. Instead she wondered what Dar and Jack's rooms looked like.

"Is there somewhere to do laundry?" she asked, realizing that some of the clothes she'd moved from the floor of her apartment into her bag probably didn't pass the sniff test. A vampire at the laundromat just didn't seem right.

"You have to get a hamper," Jack said, pointing. "There's a room on the other side of the basement, beside the kitchen. Leave the hamper outside your door during the day, and your clean laundry will be returned by evening."

"Who washes the clothes?" she asked, peering into the shadows, half expecting some mythical currying creature to appear. She let slide her curiosity about a kitchen for vampires.

"The staff," Dar said. "Familiars we trust enough to care for us while we sleep."

"Familiars?"

Dar didn't answer. Instead he looked at Jack then back at Mina. "You're looking a little pale," he said. "I think it's time you met some of the others, vamps and familiars. The night is young, so most of the hive should be around."

Mina was still trying to wrap her head around the idea of the undead having staff as she followed Dar and Jack upstairs.

"This is Sanctuary," Jack said. Mina couldn't tell if the wave of his hand indicated the building or the people gathered there. The space was less imposing at night. Warm light flickered, cast from sconces on the pillars and candles set in giant chandeliers, and pooled between the shadows. Even nearly empty as it was, the echoing seemed dampened, more muffled than during the day. A handful of people were gathered there.

Mina looked at the assemblage. A pair were sparring with what looked like real, unblunted swords. A few more were playing video games that seemed to involve a lot of shooting and bloodletting. Others were just lounging – chatting, reading, snogging. Mina was surprised by the variety, especially the ages; they weren't all young. But they were all fit: muscled or wiry, strong or agile. And they were all tattooed to one degree or another.

Every one of them stopped what they were doing, almost in spooky unison, and focused their intensity on her as she entered the halo of light in the center of the sanctuary. Mina felt herself shrink a little. There were eleven people in all, not including her, Dar and Jack – eight vampires and three humans, though she didn't know how she knew that. One of the people was Sam, her boss.

Her breath caught in her throat. She opened her mouth to speak, but couldn't find any words to put to her thoughts, or maybe no thoughts to put to words.

"This is our hangout," Jack said. "It's where we train, and where we gather when not on duty."

Mina took a deep breath and stood up straighter as Dar led her into the middle of the group as they gathered around her. She resisted the urge to back up, to keep her line of retreat open. She felt Jack's presence over her right shoulder and let out the breath she'd been holding. Mina's mind caught up to what Jack had said, and she was about to ask 'what duties' when Dar spoke.

"Everyone, meet Mina. Mina, everyone." Dar went through a roll call. She tried to commit faces and names to memory, as heads nodded or hands raised.

"Tana." The woman indicated inclined her head. Mina noted the lion-like creatures rendered in black ink on each shoulder, exposed by the black tank top. She seemed to have stopped in the midst of some kind of kata, and now stood poised, with her weight on one foot, as if to pounce. A swathe of silver in her dark hair and faint lines around her almond eyes hinted at a greater age than first glance betrayed. She was willowy with freckles strewn like stars across her pale cheeks.

"Adeh." The man smiled at her, a smile that spread from his lips to his ruddy cheeks to his black walnut eyes. His smooth skin was the colour of weathered bronze, rich and warm. He had geometric tattoos on his forearms, that almost looked like braille, but Mina was more intrigued by the scarification along his collarbone, exposed by his white V-neck shirt.

"Alex." The man nodded towards her, without smiling. Mina tried not to gawp: except for face and hands, he had lettering tattooed all over his body, in a hundred different scripts, an epistle in flesh. Short and wiry, he had been sparring with Simon when she'd come up – a bit of a mismatch but he had been holding his own, with sinewy capoeira moves.

"Simon." She nodded curtly towards Simon, the Chest, having met him in her earlier attempt to escape. He didn't seem to be holding a grudge about her plan to mace him. He was built like a rugby player; Cam would have been all over him.

"Hiya," he said. Mina could see the raven's wingtips peeking out from under his tank top.

"Alisha."

"Call me Sha," the woman corrected. Her chestnut hair, cut in an asymmetrical bob, fell over one side of her face as she spoke. Falling cherry blossoms descended along one arm, and Mina wondered if they had anything to do with the Arabic script that cascaded down the other.

"Bee." The woman tipped her head as she was introduced to Mina. She was tall and wiry, muscles clearly defined on her bare arms. For some reason Mina thought alley cat. Her expression was open but gave nothing away. Her tank top stretched taut over a flat chest. A pink mark on her shoulder stood out against her cool mahogany skin. Mina didn't see any tattoos but, judging from their prevalence, she was sure she had them hidden somewhere.

I just need to get her out of her clothes to ferret them out, Mina thought. A small smile crept into Bee's lips. Mina felt her cheeks flush and quickly looked at the next person Dar indicated, hoping mind-reading wasn't one of the vampire superpowers.

"Astrid." The woman reached out to shake Mina's hand with vigor. Slender dragons, rendered in vivid colour, snaked around the woman's wrists and up her arms, disappearing under loose sleeves above her elbows. A riot of wavy black hair cascaded over her shoulders, and her sweater fell off one shoulder to reveal the translucent ivory skin underneath.

"Last of all, Quinn." With his red shirt highlighting the blue in his skin, the man looked like a ghost, with a translucent skin and silver blond hair. A pair of startlingly blue eyes looked at her as he nodded a greeting. One forearm had a Celtic cross tattoo, the other a thistle and a woman's name: Magrit? Those stunning eyes looked sad and he didn't smile.

"Now that you've all been introduced, those of you on duty can head out," Dar said. He turned to Mina, while most of the others filed over to the cabinets in the arcades and started pulling out weapons of all sorts, many Mina had never seen before.

"What are they doing?" Mina asked, watching guns and knives and weapons she couldn't name disappear under jackets, and into boots and waistbands.

"That's the second part of tonight's lesson. Have patience. First, the familiars." Dar nodded at the humans who had hung back during the introduction of the vampires. "At the moment, Brett, Sam and Nicole are gracing us with their presence." Mina eyed them: it was unnerving that she'd known they were there, behind the vampires, their pulses throbbing in her ears with a different timbre.

Dar's eyes fixed on Sam, and Sam stepped towards them. Mina felt a jolt of anger as he approached. *What other lies lurked beneath his amiable face.* "I quit."

Sam had the good grace to look away.

Dar's eyes traveled from Sam to her. "There are others, they come and go, and haunt our haunts in the city. Then there are those who take care of us during the day. But they all have this tattoo on their neck." Dar stroked Sam's neck.

Mina had wondered about the blocky sigil, incongruous amongst Sam's other tattoos. "To mark you as property?" she said, hoping the words stung.

"To protect," Dar said, his voice hard. "It marks our responsibility of care. And some say there's magic in it."

Mina looked at Dar then her boss – former boss – then at the other two familiars. Like the vampires, they ran the gamut. Brett seemed very all-American, clean cut, jeans and T-shirt, the only sign of something different about him being the tattoo and a depth to his gaze. Sam was still decked out in his bespoke vest and dress pants, the cuffs of his tailored shirt rolled up to reveal the vines climbing his arms. Nicole tended towards goth – dark clothes, dark hair, dark makeup, with various piercings and more tattoos than just the one on her neck.

Although Mina felt rude talking about them when they were right there, she leaned towards Dar and asked, her voice low, "Why are these...familiars here now, if not to work?" Though she could think of a few things to tell Sam to do.

Dar looked at her, his dark eyes forcing her to look at him. "Like I said earlier, you're looking a little pale." He turned back to

Sam, who loosened his tie as Dar stepped up to him. Dar placed a hand behind Sam's head and drew him close, looking at Mina over Sam's shoulder. Her pulse quickened as she watched them share a hard, dry kiss before Dar's full lips moved along Sam's jaw and down his throat, now exposed. Sam leaned his head back, lips parted. Dar turned slightly, moving them both so he could fix his eyes on Mina as he sunk his fangs into the skin of Sam's neck. A small sound escaped Sam's open lips. Dar drank for a long minute then ran his tongue over two small puncture wounds in Sam's neck. Sam brought his head back up and looked from Dar to Mina with glassy eyes.

Mina's stomach twitched. Her mouth opened and closed. "But...."

"But what?" Sam said, slurring his words slightly. He pressed against Dar. "You're a vampire now. Accept it: you need to drink blood to survive. And we offer ours freely."

Dar beckoned Nicole to them. There was no need for her to loosen anything since the top she wore already had a plunging neckline, the dark fabric framing an overflowing decolletage. Mina swallowed hard and ran her tongue over her own growing fangs.

"You don't have a fridge of blood somewhere, like a blood bank?"

"We tried that, once the technology was available. It nearly drove the early testers crazy. Yes, it will keep you alive temporarily, but there is something about fresh blood that calms the beast within."

"What about the blood I drank earlier, in the cup?"

"Taken from a familiar. As I said, it will keep you alive. But not by much."

"So I have to drink from the familiars?" Mina asked, searching for more questions to ask.

"Does that seem so bad?" Dar said, gathering Nicole's hair and pulling it back over her shoulder to reveal her neck. "When you're hungry, you drink before the hunger consumes your judgment. If there are no familiars near, you find someone in some dark corner of some anonymous club and take a little sip. The person won't realize what's happened, and may even enjoy it."

"Hmmph. I've heard that one before."

Nicole took Mina's hand in her own. It was warm, soft and dry.

"Why don't you take her somewhere more private?" Dar said, looking at Mina, though his head was cocked towards Nicole. "Jack, go with them."

Nicole led Mina to a divan set in a dark corner of the narthex and sat down, patting the seat beside her. Mina sat down. Jack stood in front of Nicole, who tilted her head to the side, exposing her neck, as he ran a hand through her hair.

"For the neck, you want to bite here," Jack said, stroking a spot on Nicole's neck just below the tattoo with his thumb.

Nicole's kohl-rimmed eyes held hers.

"But the neck's not the best place to bite until you're more experienced, until you can aim for the jugular – the brain kind of needs the oxygen the arteries carry." Jack slid to his knees. Nicole's short leather skirt slid up as she shifted to make room for Jack, exposing the garters that held up her fishnets. "Until you can tell the difference between the veins and arteries, and control your hunger, extremities are better. Arms, legs."

Jack ran a hand along Nicole's leg as he lifted her ankle. He looked at Mina, as he whispered his lips over the torn stocking.

"But avoid the inner thigh. You don't want to risk hitting the femoral artery."

He gently placed Nicole's leg back on the floor, and she turned to Mina, running a hand through Mina's hair to the back of her neck and drawing her close. She kissed Mina, prodding Mina's lips open and playing her tongue across Mina's fangs. Mina kissed back with a force that surprised her. Nicole's free hand ran softly over Mina's chest before coming to rest on her shoulder. Nicole pulled away, pulling the hand away and cocking the wrist so the pale inside was inches from Mina's lips. The breath caught in Mina's throat and blood pounded in her ears.

Mina hesitated.

"It's okay," Nicole said, as she lay back against the wall. She ran her hand through Mina's hair and nudged Mina's head closer to her exposed wrist. "I want you to bite."

"Go ahead," Jack urged quietly, startling Mina with the intrusion. "You have to drink or you'll go mad and become a danger to yourself, to people on the street and to us. We don't hesitate to take care of our problems."

Tentatively, Mina stuck out her tongue and kissed the soft flesh on the inside of Nicole's wrist, like she'd seen Dar do to Sam's neck. Nicole let out a sigh and shifted on the divan. Despite her inexperience, Mina could tell where blood flowed beneath the skin, where it was closest. She almost thought she could hear it, like a trickle of sand in an hourglass.

"That's right. Find the vein, hone in on it, and sink your fangs into it." Jack's warm breath tickled her ear. She hadn't realized that he'd come to sit behind her.

Mina did as she was told. The blood filled her mouth faster than she'd expected. It started to dribble out the sides until she remembered to swallow and fasten her lips to Nicole's wrist. Nicole let out a moan through parted lips. Then the throbbing of blood in Mina's ears drowned out further sound.

"Enough," Jack said. Mina barely heard him over the pounding in her head, and the slowing trickle of sand through the hourglass.

"Stop!" Jack hauled her back. She reeled against the end of the divan, one palm pressed against the stone wall as she tried to steady herself, the other hand on her chest, where she felt her breath, ragged and shallow. Catching her breath, she ran her fingers along her lips, noting the smear of crimson when she pulled them away.

"You have to learn to control the blood lust," Jack continued, his face inches from her own. "Right now, your thirst is vicious. You're starving. Don't do that again. Take small meals, every day. It's easier on the familiars and it keeps the edge off, allowing you to control the hunger rather than it controlling you."

Jack turned to Nicole, who lay sprawled out on the divan, and pressed his lips to her wrist. "Are you okay?"

Nicole nodded languidly, her eyes half closed, her mouth half open.

Looking at her, Mina was overcome with a heady mix of horror, shame, guilt and desire. She wanted to cry or throw up or both. "Oh god, I'm so sorry."

"Don't be." Nicole got up, a little wobbly, and kissed Mina again, gently this time. "It was your first time. And it was good for me. I hope it was good for you."

Mina's throat started to tighten again, as it had when she'd drunk from the cup. She ran a hand over her stomach, and nodded. Nicole smiled then sauntered into the nave.

"That blood's a gift," Jack said, giving her a hand up. "Don't throw it up."

"I'm not going to puke," Mina said, trusting herself to speak, but still wrestling with the heaving in her stomach.

"Some of us do the first time," he said as he turned and followed Nicole.

"Did you?" she asked Jack's back. Jack's back didn't answer.

BACK IN THE SANCTUARY, Jack handed her over to the tall vampire with skin the colour of deep, rich sepia. The woman stood in the center of the cavernous space, a long bamboo staff slung across her shoulders, her wrists resting on either end. Mina's eyes traced the carving of muscles under her slate gray top and tried to remember her name.

"Bee," the woman said, holding out her hand. She had long pianist's fingers. Her voice had a leftover lilt, redolent of cinnamon, cloves and allspice, and her almond eyes smiled at Mina. "You'll get our names down soon enough."

"You'll wish you could forget Bee's before long," Jack said.

"Why?" Mina's eyebrow arched. She looked from Jack to Bee.

"She's going to induct you into your duties." Jack started to walk away.

"Where are you going?" she asked.

"Are you my keeper?" Jack said, half turning.

"No." Mina shrugged. "I just figured you were mine."

"I have work to do. It doesn't involve babysitting."

Mina's eyes narrowed, tracking him as he disappeared into the shadows. She turned back to Bee with barely time to register the staff arcing towards her calves. Unable to throw her hands out to catch her fall, she landed on her back, the wind knocked out of her.

"What the fuck?!" she said from the floor.

"Welcome to your new life," Bee said, holding out a hand to help her up.

"What?" She looked at the offered hand before taking it and pulling herself up. "The biting I get," she said, her cheeks flushing. "But you knocking me on my ass, not so much."

"We're foot soldiers in the battle between, well, sort of good versus mostly evil. A fight more ancient than any of us alive now know. You met the Necrophagos, yes?"

Mina nodded, as she circled one ankle then the other. "Em and Ivan."

"That is what we fight: the creatures that subjugate, that revel in bloodshed, that embrace the void – the wicked who care not for redemption. We fight these things, protect the world from them, kill them when required. You're expected to do your part in exchange for your place in polite vampire society."

"But someone mentioned a truce?"

Bee tilted her head, and spun the staff in slow figure eights. "More a ceasefire. For both side to bury their dead. Figuratively speaking."

Mina's lips rounded, thinking of all the empty rooms downstairs. "You said things? Plural?"

Bee nodded. "The Necrophagos are one thread of evil in a larger tapestry. But that's a long lesson, one for another night. Tonight I need to teach you the basics of staying alive."

"But the Necrophagos are vampires, like you." Mina's eyes narrowed. "Like us."

"They're vampires, but not like us. They're the ones who chose the perverted path. Most are smart enough to moderate their proclivities: they don't need a light shone on their dark corner any more than we do. But they were often reprobate humans. As vampires, that tendency is amplified and they're capable of much greater harm."

"So what, they were killers in their former lives?"

"Some were, yes. Some were rapists, or paedophiles, or torturers of small kittens. Some just enjoyed inflicting mental or emotional pain. And for some, the Necrophagos just found them before we did, gave a young, confused vampire answers and a place in their new world. It takes a fierce fortitude to break from their clutches."

"So you fight them."

Bee nodded slowly. "But it's more than that. Eventually the shadow of evil falls over us all. It's in our vampiric blood, the parasite that infects us. We fight the Necrophagos as a way to fight the wickedness in ourselves."

"I'm not wicked. I have a hard time killing a spider."

"You shouldn't, those things are evil – you can see it in the way they move, clickety clack." Bee frowned as her fingers moved with her words. "But, to paraphrase Solzhenitsyn, everyone has a corner of evil in them. Especially us. You're once-bitten, newly turned. But the infection is insidious, it grows and spreads without you realizing it. As it ages, or when you're bitten again, it's distilled, strengthened. You become dracul, and the siren song of evil becomes stronger, harder to ignore."

"So Em and Ivan have been bitten three times?"

"What? No. They just chose the wicked way right from the start. But eventually, by time or by teeth, you turn into a nosferat.

Then the plague is irresistible. You become Necrophagos, whether you want to or not."

"What happens then?"

"We kill you, if we can."

Mina's head shot up. She looked at Bee, searching for some sign that the woman was kidding. She didn't find one.

"I suggest leather," Bee said as she started towards the far end of the arcade.

"What?" Mina's head reeled as she tried to make sense of the woman's words.

"Clothes," Bee said, as if that explained it. Mina just shrugged. "Most of us wear leather when we go out. Harder to bite through."

"Not because you think it makes you look cool, then?"

Bee didn't answer. Instead she opened a drawer. Inside, objects of black leather and dull metal were laid out neatly on blue velvet. Bee reached her hands towards Mina's arms. She jerked away. "Good reflexes but I'm not going to hurt you." Mina forced herself to relax and let the woman place her warm hands around her wrists. Bee grasped them gently, one in each hand.

"What are you doing?" Mina asked, her voice raspy.

"Measuring," Bee said as she ran her thumbs along the inside of Mina's wrists, before abruptly letting go and examining the contents of the cupboard. She pulled out a pair of leather cuffs, about 5 inches long, snaked with matte metal whorls, and snapped one on Mina's right wrist.

"What is it?" Mina asked, running her fingers over the patterned surface.

"A brace."

"A brace for what?"

Bee ignored her question and grasped her hands instead. "You've got skinny wrists. You need to strengthen your forearms."

"But why? Why the braces?"

"Insurance. Protection for the most exposed bits against teeth and blades."

"Seriously? I'm going to look like an extra from some low-budget sci-fi fantasy flick."

Bee ignored her. "Now for tonight's lesson." She walked over to another cupboard where she opened a drawer and pulled a short sword out of its scabbard. A stout hilt wrapped in worn leather gave way to a blade that tapered to a vicious point.

Bee ran her hand along the flat, a smile at the corners of eyes. "My first. From when I first learned to fight with a sword. Still my favorite." Bee grabbed the oil and rag from the cupboard, and tucked these under her sword arm. In her free hand, she grabbed a couple of wooden clubs and walked back to the centre of the large space. Mina followed. Bee motioned with the blade. "Squat."

Mina started to lower herself to the floor, making like her grandmother weeding between the rows of cabbage in the garden.

"No, like you'd sit in a chair," Bee said.

Mina looked at her sideways.

"Like this. Butt back, not down." Bee lowered herself into a squat, knees at an almost 90 degree angle. "Arms in front, shoulder width apart. Focus on that picture over there." She indicated a painted icon with the sword. "It'll help with your balance."

Mina did as Bee had demonstrated, reaching her hands out. "How does this teach me sword fighting?"

"Who said anything about sword fighting? You're learning to fight, period. This lesson is about focus and perseverance in the face of discomfort and pain."

"By squatting?" Mina looked at her so-called teacher.

"Just wait," Bee responded then walked behind her, shuffling around out of sight.

Sure enough, her quads and shoulders soon started to tire, and she had to work to stay in position. She heard scraping behind her. She tried to peek over her shoulder but her balance started to waiver.

"Focus," Bee said. "Maintain position. Look at the picture."

There were more sounds behind her, but Mina kept her eyes mostly forward, trying to peek over her shoulder every once in a while to catch a glimpse of Bee's maneuvers in her peripheral vision.

"Arms up." Bee prodded Mina's left tricep with the tip of the sword, before placing a stool beside her. Some tension went out of Mina's face and she sighed.

"Not for you," Bee said. The look of relief on Mina's face turned to a grimace. Once more Bee disappeared, returning with a bowl full of water which she placed in Mina's hands. Her aching shoulders screamed at the added weight, her arms lowering a little. She looked at Bee out the corner of her eye as the woman came to perch cross-legged on the stool. Bee held a club in each hand; the sword, back in its sheath rested across her legs.

A flicker of movement caught the corner of Mina's eye. She turned her head and strained her eyes towards Bee as much as she dared, without upsetting her precarious precision. She realized the woman was juggling the clubs. While she squatted, the muscles in her thighs spasming. She looked away, her lips tensing, and shifted a little, trying to ease the burning.

With a whisper, one club swung around, coming to rest a hairsbreadth away from Mina's shaking knees.

"What the hell?" Mina said, shifting so a slurp of water ran over her hands. "You almost hit me."

"Mmhuh, and it'll be your knee next time." Bee returned to juggling the clubs, tossing, catching and whirling. "Squat. Quietly. I'm trying this meditate in motion thing Jack does."

Mina glanced at her, but Bee's focus was on the clubs. Her legs started to shake, joining her arms, and her glutes protested. "How much longer?"

"Until I say so."

"I can't." Mina's butt inched towards the floor. "Ow!" she yelped as a club smacked her glutes. She started to stand up but stopped when she felt the other club come to rest against her knee caps. Water sloshed down her arms.

"Yes, you can. If you want to give up, you can stand or sink to the floor; I promise it'll hurt either way. But you'll heal."

Mina's legs shook, and she was sweating as a club thwacked against her backside again. She wanted to kill Bee; she told her so.

"Good," Bee said, returning to her juggling. "Use your anger. If it helps you stay focused, you can hate me all you want."

Her arms were numb and more water sloshed down them. It made the bowl lighter, and more slippery; she didn't think Bee would appreciate being doused with water. She smiled at the mental picture.

"You're a sadistic bitch."

"Reach," Bee said. "Push through the pain and the weakness. They're remnants of your old life. Stop acting human. Focus on your new life."

"I want my old life back." Mina's cheeks flushed under their sheen of sweat.

"You can't have it back. Deal with it."

Mina bared her teeth at her, like a lioness over her kill. "I hate you."

"So you say," Bee said, not taking her eyes off the whirling clubs. "Be careful. Baring your teeth at another vamp is a challenge that can't be ignored."

Mina kept her teeth bared and growled at her, and Bee finally stopped and looked at her.

"Yes, growl like the beast you are. You're a vampire, like it or not. Embrace it and the strength, speed and agility it gives you. If you don't, you won't be human or vampire. You'll just be dead. As you will be if you ever bare your teeth at me again."

Mina pressed her lips tightly together, and focused on the painting. It was some ornate icon, all silver and gold, though the subject matter didn't seem all that holy. A silver-armored vampire leaned over a golden, helmetless knight. The vampire looked at Mina with black eyes. Red ran down its chin and pulsed from a wound in the knight's neck.

A few more minutes and Mina had sunk a few more inches. She gathered all the strength she could find in her newly immortal skin. But still she sank, her thighs burning.

She grunted, then yelped, like a kicked dog, when a club tapped her shins.

"How long can you withstand the pain without making a sound?" Bee asked. Mina didn't answer. Thankfully she didn't have to stand it for much longer.

JACK STOPPED SHORT, keeping to the shadowed entryway. Mina was haloed in a circle of light, a sheen of sweat on her forehead, legs quivering with the effort of staying in a squat, while Bee kept watch beside her. Bee's eyes appeared closed but Jack knew that she was watching the impact her lesson was having on her hapless pupil. Mina seemed to be holding up better than most: she still held the bowl, not having smashed it against Bee's head, and kept the pose despite shaking arms and legs.

Her yelp broke his reverie, and he rocked forward onto the balls of his feet. Then jumped back as the door behind him banged open.

He spun around to face a pair of vampires – Sha and Adeh – carrying something, someone between them that dripped blood across the tiles.

Bee jumped up, dropping sword and staff. "Dar!" she shouted into the shadows over her shoulder as she ran towards the door.

A clatter sounded behind him, causing Jack to turn back to the sanctuary. Mina had dropped the bowl, splashing water over her feet, up her legs. Now she was swinging her arms, as a soft moan escaped her lips. She stood mostly straight and hobbled towards him as Dar came striding out of the depths behind the altar. Sha and Adeh placed their burden down on the floor. Jack finally looked closely at what they carried. He couldn't see the face as Bee leaned over the body, but he saw the tattoo of a thistle twined with the name Magrit: Quinn.

Blood pulsed from a ragged gash in his throat. Jack sensed Mina coming to stand beside him, unsteady on her feet.

"What happened?" Bee asked.

"I don't know," said Sha.

"We sensed something, another new vampire maybe," Sha continued, glancing at Mina. "We split up to search but couldn't find it. It was muddled, like I was hearing it through water. Eventually, we regrouped. Only, well, Quinn didn't. We found him like this. Torn into, bleeding out."

"You're vampires," Mina said, the words coming slow and thick. "You're supposed to heal."

Dar looked at her. "Call the others in," he said to Sha. "And Jack, get her fed and to bed before she passes out." He nodded towards Mina as he spoke.

Mina leaned into Jack as he led her to the other end of the nave, trailed by Brett.

"It looks like you could use a drink," Brett said as they reached a quiet corner.

Jack could hear the blood pounding in Brett's veins, with Mina's pulsing slightly off tempo. Mina licked her lips and nodded. Brett took her into his arms as her knees gave way, and she sank into his embrace. Jack took a step back, arms crossed over his chest, and watched. Mina pressed her hands weakly against Brett's chest, her arms shaking as he lifted her up so her mouth was just above his collarbone, one hand across her back, the other on her ass.

Jack's jaw clenched as Mina sank her teeth into the vein that pulsed just underneath Brett's skin, below the tattoo, totally forgetting Jack's instructions to aim for the extremities until she knew her way around the major veins and arteries. Jack watched carefully, considered what would happen to Brett if she drank too much, but it seemed she was able to control herself this time: when she'd drunk enough, she slowly pulled out her fangs and kissed the puncture marks lightly. Jack's lips tensed.

"Thank you," she whispered against Brett's neck.

"No problem," he said, sliding her gently down his body until her feet were on the ground. Though he still held her close, helping her stand on unsteady legs. "It's what I'm here for."

"Though I'm sure it's not all you're good for," she said, her words slurred.

"Maybe I can show you sometime what I'm best at."

"Come on," Jack said, stepping forward and placing his arm around Mina's waist. "Time to get you to bed."

"Maybe Brett would like to come," Mina said, her head lolling back to look at Jack.

"I'm sure he would, but he's a gentleman who doesn't take advantage of impaired women." Jack looked hard at Brett, who took a step back.

Jack took her back to her room where he helped Mina out of all but the final layer of clothes, after finding that Mina's stiff arms were unable to manage the fine motor movements required to work buttons and zippers. Clad in her underwear and tank top, Mina crawled into bed.

"By tomorrow, you should be back to normal," Jack said, as he pulled the blanket over her.

"What's normal?" Mina said quietly.

Jack ignored the question, instead tucking an errant hair behind her ear. "And your thirst should be stabilized."

"Hmmm." Mina turned her face towards the wall.

"Good night," he said, standing up. "Or good morning, near enough."

"Can you turn out the light on your way out?"

RETURNING TO THE SANCTUARY, Jack found Dar kneeling beside Quinn. Jack crouched to join him, and turned Quinn's head to the side to examine the wound. The body was already cold and stiff. The dark crimson of the drying blood stood out against the ashen pallor of the skin. The blank eyes stared at the stained glass ceiling. Viscous blood pooled under the body.

"I've never seen anything like it," Jack said. He looked up at Dar.

"Me neither," Dar said, running his hand over the face, closing the empty eyes.

"The lupines tear your throat clear out," Jack said. "The incubi, the succubi, they're not capable of doing this to one of us; they need time to do this kind of damage, time we'd never give."

Dar shook his head, his uncoiffed mohawk falling over his face. "I've already gone through the catalogue of creatures in my head. Nothing I know of could do this to a vampire. Nothing would: anything capable of killing us would take the direct approach."

"And that's the other thing." Jack looked into Dar's deep brown eyes, then they both looked at the body.

"It shouldn't have killed him," Dar said.

"No. As Mina said, he should have healed."

"I don't like it." Dar's lips were thin. "I don't like having this thing here," he said, waving a hand towards the body.

"Do you want me to set up a day watch?"

"Always the warrior," Dar said, placing his hand on Jack's shoulder.

"I was born a warrior, son of warriors."

"Yes, set up a day watch. I don't want our familiars to have to face whatever did this."

"You think it will come out in the day?"

Dar shrugged. "We don't know."

"I'll take first watch," Jack said.

"While I figure out what to do with the body." Dar used the hand on Jack's shoulder to push himself up.

Jack stayed crouched beside the body.

CHAPTER SIXTEEN

WHEN MINA WOKE UP, she was still lying on her bed in her cell in her underwear. The tears had dried, but left crusty accretions at the corners of her eyes. Her back ached as she turned her head toward the room and looked at the bare, gray walls and the rough concrete floor. She looked at the small window high up the wall, painted black to block out the sun, though a few scratches let in shards of light. She looked at the armoire, worn around the edges, and empty except for her leather jacket and a spare set of bedding.

Home.

The few things she'd collected from her apartment were still in her duffel bag. She lay on the single bed with its itchy wool blanket. She rolled on to her side, back towards the wall, her cheek on the hard pillow.

The silent tears came again, against her will. She had no idea what she'd tell her brother, let alone Cam.

Hey, guess what, I'm a blood-sucker. She knew Dale worried about her, the prodigal child. And now she could never return to the fold, to the path her parents had hoped for her. He'd always been the good son: he'd gone to medical school, married a good Korean girl, had 2.5 children (if you counted the terrier as half a kid, which they did). She, on the other hand: she'd left home, gotten tattooed and, worst of all, gone to art school. She was definitely not a good catch for a nice Korean boy. Even if she weren't one of the undead.

Eventually the tears slowed to a trickle then stopped. Mina looked at the stone wall for a while longer, before getting up, drying her eyes, and rooting around in her duffel for some mostly clean clothes, settling on a pair of skinny black jeans and a T-shirt. After getting dressed, she sat down on the bed and picked up the black and white photo she'd taken from the apartment: a man and woman walking down a beach, arms around each other, a teenage boy smiling broadly, arms wide, and a quiet girl holding a shell, looking directly at the camera. Her family's last vacation before her father died. She sighed and put the photo on the desk.

Opening the door to her room, she wondered where the showers were; she assumed vampires still needed to shower, given her own funk at the moment, but she didn't care enough right then to go looking.

Instead, she headed upstairs. It was quiet and dusky, lit only by slanted shafts of light filtered through stained glass. She pegged the time as 11ish. Motes of dust drifted down from the ceiling on waves of sunshine. At first, she thought she was alone, the only sound the soft padding of the soles of her feet across the cold marble and faint orchestral music.

Then she saw the body. It was grayer now than it had been when Bee had led her away in the dark hours of the morning. Despite its pallor, the vampire looked more alive now in the weak sunlight than he had in the artificial lights of night. As she shuffled closer, she saw that the blood pooled beneath him was still tacky, though the wound looked less vicious.

"Any ideas?"

Mina spun around, and lowered her center of gravity. As Jack approached from the shadows, have risen silently from Bee's stool, she breathed deeply, forcing her heart into a more normal cadence and her body into a casual stance.

"Hmm? Ideas about what?" she said, finally pegging Jack as the source of the humming in her blood.

"What kills an immortal in a way that's not accounted for in the Hierarchy?"

"It wasn't another vampire?" she asked, her voice swallowed by the empty space.

"No, we use weapons: silver bullets, neck-severing blades, ash stakes," Jack said, his voice equally muted. "Not teeth and claws."

"So what uses teeth and claws?"

"Creatures of the forest, of the earth, the Werekind maybe. But the full moon is passed, and they don't leave bodies around to be found. They don't tear a chunk out of you; they tear you apart."

"Oh." Mina looked at the body, then back at Jack. "Maybe it was interrupted?"

"They tear apart anything that interrupts them. And if they don't tear you apart, you live, you heal." Jack nodded towards the body. "Does he look alive?"

Mina looked over the body. His skin was ashen, his face sunken. Even his lips were gray, and his fingernails blackened. He had definitely not healed. She thought about what Jack had said, then looked back at him quickly.

"So you're saying you don't know what killed him?" In that moment, Mina felt more fearful of her new life than she had as of yet.

But only for a second – then that fear was eclipsed by terror. The body opened its eyes and grasped at the air with a clawed hand. Mina jumped back. Jack pulled out a gun, silencer already in place. The body looked at Mina, its eyes completely black in its gray face. It bared its teeth, all of which were sharp and pointed, not just the long canines of a vampire. It rolled over, onto hands and knees, and its upper lip and nose twitched as it smelled the world around it. When it stood, Mina heard tearing, the clothes no longer fitting the extended limbs and contorted torso – it towered well over six feet, taller than Quinn had been. Those limbs lunged at Mina. She dove out of the way, rolling herself to standing, relying on muscle memory from long ago martial arts lessons: she may not have remembered much but she remembered how to fall.

When Mina evaded its grasp, the creature turned its attention to Jack. A fraction of a second later, a bullet entered its chest. The creature howled but continued its advance. Only when Jack fired four more shots in quick succession did the creature spin on its heels and flee towards the doors, the wood splintering as it hurtled through them like a bowling ball. Mina and Jack both gave chase but by the time they reached the broken doors, it was loping along the rooftops down the street, blending into the twilight.

"What just happened?" Mina asked as others, drawn by the creature's howl, joined them on the porch.

"I don't know," Jack said.

DAR LOOKED AT THE GROUP gathered in the nave just before nightfall. Tense, edgy and serious: that would keep them alive or lead to the knee-jerk reactions that meant death. He racked his brain for something to give them some peace of mind, but his tense, edgy mind came up empty.

"We patrol in groups of at least two, and you're never out of sight of each other." Dar divided them up into groups and handed out patrol assignments to all except Bee.

"What about you?" Jack asked. "You just said we shouldn't be alone."

"My errand isn't as dangerous," Dar said. "I need to see the priest."

"Why?" Mina asked, only half aware that she'd said it out loud until the others looked at her. She scanned the faces before returning to Dar. "Why do you need a priest?"

"To reconsecrate our home. Quinn was one of the invited. It's possible that, whatever he is now, he could come back. Hopefully reconsecration will keep him out."

"Hopefully?"

"Hopefully."

"And priests do that, bless the nests of vampires?"

"Some priests do."

"Like the priest who served me up to Jack," Mina said, looking sidelong at Jack before returning her attention to Dar.

"Priests like Father Pietro, yes," Jack said. "Ones who realize that stubborn doesn't equal bad."

"Priests who realize that there's more than one kind of vampire," Dar added. "Who know that not everything that goes bump in the night is evil. And after the priest, I need to see the Librarian."

"There's an unknown creature killing out there, and you're going to the library?" Mina said.

"Not to the library, to the Librarian. Now form up and head out."

"Make sure you take blades," Jack said, as he moved towards the weapons cupboards "Silver bullets just seem to make it mad."

"What about me?" Bee asked Dar. He looked at Mina.

"Continue Mina's training."

"But...."

"Accelerate it, push her as hard as you can. Skip the Shaolin 'break you down so I can build you up, meditate your way to being a warrior' part. We need you both out there as soon as possible."

Bee looked at Mina, the woman's face unreadable.

"HAVE YOU HAD SOMETHING to drink?" Bee asked Mina when they had the sanctuary to themselves, the others gone on patrol and the familiars off in the bowels of the building.

"No." Mina shifted from one foot to the other. She had decided to forgo the drink, not quite to terms with that part of her new life yet. She couldn't bring herself to sidle up to a familiar and ask for a sip of their blood.

"Your mistake. Take this." Bee threw a wooden stave at her.

She grasped it out of the air. "I'm supposed to fight a monster with a stick?"

"Sometimes, yes. Sometimes a stick is all you have."

"My dad had more fire power when he went looking for monsters under my bed." The image of her dad on his hands and knees with a baseball bat surfaced from the cool, deep pool of memory.

"Overkill. Creatures that hide under beds are scared of their own shadows." Bee picked up another staff, tested its weight, and turned to face her. "Hit me."

"What?"

Bee arced the staff low in one hand and swiped at Mina's legs. Mina was on her ass before she realized what had happened. This was not the first time she'd wished she was a little less bony.

Bee took a step back. "Up."

"Huh?"

Her mentor took a deep breath and spoke slowly. "Get up and hit me."

Mina got to her feet and looked at Bee warily. Years of kumdo lessons, the Korean way of the sword, made her hold the staff with both hands together, like she would a bamboo jukdo. She pulled the staff back over her shoulder and swung at Bee: *chwa pegi*, a strike across her torso. Bee grabbed the far end with her free hand and sent the butt into Mina's abdomen. She managed to stay standing despite wanting to throw up.

"Too slow if you're going to try something like that. And staffs are too long for that kind of strike. Keep it in front of you, hands apart until you're ready to strike." Bee demonstrated with her own staff. "And don't advertise your moves so blatantly."

As Bee circled around her, Mina watched her moves, keeping herself facing her opponent and her centre of gravity low. She moved her hands shoulder-width apart, one facing up and one facing down, to match Bee's stance.

"Better," Bee said as she watched Mina change her posture and mirror her own movements. Mina flushed.

"Now hit me," her teacher said.

"I'm getting tired of hearing that."

"So stop complaining and do it."

Mina tried again. She drove the left end of the staff towards her opponent, with more speed and force this time, surprising herself. The right end hit her shoulder when her teacher blocked the move. Bee's staff hit her hand, channeling the force into her fingers.

"Bloody hell!" Mina dropped her staff and shook her hand out. "You almost broke my hand." She looked at Bee, hoping her face conveyed how pissed off she was. She saw a total lack of sympathy. She scooped up her staff, keeping her eyes on Bee. "Right. I'm a vampire. I'll heal."

"Maybe you're not such a slow learner after all," Bee said as she started to circle again. "You will heal. Unless I stabbed you through the heart with the sharpened end of one of these. Ashwood kills."

Mina prepared to strike again. Her lips pursed and her nostrils flared. She watched for an opening as Bee moved around her, arcing her staff in a blur of movement. Mina wanted to wipe the sweat off her forehead, somewhat disgruntled that vampires sweat, but didn't dare drop her guard.

As she focused, the blur seemed to slow down, to coalesce. She realized that Bee's swinging wasn't random. Her teacher was showing her what to do, if she paid attention and picked out the threads. Like Bee said, Mina was a quick learner, especially when it came to the physical, and within the hour, she'd managed to strike Bee. Looking at the chagrin on Bee's face, Mina took it as a victory, even though she would be covered with bruises from all the hits Bee had landed. In the second hour, Mina's previous victory was outshone when her teacher ended up on her ass. Her celebration didn't last long when Bee took her gloating as an opportunity to knock her feet out from under her.

And the night didn't end there. After a quick break, they continued for a few more hours, with staffs and grappling, until the others returned for a midnight snack and roll call. Mina was so engrossed in sparring that she didn't realize that the audience had grown beyond the three familiars who had followed them back from their earlier break. It was only when she knocked Bee down for the second time that night that the smattering of applause cued her into the gathering crowd. She looked around to see a group of seven watching them. Including Jack.

"How often have you been taken down on the first night of sparring?" Jack asked, looking down at Bee.

Bee didn't respond. Instead she held out her hand for Mina to help her up.

"Good job," Bee said. "We've done enough for now. Take a break. Then I think we can step it up to blades."

Mina bowed, falling back into years of habit, causing Bee to smirk. She headed downstairs, away from the crowd of relative strangers. Once in her room, she stripped off her sweaty clothes. She was digging through her duffel bag for something fresh to wear, noting that she needed to head back to her apartment soon, when she heard a knock on the door. She stood behind it, opening it a crack, aware that she was half-naked.

"I thought you might be thirsty."

Mina smiled and opened the door all the way. Brett flashed a toothy smile back, stepped into her room and closed the door behind him.

CHAPTER SEVENTEEN

DAR FOUND FATHER PIETRO at confession.

"Forgive me Father for I have sinned." Dar looked through the screen at the priest he had known since the man's early days in the cloth, a rising star in Rome, recently out of the seminary. And still disbelieving the knowledge a senior priest had just shared with him, that the handsome, young foreigner lighting a candle was over two thousand years old. Dar had bared his fangs and turned the priest's world upside down. Pietro had tried not to like him as he wrestled with that new knowledge of a demon-haunted world.

"I'm sure you have, Dar. But what brings you my way?"

"Are you free? Can we walk and talk? I need a priest at the Sanctuary."

"That doesn't sound good."

"No, it's not. Bring some holy water."

"Let's walk then."

Father Pietro found another priest to take confession. The young man looked Dar over with a wrinkle on his eyebrows and a flare to his nostrils. Dar gave him his most lascivious smile, like a rent boy looking for a john. The young priest flashed wide eyes to Father Pietro but silently did as he was asked. Then the two of them headed out into the leaden, drizzly day.

"I didn't expect to see you again so soon," Father Pietro said. "You haven't lost your newest recruit to other side, have you?"

"Mina?" Dar shook his head. "No. She's still with us. Though perhaps not one of us yet."

"How is she?"

"Bee says she's a quick learner. A natural fighter."

"Not what I asked," the priest said.

Dar sighed. "She's stubborn, and reluctant to accept her new life."

Pietro barked a dry laugh. "Ha, it's only been three days since her world turned upside down. How long did it take you to accept the change?"

Dar glanced at the priest. "I don't know that we have that kind of time."

"I like this one," Pietro said, fingering his crucifix. "So, if not that, then what brings a heathen like you to my church today?"

"Quinn's dead." Dar turned up the collar of his wool coat and tightened the cashmere scarf around his neck. "Sort of."

Father Pietro was quiet for a minute. Dar knew that he had counseled Quinn after his turning; at one point Quinn had been bound for the seminary himself. Before Magrit.

"Sort of?" Pietro said. "Death isn't usually a sort-of kind of thing."

"I'm sort of dead." He looked at the priest sideways.

"Fair enough. Why is Quinn different?"

"He was attacked, lacerations in his neck and shoulder." Dar scanned the street. "It shouldn't have killed him; even as bad as it was, he should have healed."

"But he didn't."

"No. He was most definitely dead."

"Was?" Pietro asked, his eyebrow arched.

Dar nodded slowly, scanning the sidewalk ahead of them, glancing over his shoulder. "Until this morning, when he arose. Changed."

"Changed how?"

"Not in a good way, Pietro. He was ashen, his eyes black, all his teeth pointed. And he was faster, stronger." Dar paused. "He got away from Jack."

"Really? Unusual." Dar nodded and Pietro continued. "Any idea what happened? What he changed into?"

"No, it's not something I've seen before. And I've seen a lot." They walked in silence for a bit. "I gather it doesn't ring a bell with you?"

Father Pietro shook his head. "I can ask around though. Someone in the order might have some clue. And this is why you came to me today?" the priest continued as he entered into the Sanctuary.

"Yes, I'd like you to reconsecrate it in the hope that it will prevent the thing that was Quinn from coming back home unannounced."

HE SHAMBLED THROUGH the overcast alleyways and back streets, scratching his shin as he tore away the fabric that bound it. He kept quiet, trying to ignore the burning in his chest where scabs were forming over wounds that were still raw and oozing. He was having less success ignoring the gnawing in his belly. His serrated teeth gnashed.

Food. Flesh. The wound would heal. He just needed to find food without getting hurt again. Though the pain and the hunger cloaked his mind, he did recall one thing: he was a hunter. He stopped. He stilled. He listened to the world buzzing beyond the shadows. He heard the shuffle, the breathing in and out, the easy thump-a-da pulse of prey unaware of a predator. He shifted closer to the edge of the shadows, not quite touching the light. He lifted his chin and sniffed the air, scenting the sweat and metallic tang of food. He turned his head at a faint scratch. He smelled the air again, mouth open, lips taut.

This sound was not food. He inched into the void between the buildings. His black eyes sought out the faint traces of cloudy light and neon that seeped into this dim crevice. He saw something move further along the way. Gray against black.

His nostrils flared as he smelt the air. The source of the sound stopped, and turned its head partway back. He stood as still as stone, poised on the edge of fight or flight. Slowly the thing turned its face to him, dragging its cargo around. He sniffed and inched closer. It sniffed and inched closer. He tilted his head this way, and it tilted its head that way. A mirror image of himself.

His black eyes narrowed and the tension in his mouth eased as he crept up to it and smelled it face, his movements mimicked by the other creature.

His eyes slid sideways, downward to its cargo. The creature aped his movements, every muscle tense. A pause, then the tension eased slightly as the creature shifted, in an unmistakable offer to share its meal.

CHAPTER EIGHTEEN

DAR KNOCKED AGAIN, harder, on the door of the basement apartment in the old brownstone. Finally, he sensed movement on the other side and waited with the stillness of a corpse. A few minutes later, he felt a pause on the other side of the door then heard various latches being drawn back before the door opened a crack.

Two rheumy eyes, their piercing blue faded to soft cornflower, peered at him from behind a pair of thick glasses. The man's head bobbed on a lanky, neglected frame, though Dar could still see the finely carved features beneath the thin skin and white stubble. The man's hands, covered in ink stains, came up to his head and dug through wild silver hair until they found what they were searching for. He swapped the thick glasses for a slightly less thick pair.

"Darius." The man scratched the stubble on his jowl. "Long time no see. Why are you darkening my doorstep this day?"

Dar felt his guilt at avoiding Rhys gnaw at his stomach. People called Rhys the Librarian; Dar knew he would be happier if they'd called him hermit and left him alone.

"Hello to you too, Rhys. I was hoping you could help me solve a puzzle." He watched Rhys' curiosity battle his reluctance. But Dar knew the Librarian's weakness: curiosity always won.

"Come on in then. I suppose the place is due for another sprinkling of holy water, though it means calling a priest." Rhys' voice faded to a mutter as he led the way down a long hallway. He said that every time, though he never left Dar standing on the stoop. "Maybe try a rabbi this time. Might have more success."

Dar glanced over his shoulder then followed Rhys into his apartment. Piles of paper and old books formed a maze. Dar expected to find Rhys buried under all the stuff one of these days.

Rhys' green-eyed cat hissed and swiped a taloned paw at Dar from the top of one of the stacks. Dar hissed back. The smoky cat glared at him then seemed to decide on an uneasy truce, saving itself to fight another day. It found another perch from which to eye him. Although it refrained from hissing, a low growl escaped from deep in its belly.

"Grey's always been a good judge of character," Rhys said without looking back. They arrived at what served as Rhys' desk. The only difference between this space and the rest of the apartment was the chair and the slightly shorter piles of books and papers that covered the surface. A small oil heater sat beside the desk. Rhys bent over one of the stacks and shifted some of its contents to another pile until a chair appeared, disturbing a layer of dust and cat hair.

Rhys coughed into the sleeve of his sweater. "Have a seat then."

Dar took the proffered seat and crossed his hands over his lap. He wondered what was up with his old friend: Rhys was in a mood, even for him.

"I'd offer you some tea but since you'd get no pleasure out of it, it'd be a damnable waste. I hope you don't mind if I enjoy a cup." Dar said nothing, just inclined his head. He watched as Rhys filled a tea-stained cup from a tea-cozied pot that had been hidden behind one of the heaps on his desk. Eyes closed, Rhys took a long sip of the steaming black tea, his fingers wrapped around the china. Finally, he opened his eyes and looked at Dar.

"So what's this puzzle then?"

Dar explained what had happened to Quinn: how he'd been attacked minutes after being separated from the others and died of injuries he should have survived; how they'd brought him back home; and how he had risen, changed.

"Quinn?" Rhys said, scratching a note on a scrap of paper. "He's a new one?"

"Not the point, Rhys." Dar sighed and started to lean forward then thought better of it as the chair teetered. "What kills a vampire when it shouldn't die? What caused him to change like that?"

"You don't know?"

"No. That's the puzzle. Do you?" Dar watched as the gears clicked behind Rhys' watery blue eyes.

"No." Rhys made another scratch on another scrap then blew on his tea. "It's just rare to hear you admit there's something you don't know."

"That's why I'm here. You're the one person I can turn to when there's something I don't know."

"Oh, flattery will get you everywhere. Always did." Rhys let a small smile slip out, then lifted the cup to take another sip of tea. "No, I don't like this. If you're here, it means Matteo may soon be haunting me."

"Don't invite him in."

"Well, yes," Rhys said. "That's all well and good. But I do go out, you know. I don't just sit here waiting for you to call."

"So you don't know what this is, Rhys?"

"Hmm? Not a clue. Off the top of my head." Which he proceeded to scratch. "Now let's see. There's the *Vampiricon* – the encyclopedia of all things bloodsucking." Rhys put his cup down and tottered over to one of the many piles and placed a hand on top of it. "No, not there. Where did I put you?"

He scratched his jowl and looked around, pointing at piles with an inky finger and making indeterminate sounds. "Ah, of course," he said, pointing at Dar. He moved towards Dar and bent double, surprisingly flexible for his age. "Up, up, old man."

Dar looked down and saw Rhys reaching for something under the back leg of the chair. He stood up as Rhys pulled an enormous volume, about the size of a small tombstone, out from under the chair.

"Got that chair off the street, if you can believe it. Has a broken back leg that needs fixing. But this is the perfect size to prop it for now." He placed another book under said leg, then let go of the chair, which teetered precariously but didn't fall.

"Hmm. Hold this." Rhys handed Dar the book while he dug around for a couple more to prop up the chair.

Dar looked at the ancient book. Faint traces of gold still graced the smooth brown cover. The title was in Arabic, a language he'd never learned to read. He'd left Persia before the Arabs descended from the west. He supposed he should take a stab at learning more than a few passing phrases, since it seemed like the language was here to stay. He stroked the cover then opened it to an intricate illustration of a lamia gorging on her dinner, said dinner lying limp in her arms. Iridescent green scales covered her naked body, and gold thread and gems were woven into her black hair. Her lips were the same shade of red as the wound in the man's chest. Her face was soft but her eyes fierce. She looked like someone he knew, if he stared long enough maybe he could work out who. The book snapped shut, Rhys' sun-speckled hands on Dar's. Rhys took the book from him.

"Greater men than you have gotten lost in these books."

Rhys sat down and Dar followed his lead, carefully, as the chair now listed slightly to the right. The Librarian's mouth moved silently between absent-minded sips of tea, as he opened the book and flipped through the pages, pausing even now and then to caress a page with his fingertips.

Dar sat still as stone for ten minutes, his features smooth as marble. For another ten, he picked up and put down all of the books within easy reach. "Anything yet?" he asked when his patience petered out.

Rhys' head shot up. "What? Oh, no. Very interesting stuff. But no, no answer to your puzzle. This could take a while. And the answer might not even be here. I might have to search other books, scrolls, the Interwebs even." He indicated a dusty square on his desk that Dar realized was a laptop. "There's a surprising amount of information out there on the things that hide in the dark."

"Maybe I should come back?" Dar said, as Rhys returned to scanning the book.

"Hmmm?" Rhys looked up again, his eyebrows pulled together. "Oh yes, that would probably be best."

"Call me if you find anything." Dar handed him yet another card with his phone number on it, even though he was sure he'd given him a hundred already. He placed his hand on Rhys' head, feeling the warmth through the silver hair, before letting his hand fall to his friend's bony shoulder. "You do still have a phone, don't you?"

"Oh yes, of course. It's even one of those new-fangled wireless things," he said as he patted an empty pocket without looking up from the book.

THE CREATURE THAT HAD been Quinn followed his new companion to its lair, staying a step behind and off to the side, where it could keep an eye on him. Its head stayed cocked to one side, its catch held on the far side, away from him. Every once in a while, the cargo hit a bump and made a sound. He could smell it. His stomach gnashed at his intestines.

But he made no move towards it. Not yet. Two hunters were better than one, even though it meant they needed to share their meals. He wasn't sure if it realized that yet. So he shuffled after it, making small gurgling noises. It led him down into a dingy basement that was dank but out of the unrelenting rain. And it was dark, without the snakes and shards of piercing light cast by the wet night.

It laid its load on the moist cement, and crouched over one end. The juicy end, with the tastiest bits. It looked at him, its black eyes glinting red in the faint emergency lighting. It sunk its teeth into the flesh of the neck and tore off a piece, all the while keeping an eye on him. It gnawed and rended flesh from bone. He crouched at the far end of the body and shredded sheer fabric from flesh with his fingernails. A sound rumbled deep in the other one's throat but it made no move towards him. Slowly he raised the leg to his teeth and tore in. He had to rend through stringy sinew but it was food.

And so they shared their first meal together, wary but accepting, both sated. For now.

CHAPTER NINETEEN

MINA LICKED THE LAST few drops of blood off of Brett's leg, before snaking her tongue up his torso on her way to his lips. Maybe she could get used to this life after all. Brett smiled at her as she knelt over him, drops from her still wet hair falling on his slick chest. She smiled back, images of the shower he'd helped her find flashing through her mind. He started to run his hands up her back. Mina groaned before placing her hands over his and pushing them back down by his sides.

"Mmm. I need to get back before Bee comes looking for me," she said.

"Why? She might want to join us."

Mina arched an eyebrow, and her lips twitched at the thought.

"What?" he said. "It'd get you out of training."

"You know, with Bee, I don't think it would." Her smile fell away. "Besides, I have a feeling I might need to put the training into practice soon. There've been rumours of more attacks. On people. Not just vampires." Slowly, languidly, she got up. Once dressed, she threw a smile over her shoulder at the still-naked Brett. "Take care out there," she said before heading out the door. She found Bee in the narthex talking to someone she didn't know, though she knew in her blood that the someone was not a vampire – she felt the buzz in her veins, overlaid with a pitter pat percussion she associated with Bee. A familiar, Mina thought, noting the tattoo on the man's neck when he turned his head, his long hair falling away.

"You look refreshed, if not rested," Bee said, her dark eyes travelling over Mina. "Have you met Ari?" The man's hand dropped from Bee's arm as he gave a curt nod of greeting, causing his dark curls to flop forward again. "Ari, this is Mina, our newest vampire." Mina tilted her head and smiled. Ari responded with a small upturn of his lips that didn't reach the bright blue eyes rimmed with black eyeliner.

"Time to get back to work," Bee said. She ran her hand down the man's back. "See you later, Ari?" The man's lips bloomed into a full smile that revealed perfect, white teeth. This smile did reach his eyes.

Mina followed Bee to the nave, glancing back at Ari. The smile was gone. He looked at her with narrowed eyes before turning to go.

Bee walked to the arcade and opened a drawer. The contents shone even in the dim half light. Mina reached a hand out, lightly running her fingertips along the cold metal of a simple, single-edged sword, following its slight curve to a double-handed, leather-bound hilt, which she made to grasp.

"Not yet," Bee said. "We work with the short blades first. Much more useful in the city. But you have good taste: that katana was made by a master swordsmith."

She handed Mina a pair of sai. Mina grasped a cord-wrapped handle in each hand, keeping her fingers on what she presumed was the safe side of the prongs, away from the long hexagonal shaft that tapered to a point. Bee soon disabused her of that notion with a rap on her knuckles.

"Ow," Mina pulled her hands in.

"Not like that," Bee said. "First position is always defensive. The baton...." She stopped when Mina's head tilted sideways. "The pointy bit, or baton, should be back along the inside of your arm, your thumb around the inside of one prong, your fingers around the outside of the other. That way, if someone attacks, you just lift your arm." Bee positioned Mina's arm, first with forearm and elbow out to the side, then in front of her forehead. "The blade strikes the sai instead of you. Stay still." Bee stepped back and aimed the pointy baton at Mina's arm. Sure enough, when it struck this time, the sting was lessened...though still there, the reverberations of metal on metal travelling along the length of the sai instead of into her bones. Following fast on the lesson of first position, which Mina was pretty sure Bee had made up, the other uses of the sai blurred one into the next. She found her cadence, growing accustomed to their weight and balance, and used them as an extension of her body, from toe to finger tip, spinning and flipping them as she and Bee danced around each other, looking for gaps in each other's defense, places to strike and jab.

After an hour of this, Mina felt she needed another shower, her skin slick and the hair on her neck damp. She was grateful for the cording around the handle. It chafed her hands but her sweaty palms kept their grip. In that moment's distraction, Mina let her guard down and Bee drove the pommel of a sai into her solar plexus, finding that space between sternum and navel. Mina had the breath taken out of her, and Bee took the hesitation to hook her left leg around Mina's. Mina went down on her knees, grasping the hilt of the sai. She looked at Bee's feet as the other woman paused to convey some lesson, her sai at her side. That's when Mina drove the pointy bit of her right sai at Bee's exposed abdomen where the tip made contact. Bee managed a step back while Mina, from her crouch, twisted back and around, kicking her left leg out and sweeping Bee's feet from under her.

"Fuck!"

The profanity cut through the rush in Mina's ears. She stopped and turned to her teacher; she hadn't heard Bee swear as of yet. The other woman looked at her, eyes narrowed.

Mina's eyes widened, and a flutter rose in her abdomen. "Sorry. I got carried away."

Bee shook her head slowly. "Don't be sorry. You need to be deadly to survive in our world." Her teacher gave her a small smile as she pressed a hand to her abdomen. "It just usually takes a little longer to get my pupils to this point. Besides I'll heal. I'll bruise but I'll heal." Mina tilted her head and arched an eyebrow. Bee's smile became larger.

At that point, they replaced the sai with a pair of daggers. These Mina practiced throwing, though not for long. After the first few errant blades, she found their balance and hit the target time after time.

Then came the long blades. Bee handed her the sword she'd admired earlier, along with a leather gauntlet for her forearm.

"This is real," she said, her voice quiet, as she looked at the ghostly blue blade. She'd only ever used bamboo, wood and blunted metal in the kumdo classes her father had signed her up for.

"Yes, and sharp."

"How do we keep from getting hurt?" She remembered the heavy armour she'd had to wear as a teenager, and that was against bamboo.

"Try not to get in the way of the blade," Bee said.

Mina laughed but when she looked at her, she saw no sign that Bee was joking.

"Try to avoid the head and the heart when we spar. There's no silver in the blade, so if you get hit elsewhere, it won't poison you. It'll just hurt like hell."

"But I'll heal." Mina's lips pulled down.

"You're starting to get the hang of this," Bee said, then sank back into the ready stance: right foot forward, left heel raised, sword grasped in both hands, point towards Mina.

After another sweaty hour and a half, Bee called a stop to the training from where she stood with her back against a pillar and the point of Mina's sword at her throat.

"I think you've got the basic idea of the blades," she said, pushing aside the sword tip, looking at Mina with tight eyes and a furrowed forehead. Mina felt the sting of the cut across her thigh, bemoaning the wrecked pants, and doubted she had the hang of it.

"Tomorrow night: projectiles." Bee walked over to the arcade and opened another couple of cupboards. Inside the first cupboard were blow guns with barbed darts of wood and metal, then came crossbows and bolts of assorted sizes and styles. The last one contained guns, great and small. Mina ran her fingertips lightly over one of the guns. Bee slapped her hand away.

"Tomorrow. And we start with non-explosive projectiles. Now, the sun's almost up. Time for bed."

"But why put off until tomorrow what we can do today?"

Bee didn't respond. She just looked at Mina for a few seconds, the furrow returning with a frown, before turning and heading towards the stairs.

A SCARLET FEVER

Dar was the last to return to the Sanctuary, sliding in just as the first rays slid over the horizon.

"Aren't you cutting it a bit close, old man?" Jack asked as he shifted from the shadows and followed Dar to join the others on the dais. Though Darius would never say, Jack had seen how the sun affected him more each day, more than the others.

"I thought you liked taking risks," Dar answered.

"Only if the risks get results. What did you find out?"

"Before we get to the debrief, I'd like to hear how our newest recruit is doing on her accelerated training program." Everyone turned to Bee.

She grunted. "I'm sure you've all heard that she managed to knock me off my feet."

"On your ass, you mean?" Simon said with a grin. Bee ignored him.

"She's doing well then?"

"Beyond well. She has the most raw talent that I've seen in a very long while." Bee looked at Simon, her penultimate trainee. "Sorry." Bee shrugged, a small smile creeping into her lips. "And she learns at a phenomenal speed." The smile slipped from her face.

Dar nodded. His mohawk followed the bobbing of his head, and the rings in his ears, brows and nose glinted as they caught the light. "Now, what about the creature?"

Jack spoke first. "I followed the police, listened in on their conversations. People have disappeared, most of them homeless, but enough that the police are noticing. Mutilated corpses turn up a few days later. They haven't a clue what they're up against."

"Simon and I went downtown, chatted with the kids there," Sha said, her voice small in the open space. "The street kids are scared, talking serial killer."

"The homeless are the same," Adeh said. "They know there's something out there, they just don't know what. But they weren't talking serial killer; they say monster. Of course, everyone just thinks they're off their meds."

"The Necrophagos seem to be in the same boat as us," Elijah said. "We crossed paths with a few of them last night. They weren't very forthcoming, but they looked like they were searching for something."

"They spent a lot of time looking in shadows, checking over shoulders," Fatima added. "Just like us."

"We're all on duty again tomorrow night," Dar said. "Until we figure out what this thing is, and how to kill it."

"Any luck on that front?" Jack asked.

Dar shook his head, frowning. "Nothing. The Librarian is on the hunt. But he didn't know. Neither did Pietro." He looked hard at his hands, as if the lines of his palms held the answers. "No one knows what this thing is."

CHAPTER TWENTY

DESPITE THE FACT THAT it was an unseasonably sunny day outside, Rhys' apartment was dark except for the blue glow from the computer screen, reflected in his glasses, and the green cast of an old banker's lamp.

He lifted the dainty, flowered teacup to his lips, once again forgetting that he'd already finished it. He lifted the cozy from a teapot that matched the cup, right down to the chip on the rim. He swirled it around, frowning when he didn't feel the ebb and flow of liquid amber. The tea would have to wait – a contented cat purred on his lap and he was following a thread that might disappear if he let it go. He found the Web aptly named: he could follow delicate filaments to troves of information, then get snared in the tendrils or find them destroyed under his touch.

He reached for the mouse to scroll down the page he was on, seeking a link, a tasty tidbit that would lead him along some interesting new thread. He lifted his glasses and rubbed his nose then returned to scanning, his eyes flitting over lines of text until they found something to latch onto. He scratched Grey between the ears, and was rewarded by renewed purring. Otherwise Grey showed no signs of rousing. Rhys picked up a pencil, tapped the desk, then put it down. He scratched behind his own ear. He lifted the teacup to his lips, avoiding the chip. His brow furrowed. He scrolled down. He put the still-empty teacup back on the desk.

He stopped, and went still for a second before he clicked the link. The page loaded, line by agonizing line, until an image appeared, taken from an ancient manuscript. Rhys started scanning the lines of text in an archaic script but the movement of his eyes across the screen soon slowed. A pit formed in his bowels. Grey shifted and started pawing his stomach.

There would be no tea for a while yet.

CHAPTER TWENTY-ONE

UNABLE TO SLEEP, MINA headed upstairs. She was getting better at avoiding the creak in the stairs, or she was stepping more lightly, despite the boots. At the top of the dark stairwell, she listened, her ears keyed for any sound. All was quiet except the thrum of her pulse in her ears.

She needed to get out. Not for good, just for a bit. To be alone. All these people, all the time, it made her skin crawl and her blood itch. One reason she and Cam made good roommates: they left each other alone often enough.

"Fuck," she whispered. She needed to call Cam. But not here. She took the last step, focused on the door, her means of egress, ignoring the jumble in her brain, the buzz in her veins, the percussive brass in her ears.

Dusty shafts of blue light cut across the open space. Mina stopped short.

Jack swirled in and out of the spears of light, causing eddies in the dust, practicing a kata of some sort. His moves were liquid. But watching the muscles of his bare torso tense and flex, Mina didn't doubt they could be as hard as ice.

His feet made only a soft shush on the marble floor. As soon as Mina stepped into the cavernous space, he stopped and turned to face her, even though she made no sound to betray her presence. His dark eyes traveled over her. She shifted.

"Sorry," Mina said. "I didn't realize anyone was here."

He watched her for a second before answering. "You should have," he said as he stepped up to her. "Get out of your head. Listen to your heart and you'll always know when a vamp is near." She tensed, holding her breath, until he reached down to the chair beside her, grabbing his shirt. "Still trying to escape?"

Mina slowly moved her head from side to side. "No. I just need some breathing space." She pulled her phone out of her bag. "And I need to call my roommate before she calls the police."

He took a step away. "So you're settling into your new life?"

"I wouldn't say settling." She paused as he pulled the black T-shirt over his head. "But maybe accepting." She stepped into the muted halo of light cast by the starry stained glass dome.

Jack nodded, and stepped aside as she passed him. "Good enough. Though it's better if you die."

"Excuse me?"

"Easier on you and safer for your loved ones if you're dead to them," he said, looking at the floor.

An image of Dale, Hana and their kids rose to the surface. "I doubt my funeral would be easy on them."

"Easier, not easy."

"If you say so." Mina paused at the door, recognizing the source of an itch at the back of her brain. She turned back to him. "Why is it always so quiet in here?"

Jack went still. "What do you mean 'so quiet'?" he asked, in carefully measured words.

Mina shifted her weight from one boot heel to the other. "I mean, I hear you and the others. But, well, I know it's massive stone and all, but it's mid-afternoon outside that door. I guess I expect some street noise to seep in. But it's like a cave."

"You don't hear the street?" he asked, as he stepped close again.

"No?" Mina started to shake her head, but stopped when he grabbed her arm in iron fingers. "Ow! Would you all stop doing that?"

"Don't mention this to anyone else," he said, his voice low and hoarse, his face impossibly paler, as he looked over his shoulder towards the stairs to the basement.

"What's the big deal?" Mina's hackles started to rise, and she pulled her arm free as he loosened his grasp. "I'll mention it if I feel like it."

"Let's go for a walk," he said, as he slid on his flip flops.

Mina started to protest but the look on his face stopped her.

"You wanted to get out," he continued. "Let's get out."

Mina let him lead her outside, past the gates onto the street without a word, not even to correct him – not even to say that she had wanted to get out to be alone.

"Will you tell me what this is about? What's wrong with it being quiet in there?"

"The fact that it wasn't?" he said. "It was muted but not silent. I could hear the police sirens, the taxi horns, the jackhammer down the street." As he mentioned the sounds, Mina heard them too, as if someone had turned them on just then. "You shouldn't be able to filter like that, being a new dhamphir. I have to work to do it, even as a dracul."

"So?"

"So you were doing it without even realizing, let alone trying. That's something even most nosferata find difficult, to shut out extraneous sensation."

"Oh." Mina still wasn't entirely clear on this Hierarchy thing.

"The others might suspect you've been bitten again, even that you're a nosferat. Then they'd have to kill you."

"Oh."

"Yeah. Oh."

Mina pursed her forehead. "Well, it wasn't completely quiet," she said. "Now that I think about it, I did hear your song, and the songs of the other vampires, like they were through water."

"My song?"

"Yeah, your blood song. You told me about it, the buzzing."

"Buzzing, yes. More a sensation than a sound." Jack stopped, forcing her to do the same. He took her wrist gently this time, and looked at her. "And it's the same for every vampire. Different for Were, for demons, for each category in the Hierarchy but not each individual."

Mina nostrils tensed as she tried to think of something to say. Unsuccessful, she started walking again, and Jack kept beside her. She felt the imprint of his fingers on her skin, even though his hand was no longer on her wrist.

They walked down the road for a few minutes, accompanied only by the sound of Mina's heels clacking and Jack's flip flops slapping on the pavement. Mina forced herself to open her ears to the noise around her, but then the sounds became overwhelming and she had to shut them out, just picking out the useful sounds from the cacophony.

"I'm not. A nosferat, I mean. You know, I haven't been let out on my own yet."

"We don't know what happened to you before we found you."

Mina started to respond, but changed topics instead. "I need to go back to my apartment. To pick up a few things. I need to tell Cam something."

"Give me time to get properly dressed and I can go with you. If you want."

Mina nodded. She found she no longer wanted to be alone.

MINA'S PHONE RANG AS she and Jack wended their way along the city streets towards her apartment, the sound snapping the silence that hung between them. She felt Jack's eyes slide her way behind his dark sunglasses. She realized now, during these lengthy daylight excursions, that he wasn't trying at cool with his mirrored aviator shades; she'd forgotten hers and a knot of tension was settling in between her eyes. So not totally impervious to sunlight.

She dug her phone out of her bag: Cam returning her call. Mina had called and left a message for her roommate as soon as she and Jack had left the Sanctuary. She barely had time to eke out a 'hi' before Cam stopped her.

"Where have you been?" Cam said, her voice abnormally even, before switching into overdrive, her voice getting louder with each word. "Do you realize that I've been worried sick? Do you care?"

Mina cringed, recalling how Cam had seen her through her mother's illness and death. She glanced towards Jack, sure he could hear the words that stung her ear. She pulled the phone away from her head as Cam added a few choice words in Italian; Mina didn't need to know the language to understand what Cam was saying.

"Why haven't you called?" Cam added, in a slightly quieter voice, having vented.

"Sorry, I...." Mina started to bite her lip, before the copper tang reminded her of her budding fangs. She scanned the street ahead, pausing as a bus up ahead disgorged its passengers. She avoided looking at Jack. "I went to my brother's, hoping Hana could nurse me back to health." Mina slowed her pace as she neared the gaggle of commuters; Jack followed her lead. "I left a note."

"That's no reason not to call. Would your brother let me know if you died?" Mina didn't think 'yes' was the response Cam was looking for. Her friend's voice softened slightly as she continued. "I was worried."

"I'm sorry, I was just so sick, with the vomiting and the shaking. Not good...."

"I'm pre-med," Cam interjected. "Really? You don't think I can handle a little upchuck."

"I didn't want you to catch it, with mid-years coming up."

"Fuck the tests."

"Says the one who aced the MCAT after a night of partying."

"Exactly. I could have shown up as patient zero in the zombie apocalypse and passed. So you're coming home?"

"Um." Mina stopped to nudge at something of sudden interest with the toe of her boot. "I was just going to swing by later and pick up some things." She felt Jack's presence beside her. "Something else has come up. How about we go for coffee? I think I can handle that."

"That doesn't sound like a yes," Cam said after a moment's pause. "The shop on St. Frank's Square? 10 minutes? It's on my way to the library and I think there's some seasonal music or something."

"Sounds good. Ciao bella."

Mina finally looked at Jack as she dropped her phone back in her bag. "St. Frank's, 15 minutes," she said. "I'm meeting Cam for coffee."

"I don't think that's a good idea."

"What? I'm supposed to just disappear? Leaving my friends, my family, wondering?" Jack didn't answer so she started walking, turning right at the corner. The church spire rose over the red-brick townhouses in this gentrified strip of downtown. "I'd like to talk to her alone, if you can make yourself scarce."

"You shouldn't drink coffee. It'll make you sick."

"I can fake it."

"For now."

CAM WAS LATE, A HABIT that still irked Mina even if she'd come to accept it, so 20 minutes later they ordered their coffees and made their way into the busy square. Sure enough, the winter festival had started without Mina realizing it. This Christmas would be very different from the last one. She caught herself wondering what vampires drank as they strung lights and draped garland.

The square was full of people, despite the damp chill. A band was warming up on the small stage, but the music usually didn't start until after sunset. Then she noticed the slate gray deepening to charcoal; it was later than she thought.

"I think I see a sliver of a planter over there that we can park ourselves on," Cam said, leading the way through the herd of people.

"Darling." A voice slithered out of the crowd. Mina looked at the owner of the hand that had caught her arm. There was a twinge of recognition in her gut as she took in the blond hair pulled back in a severe ponytail, the smooth skin and overly red lips. "How are you? You still look like hell."

A moment later it hit her, and the twinge of recognition stabbed at her intestines. The woman from the alley beside the church, from the night Jack had caught her: Em. Tonight she was dressed as a biker babe, all in black leather and denim. Cam looked from her to the woman.

"Is this your...roommate?" Em asked. Mina stayed silent, but slid slightly sideways, edging between her and Cam.

"Yeah, I am," Cam said over Mina's shoulder. "Cam. And you are?"

"Nice to meet you Cam. Emily. You can call me Em. Your roommate and I met at the hospital the other night. Misery loves company, you know?" Emily walked around behind Cam, who took the opportunity to make a face at Mina. Mina shook her head. Emily eyed Mina over her friend's shoulder, and gave her a toothy smile. "She didn't mention that her roommate was so hot."

Mina's heart paused. Emily's eyes flashed red in the descending darkness as she scanned Cam's throat, exposed by the haphazard updo her roommate had tried to tame her curls into. Emily's mouth opened as if to say something more, but Cam turned to face her, and Em's lips morphed into a smile, which Cam returned a little too readily for Mina's liking.

"Let's go," Mina said, grabbing Cam's hand and dragging her away.

"Take care of yourself," Emily said as they walked away. "You look a little anemic."

"You were a bit rude," Cam said, glancing back at Emily with a look she normally reserved for football players. "She seemed nice."

"Not really," Mina said as she steered Cam towards the planter, glancing back to see Emily watching them as she pulled her phone out of her pocket. "A bit of a bitch actually." Mina hoped the woman could read lips.

"Pity." Cam smiled into the foam of her latte, eyes on Emily.

"Are you okay?" Mina asked, scanning Cam's face and neck. "You didn't catch what I have, did you?"

"I'm fine," Cam said. Mina watched her friend's eyes slowly focus on her. "So why didn't you call sooner?"

"I was so sick, like I never am," Mina said before taking a sip of coffee without thinking. Her stomach clenched, and she sighed. At least now she understood why. She put the cup down on the planter and scanned the square filled with people. Her skin itched. "I still feel a little queasy."

"You need to eat more of that soup your mom...." Cam stopped, her eyes flashing back from the crowd to look at Mina, her smile falling. She looked down at her coffee. "Sorry."

Mina gave Cam a small smile. "Not you too. You're in pre-med. You know kimchi soup doesn't cure everything."

"It kills cooties, I swear. There've been studies."

Mina's eyebrows arched. "I'm feeling better anyway, other than my stomach still being tetchy." It twitched, echoing her words. "It might not have been flu. Maybe something I ate." Judging from the movies, that wasn't really lying. "But I might not be around the apartment for a while yet." Mina's eyes fell on the crucifix at Cam's throat and tried to tell her the truth. "There's this...." She took a deep breath and tried again. "There's a...."

"It's a guy, isn't it?" Cam's eyes narrowed on her and she gave her a wicked smile. Mina's stomach lurched, and she heard a sound like birds' wings against her eardrums.

"Guy?" She scanned the crowd for Jack, but he was staying hidden.

"The mystery man from the club. You hit it off that well?"

"The guy." Mina had almost forgotten him. "Right, yeah, kind of." As soon as she said it, she hated herself for taking the easy way out. And she knew lying now would make it that much harder to tell the truth later.

"So you've been spending time making time at his place? Wrestling with the throes of pent-up sexual tension?" Cam rolled her eyes provocatively and bit her lip. "Oh, how I love young love."

"Love?" Mina's eyebrows arched.

"Well, young lust then?"

"Yeah." Mina tried to think and act like she would have a week ago, as a wave of nausea hit her. She glanced around the square again. The flutter in her stomach grew stronger. This was something new. She looked around, feeling like she was being watched, a prickling on the back of her neck.

Jack. Coming towards them. She turned to Cam. "You should get to the library. You have more tests to study for, essays to write." Mina glanced back towards Jack, tracking his path across the square. He was striding her way, with a tense control to his movements, like he was trying hard to look like the people around him.

"Is that him?" Cam asked, her voice low, her brown eyes traveling over the nearing Jack. "I can see why you've been AWOL."

Mina smiled at Cam before turning back to Jack. He looked...afraid.

What causes an immortal to fear, she thought, then realized that she didn't know if vampires were immortal. She'd just assumed; she'd seen the movies.

"Look, I gotta go now," she said, turning to Cam.

"Sure, I understand. Just make sure you call so I know you're alive. Deal?"

"Deal." She hugged Cam, then walked towards Jack. "I'll call," she said over her shoulder.

Before Jack had a chance to speak, she gave him a hard, full-bodied kiss.

"What the hell was that for?" he said, his lips whispering against hers.

"Appearances." She looked over her shoulder and gave Cam a small wave and a smile. Jack smiled at her friend before he turned to Mina, his face dropping into tension as the crowd closed around them.

"We need to go," he said as he grabbed her arm. She jerked it away from him.

"Let go. If you all don't stop that, my arm is going to be permanently purple."

"Not likely. You're a vampire."

She stopped and looked at him, then rolled her eyes. "Right, I'll heal."

Jack ignored her as he scanned the crowd. "We need to go. Now."

"No." She stood her ground. "I'm not going to go where you say just because you say so. Why should I go?"

"For one thing, the Necrophagos want you, despite your stubbornness."

"Yeah, what's new?"

"They're here."

"So? I saw Emily earlier. I can take her."

Jack blinked. "No, you can't, and you don't seem wicked to me. They're the bad guys, remember?" Mina watched Jack's chest rise and fall as he took a deep breath. "They're the vamps of folktales and legends, the ones that kill for the sake of it, who play with their food first. Is that what you want to become?"

"No, but you said all nosferata become Necrophagos."

A commotion crept up in an walkway off the square. Mina peered into the darkness, following Jack's lead, and the nebulous flutter in her gut became an itch she couldn't scratch.

"We don't have time for another explanation of the Hierarchy at the moment. Do you feel that, that prickling in your skin, that tickle in your eardrums?" After a couple of seconds of quiet, Mina nodded reluctantly. "Something wicked this way comes," he said.

"Speak of the devil and the devil appears," Emily said, materializing from the crowd. The prickling turned to bee stings. Emily was flanked by the behemoth, Ivan, and another vampire Mina hadn't met – she was sure she wouldn't have missed him if she had: the dark eyeliner around his eyes, the series of rings in his lips and nose, and the plugs in his ears. The head to toe red leather.

Emily gave Jack a toothy smile. "The warrior poet?"

"Sorry to disappoint, but that one belongs to Shakespeare. I know you're not much for culture, but maybe you've heard of him?"

Emily pulled up close to Jack and ran her hand over his arm. Mina felt his pulse change as he tensed. "I may not be much for books," she said, "but I do love erudite muscles."

"Why do you hang around with him, then?" Jack asked, looking at Ivan. Ivan scowled but didn't say anything. Em leaned her face close to Jack's arm, her nostrils flaring as she smelled the leather.

"Back off, Em, before I put a stake through your heart."

Em took a step back. "But you already pierced my heart," she said, copping a wounded look. She pulled down the lapels of her jacket to reveal the tops of her breasts. "Why don't you do it for real?" she said, leaning forward. "You know you wanna." Jack looked from her, around the square, to the corner near the lane. She let the jacket go. "Right. Too many livestock around."

"Shh," Jack said while he scanned the square. Mina did the same; she'd heard what he had – a faint scream, quickly muffled, swallowed by the festivities.

"Don't shush me," Em said, her voice rising, before Ivan put a hand over her mouth.

"Listen," he said, ignoring her flushed cheeks, red ears and thin lips. A scream arose from across the crowd. Em slowly took his hand from her mouth and focused on the corner of the square, the entrance to the shadowed walkway.

A woman emerged from the darkness, her clothes torn and bloody scratches crisscrossing her arms. Rivulets of tears ran down her red cheeks.

"My boy! Help me...a monster took my boy!" The wailing woman collapsed to the ground. Jack started towards her but a policewoman got to her first.

The officer spoke into the radio clipped to her shoulder then asked the woman what had happened and where. The woman's answers weren't very coherent but the gist of it was that a tall, half-naked man had reached out of a dark alley and grabbed her son as they walked by. She tried to fight, to pull her son back, to hold on but the man was too strong and too fast. He'd disappeared with her son into the night.

The itch in Mina's stomach was replaced by a stone. She looked at Jack, and saw her foreboding reflected in his dark eyes and tight jaw.

"Come on," he said, and headed towards the path the woman had indicated. Mina started to follow.

"Whoa," Emily said, clasping Mina's arm with red fingernails. "You're not taking her anywhere."

"Would you people stop grabbing me!" Mina yanked her arm free from Emily's firm grasp. "He's not taking me, but I am going with him."

"Do you really want to get into this now?" Jack said to Em, nodding towards the police car that had just pulled up beside the square. This time, when he and Mina headed away, Em looked hard at Mina but didn't grab her; instead she and her entourage followed them.

"What are you going to do?" Mina asked Jack.

"I'm going to try to find the boy." Jack looked over his shoulder as he passed the gaggle of people that had coalesced around the distraught woman.

"You really think you'll do a better job than the police?"

"I get the sense that this monster is of a type and magnitude that they're not used to dealing with."

"Right." Mina gave a small nod.

"And yes, we can do a better job. One of the strengths, or weaknesses, of being preternatural – the nose of a Bassett Hound."

"Huh. That explains a few things."

"Like what?"

"Like why this city now stinks more than it ever did before," Mina said.

"Sour milk, stale sweat and a soupçon of urine?" Jack said, as they slipped into the dark alleyway, a wave of the aforementioned rising from the dank asphalt. Emily, Ivan and the pin-cushion in red leather followed a few paces behind.

Mina walked in Jack's footsteps and mimicked his actions, sniffing at the shadows. All she got was the stench of garbage and stale vomit; she tried to close her nostrils to these odors. Another smaller alley branched off to their left. There she picked up what Jack was smelling. Blood and fresh urine with a hint of feces, mixed with something else.

"What's that smell?" Mina asked, her hushed voice dampened by the grimy walls. "There's something I can't place."

"Death," Em answered, whispering over Mina's shoulder, her breath riling the hair on the nape of Mina's neck.

"Decay," Jack said.

"We shouldn't be here," Em said. "I shouldn't be here. This is not good."

"Why not?" Jack asked, looking at Em in the half-light.

"It's, there's...I just shouldn't."

Ivan looked down the alley then back at Jack. "Do you know what we know?" he said.

"Ivan," Emily said, her voice hissing through tense lips.

"What do you know?" Jack asked.

"You first," Ivan said.

The wretched smell hung in the air between them, and nobody said anything. They all looked down the narrow passage, black except for the faint shards of neon that managed to find their way here. After the initial meeting with Emily and Ivan in the square, the prickling on Mina's skin had subsided to a hum. But now it was replaced by a faint buzz in her ears, like a mosquito she couldn't see, and the itch in her gut was back.

Jack finally broke the silence. "Something new stalks the night."

"Something indiscriminate," Ivan said.

"Something terrible." Em's eyes were fixated on the alleyway as she spoke.

"Something that tore a little boy from his mother," Jack said then started down the small passage. Following their noses, footsteps could be heard in the main alley. The police had finally gotten their act together, or the woman had calmed down enough to provide useful information. The little alley they were in had no light of its own and was shrouded from the glow of the city by the tall concrete walls that loomed up on either side. However, Mina realized that it wasn't as dark as it should have been, or would have been a week ago, her eyes grasping every bit of light there was. Halfway down the passageway, Jack held up his hand as he stopped in front of a set of stairs that led down to a metal door mottled by chipping paint and rust.

No one questioned that this was the place. A malevolent odor oozed out from around the slightly ajar door.

Jack went down the stairs first, followed closely by Mina. The others were a little slower to follow, holding some whispered conversation that held little interest to Mina, but soon enough she felt Em's presence behind her.

Jack tried the door but it barely budged, only moving an inch to let out a sickening miasma of death and decay. He tried a second time, pulling with all his weight. It grated against the concrete.

"Move over," Ivan said, as he stepped down and took hold of the edge of the door. He yanked it back, his arms bulging in his leather jacket. The door rasped open on rusty hinges.

They crept forward. The rest of the group held guns they'd pulled from hidden holsters, leaving Mina feeling a bit naked.

Her foot slipped, unprepared for the slick floor, and she grabbed Jack's arm to stay upright. It took a moment to adjust to the deeper shade of pitch dark in the boarded-up basement. Dripping pipes and loose wires ran overhead. They walked a tunnel formed by derelict machinery and ancient boilers.

If it weren't for the odor, she might have thought that it was just water on the floor.

A smear of blood and human effluent, and more of it than one small boy would have, marked a path. Up ahead, where the pipes, wire and garbage gave way to open space, there was a sound. A slurping, squelching sound followed by scraping, like nails on a chalkboard. Goosebumps raised on Mina's skin.

A loud bang echoed through the basement. Mina froze. Jack did the same then tilted his head to the side. Ice shot through her veins when she realized the sound ahead had stopped. Or the source of it had moved. Jack placed a finger to his lips, and then pointed to a boiler beside them that had just thudded to wheezing life.

The noise ahead resumed and Mina breathed again. The group edged closer to the source of the sounds. As they came upon it, everyone stopped.

It looked almost like a man. A seven-foot tall, naked man. Wiry muscles snaked under its ashen skin. Pointed ears twitched on a head almost bereft of hair. A heavy brow shaded its eyes. Long, dark fingernails grew out of ten fingers and ten toes. Almost like a man. If it weren't for the large knobbly shoulder blades and the bony spikes that protruded from arms and legs. And the razor-sharp teeth that gnawed at what was left of a little boy.

"Oh my god," Mina said, not thinking, tears forming.

The creature looked up at them with eyes that were completely black, no white, no iris, just black.

"I don't think God had anything to do with it," Jack said as the creature stood up, looked at him, then at the rest of them. It froze for a fraction of a second before dodging off to hide in the maze of pipes, wire and metal, like a guerrilla in a rainforest.

"Shit," Emily said as she turned back toward the door. Beams of light flashed from the entry, followed by shuffling and a growing murmur. "Shit," she repeated.

"Don't move!" a voice said from behind the light. That was all he managed before a gray hand lashed out of the dark and black talons raked across his chest, tearing through the bulletproof vest like it was rags. The police officer looked down and let out a strangled sound before his head was twisted from his body. Blood spattered across Mina's face. She blinked against the onslaught. The thump of a multitude of heavy-soled boots echoed along the walls and asphalt beyond the door.

"There's got to be another way out," Mina said. "Animals and their lairs, there's always an emergency exit." Her voice sounded more confident of that fact than she felt.

"No," Jack said. "We need to kill this thing."

"This *thing* just tore a man's head from his body," Em said.

"Somehow I don't think we'd heal from that," Mina said, a hand on Jack's arm. "The police are here, guns versus claws equals carnage. And somehow, I don't think the guns will win." Jack let himself be turned around. "We need reinforcements."

Another scream ricocheted through the basement. Mina turned to see claws around the neck of Red Leather Jacket. Being a vamp, he had additional resources to use against the creature. He pulled out a knife and his own teeth came out, tearing at the rough skin. It made little difference. Rows of teeth sunk into the vamp's neck and tore a gaping hole. Two large hands, one on the shoulder, the other on the forehead wrenched in opposite directions. The vampire's head lolled loosely to one side, his neck broken. Dark eyes turned on the four of them.

"Maybe you're right," Jack said. The creature took a step towards him, its upper lip twitching into a semblance of a twisted smile. The sound of shots echoed along the metal pipes and concrete walls. The creature howled and spun around, dark viscous liquid seeping from four new holes in its back.

"I'd suggest we get the hell out of Dodge," Em said, tearing a board from a window with her manicured hands. "Ladies first," she said as she hauled herself out the glassless window. Mina went next, then reached down to offer a hand to Jack. Ivan tried to shove Jack out of the way, but Jack was having none of it.

"I'm not leaving you two alone with Mina."

Indeed, Mina felt Emily's fingernails scrape against skin as she grabbed a fistful of Mina's hair. Mina had some tricks of her own, and sent a spiky heel into Emily's foot as the woman tried to haul her down the alley. That just caused Mina's hair to be yanked back harder.

"What the hell, Em?" Ivan said as he finally wedged himself through the window to street level. "You were just going to leave me with that thing while you take the prize to Luca?"

"I wasn't," she said, letting go of Mina's hair.

Mina used the moment's distraction to clock Em with a sharp jab to the chin. Jack laughed.

"A little help?" Mina said to Jack as Emily's eyes narrowed and her fangs came out. Her hands closed around Mina's throat. But it was Ivan who came to Mina's rescue as he shoved Emily's shoulder, causing her to let go.

"What the fuck?" he said.

"I wasn't going to leave you down there, I just thought I could subdue her before I helped you."

"Thanks, partner."

"No honour among thieves? What say we leave the two lovebirds to their squabble," Jack said, as more shots went off in the basement.

"Whoa, no." Emily turned from Ivan. "She's ours."

"Are you hers?" Jack asked Mina.

"Hell no," Mina said, setting herself into a fighter's stance, with one foot back and her weight balanced.

"Sorry," Jack said, his head cocked, his shoulders shrugging. "You're going to have to disappoint Matteo again. Or is it Luca this time?"

Leaving the other two arguing in the alley, Mina and Jack made their way back to St. Frank's square, dodging the police who were prowling the alleys.

"Did you see the scars on that thing's chest," she asked, leaning into Jack. The pattern matched the shots he'd had gotten off against Quinn.

"Yeah," Jack said. "And I noticed that they were already scabbed over."

CHAPTER TWENTY-TWO

LUCA LAY STAR-FISHED, half-naked on the polished concrete floor of his bedroom, its cool slickness calming his fevered flesh. His head was towards the hearth, where tongues of flame licked the air but no warmth reached his feet. Other than the fire, the only light came from the black candle beside him. The small amount of light cast the corners into deep shadow, a potential lurking place for all manner of shades. The door was bolted and the thick walls sound-resistant: if anyone did happen to hear any whispers, any whimpers, any echo of his moans, they still couldn't interrupt.

He opened his eyes, his head lolled and looked into the flames, away from the terrible shadows. A shiver passed through him, against his own volition. He stayed as still as possible, waiting for the shiver to pass, the pain to abate and the lacerating whispers to subside. When he thought it was safe, he slowly pushed himself up to sitting.

"Light, low," he said, his raspy voice rising up from a raw throat. Muted lights came on, dispelling the shadows. He got one leg under him, then the other. He stood, forcing reluctant muscles to his will, the world still blurred. He walked over to the tall mirror.

His torso was covered in sweat and his hair disheveled. Dark circles rimmed his glassy eyes.

Otherwise nothing seemed different. Except for the new mark, raw and red, blazing across his chest. He traced the faint lines of the other marks over his torso, down to his abdomen, carefully avoiding the newest, which would soon enough fade to a rusty shadow like the others. He tried to decipher the pattern he was sure was there.

He'd never seen his father talk to a demon, though Luca was sure he did, when he went down into the catacombs or the vault. If it had hurt, his father never showed it afterward. If Luca had known the pain, he might never have done it the first time. But the voice had been so seductive.

He assumed the voice belonged to a demon, though he'd never actually seen its face. From what he'd heard of them, he wasn't sure he wanted to. All he ever saw was a glimmer of darkness at the edge of his vision, a coalescing of shadows.

But the voice spoke in vivid colour, painting a horrible, wonderful, phantasmagoric picture in his mind's eye. It spoke of power and dominion, and he learned many wondrous things, like how to control the bestial army it was creating. And there was the promise of more knowledge, tantalizing tastes of power, but so far everything else was Sisyphean: one step forward only to be assaulted by a wave of ire and impatience from his shadow.

The whispers had been wrathful tonight, still fixated on this wayward dhamphir, but Luca had managed to placate them. He'd have her in hand or dead soon enough. Especially with the new guard the voice had promised him, all wiry muscles, taut tendons and fathomless hunger.

Luca looked at his reflection again. The sweat on his skin glistened in the firelight and the raw mark was already starting to heal. He ran a hand over the muscles of his torso and smiled.

He hadn't planned on going on the prowl tonight, but he had time. And he was up for a game of cat and mouse.

MATTEO SAT ON HIS CHAIR of bones, a gift from some reprobate soul trying to save itself. In the end, he had squashed the soul and taken the chair. Anyone wicked enough to have a chair of human bones didn't deserve his mercy. He had a strong sense of justice. Besides, the man had plotted against him.

But that was ages past. Now Matteo's attention was subsumed not by the murky waters of memory but with the turbid present. His eyes were closed, head tilted down; though the lights in the room were dim, the corners lost in shadow, it was still too bright to focus. Eyes shuttered, he could scan through the record of recent events, calling up sensory memories that were clearer in the recollection than in the moment, his mind sifting through the stimuli, trying to figure out where the snag in the weft was: what was causing the unbalance in his world.

He'd heard rumours of a new creature. Something terrific and horrifying, so the flies buzzed and the rats chittered. Luca had finally admitted to making a new vampire. But just one, and just a dhampir. A nothing.

This was something different. He felt it in the vague sensation that gnawed at his gut, throbbed through his temples, tickled across his skin.

As if on cue, a tickling sensation started on his left hand.

Feeling another's presence, he opened his eyes. A spider, as if sensing a kindred spirit, had abseiled down from the ceiling and alit on the back of his hand, its black body iridescent in the low light, stark against his pale skin.

He stared at it for a moment, wondered at the creature that would dare to disturb his thoughts. Then he turned his hand over and watched it crawl over to his palm.

"You ought not to have done that," Matteo said, before closing his fingers around it. One by one, he plucked each leg from the creature's body.

"Let that be a lesson."

Matteo at least knew what he had to do with Luca.

HE PEERED DOWN AT THE mass of people, his ears twitching at their chattering. His eyes burned at the flashing of light, cold and sharp. The rain trickled from his scalp, slithering down his back to drip onto the metal roof green with age. Though it all looked mottled shades of gray under the glowering clouds.

His talons gripped crevices and crannies as he craned his neck to look at the dark alleys that snaked from the building where he had taken refuge. He whooped quietly as he looked at the darkness where his lair had been. He chittered to himself as he ran a claw over his neck, briefly giving into the compulsion to scratch an itch before returning that hand to its tenuous hold on the roof.

His head swung around and his taloned fingers tensed as he heard an echoing chitter. His dark eyes scanned the gloom, his ears flicked. He homed in on the source of the sound. On another roof, beside some metal box, hunkered another shadow like himself.

No, another two. A family.

He whooped again, softly, from deep in his throat. He strained his ears towards the shadows. Then he heard the sound repeated back to him. He looked down at the mass of movement then turned back to the shadows. Long limbs and wiry muscles tensed and flexed as he clawed his way over the rooftops.

CHAPTER TWENTY-THREE

MINA YAWNED, A TOTAL body yawn, arms stretched skywards, back arched, as she plodded up the stairs to the nave. She'd tried to nap after returning from what was supposed to be a simple trip to her apartment. But every time she closed her eyes, her vision was filled with serrated teeth, black talons and bottomless eyes.

She'd finally slipped into a restless sleep a short time before Bee knocked on her door and told her to get up, get dressed in street clothes and come upstairs. She wasn't sure what she had meant by street clothes, but Mina donned black jeans, a black t-shirt with a faded tour logo and her worn leather jacket. She ran her right hand along the banister while holding her boots in her left.

When she entered the nave, she saw the conclave gathered. They all looked at her and went silent.

"Has no one taught you it's rude to stare?" She stared back at them.

"You might want to put your boots on," Dar said before looking back at the others. "Apparently it's rude to stare."

Mina had an urge to stick out her tongue, but she suppressed that inner child and pulled on her boots as the others turned their attention towards the weapons cupboards and geared up for the night. Dar came over to her.

"What's up?" Mina said, letting her eyes slide to where Bee was pulling ammo from a drawer and secreting it in her clothes before returning her attention to Dar. The lines around his eyes and the tightness of his lips seemed out of place on his smooth face.

"You're joining the others on patrol," he said.

Mina blinked at him. "What?"

"Part of your responsibility to the conclave: you get a home, a family, sustenance, and in return, you join our effort to protect the humans from the things that go bump in the night."

"Right," Mina said, understanding the concept but not how it applied to her.

"You're going out tonight, with Jack."

Mina looked at Jack, who was standing off to the side, arms crossed. He looked at her but the chiseled planes of his face didn't betray his mind.

"You think I'm ready?" Mina asked, even though she had her own answer. She looked down at the floor, at her boots. *I should have chosen a pair with more sensible heels.*

"Bee says you're a quick learner."

"And? That's no 'why yes, of course you're ready.'"

"You're ready enough. We need all eyes on the street until this thing is captured and killed." The others had finished arming up, holstering guns and sheathing blades, and now headed out in groups of two or three.

Jack turned to her. "Our turn."

A tingling pulse flowed through her intestines as images of her death and dismemberment raced through her mind, but Mina followed Jack and Dar over to the arcade. Jack handed her a couple of daggers and a short sword, all sheathed, then proceeded down the bank of cupboards. Mina hastily strapped the sheathes to her arms and waist. He pulled out a black pistol and a couple of magazines, and turned to hand these to her along with a holster.

Mina looked at the items cradled in her arms. "I've never fired a gun in my life."

"No?" Dar said, tilting his head. "No, I don't suppose you have."

"Bee and I didn't get that far. The closest I've come is bows and arrows in summer camp."

"Jack, take her down to the firing range. Teach her what she needs to know to not kill herself or take out any bystanders. Or you. And maybe see if we have a small crossbow or blow gun around that she can squirrel away."

"And where are you off to?" Jack asked.

"Same old, same old," Dar said. "To make sure the Librarian is focused on the task at hand. And to see if I can glean any information from less reputable sources." Mina watched Jack as he watched Dar walk out the door with narrowed eyes and a frown pulling down the corners of his mouth. Then she followed him as he led her downstairs, to a door hidden under the stairs on the far side. As Jack pushed it open, weak lights lit another set of narrow stairs that ended in darkness.

At the bottom of the stairs, Jack entered the door to the right. Dim lights came on, though they were plenty bright for her enhanced vision.

"Welcome to the firing range," he said. Mina looked down the long room. Jack took one of the targets from the pile against the wall, attached it to a clip and pressed a button to send it halfway down the range. Mina tried to make out the shape on the target, since its broad shoulders, outsized head and clawed hands were clearly not human.

"Werewolf," she said under her breath.

"Good eye," Jack said, his lips quirking into the semblance of a smile. "We'll make it easy to start. Press the magazine release to remove an empty clip." He indicated a button on the side of the handle, even though the gun was empty. "This one is set up for left-handed shooting. Before you return a gun to the cupboard, remove the magazine and pull the slide back to eject the round from the chamber." Jack demonstrated then handed the gun and a full magazine to her. "Push the magazine in with the palm of your hand – careful not to pinch any skin – until you hear it lock into place."

Mina did as she was told, breathing deeply to quiet the jangle of nerves caused by holding a gun. She heard the magazine click into place.

"Pull the slide back to load a round in the chamber."

Mina breathed into her abdomen. This wasn't as cool as it looked on TV; learning to shoot a gun meant more than making holes in paper. It meant blood and guts. And death.

She felt Jack's hands on her hips as he adjusted her stance. He squared her hips to the target and nudged her feet apart with one of his. He stood behind her and tilted his chin to her ear, his breath disturbing the hairs on her neck as he spoke.

"Grip the handle firmly, thumbs towards the target. Bend your elbows slightly. Relax." She breathed in and out through her nose, into the back of her throat, trying to quell her nerves. He guided her arms into place then stepped back and continued. "Touch your fingertips lightly to the trigger. Breathe in, exhale. At the end of the exhale, steady and squeeze."

"Oh," Mina said when she pulled the trigger and the gun fired. "Shouldn't we have glasses and ear muffs?"

"Are you going to wear them out on patrol?"

"No?"

"No." He stepped out beside her. "Try again. This time, at the end of the exhale, squeeze the trigger gently, all the way back. Use your whole hand. And don't think of pulling the trigger, it'll mess up all that careful breathing."

Mina continued firing, learning an unexpected lesson about keeping her hand away from the slide as a line of blood welled up along the base of her thumb after a careless shot. But with Jack looking on, she kept the pain to herself and kept shooting. Until she pulled the trigger and the slide stayed back. She tipped her head to look at Jack, a question on her lips.

"Time to reload."

"Right." Mina looked at the gun.

"Load a new clip into the magazine."

Mina tried to recall his earlier instructions as he pressed a button to retrieve the target. Almost all of the small holes were clustered around the chest and head.

"Huh, I think that's good enough," he said, staring at the target. "The head is the better target when it comes to the undead. For the Were, aim for the heart." He placed the used target in a bin. "Now holster it, and we'll ammo up and head out."

"What about the safety? Isn't there supposed to be a safety so I don't shoot something by accident?"

He looked at her. "Don't point it at anything you don't intend to shoot."

Mina looked at the gun, her eyebrow arched. "I don't intend to shoot anything."

Jack put his hand over hers and guided the gun down and away; she hadn't realized she'd let it drift towards him.

"You may not have a choice." He took his hand away and stepped back.

"What about the further distance?" Mina said, looking down the range, as she slid the gun into the holster.

"Don't shoot at anything that far away." He headed up the stairs.

Mina followed, trying to shrug into the holster at the same time. "Wait up. Do you really think any of these weapons are going to kill whatever is killing us?"

He stopped and turned to her. "These weapons can kill you," he said, adjusting the straps and buckles on the holster until the gun was nestled at her side.

"But I'm a vampire, I'll heal. Right?"

"It's hard to heal when your head has been severed from your body. Or a stake of ashwood is driven into your heart. Or when the silver in these hollow points seeps into your bloodstream and poisons you in a slow, festering way."

NIGHT HAD FALLEN BUT the street was ablaze with the cold light of neon and LEDs trying to lure holiday shoppers inside, out of the cold. The steady rain pooled into iridescent puddles. Cars sped by, splashing icy water onto the pavement, making Mina realize the practical benefit of her heightened reflexes and quickened reaction time, as she dodged out of the way. She wove through the crowd, following Jack's broad shoulders. He was hard to lose, the press of people parting for him.

As if they know there's a wolf in their midst. She strode after him, her boots tapping out a staccato rhythm on the sidewalk.

Mina was so focused on her quarry that it took her a few moments to realize someone was calling her name. She looked around for the source of the voice.

"Mina? Mina!"

Aunt June. Mina's left hand went to her right hip, just below where the oppressive weight of the holstered gun pressed against her side.

"Mina, where have you been? Why haven't you called lately? It's been weeks, months."

"I...." Her aunt placed a warm hand on Mina's face. June was her mother's sister, something Mina was sharply reminded of at times: a similarity in the smile, a tone in the voice, a warmth in the touch. A cold shard of memory stabbed her gut, followed by a pang of guilt. *Someone else I haven't seen since the funeral.*

"What's wrong? You look so pale."

"Nothing, nothing's wrong. I've been sick is all." Mina looked away. She couldn't see Jack, but felt him hovering nearby. She kept her left arm across her abdomen, trying to protect the bulk of the gun from wayward hugs. "I've just been really busy. School, you know."

"You mean the one you haven't been attending?" her aunt said, her voice sharp.

Mina's divided attention refocused entirely on June. "How...?"

"Someone called with some crazy message about Dale being in an accident...as if he'd be caught dead on a motorcycle...since you weren't answering your phone. I got set up as your emergency contact, remember, when we thought your mother might disown you?"

Mina had forgotten. Her aunt had actually taken up Mina's cause when her mother had objected, strenuously, repeatedly, to her intention to go to art school.

"Right," Mina said. She'd meant to update it when it became clear that, despite her mother's disapproval, she was going to continue to claim Mina as her own.

No point in worrying about it now, being dead and all, Mina thought as she shifted her weight and her left hand drifted up over the gun. *With Mom being dead and all.*

"What's wrong, Mina?" Her aunt's voice softened.

Mina glanced around, feeling guilty at the worry she saw written on her aunt's face. "Nothing. I'm fine. Like I said, I've been sick." She looked down at her feet. "Food poisoning maybe."

"Look at me," June said, channeling Mina's mother. Mina obeyed.

"Really, I'm fine. I *have* been sick. And I just needed some time to deal with things, you know? After Mom's death. To reevaluate my future." Mina bit her right thumbnail.

"And what might that future hold?"

Mina had hoped that her vague response would be enough to deflect her aunt's piercing gaze. She should have known better.

"How about I visit and we can talk about it?" Mina said.

"Hmph." Her aunt looked at her, searching, before she continued. "All right, but if you don't visit, I'll hunt you down." Her aunt placed her hand on her cheek again. Mina felt the radiant warmth. "You're so cold. I'll make some kimchi jjigae when you come by, set you right."

"Sounds like a plan." The thought passed through her mind that she would never enjoy her aunt's soup again, but she managed to keep her voice even when she continued. "Bye, Eemo."

"See you soon," her aunt said, pointing a finger. Mina watched as her aunt continued along the sidewalk before rejoining a handsome man with salt and pepper hair who Mina didn't know.

"You're better off dead," Jack said from just over her left shoulder, his breath brushing the hair over her ear.

"What?" Mina said, not really listening.

"The sooner they think you're dead, the better. For everyone."

Mina looked at him but said nothing. She looked back at her aunt, who was laughing at something the man was saying.

"It's not that easy to die."

CHAPTER TWENTY-FOUR

MINA WOVE THROUGH THE thinning crowds, still tailing Jack, still distracted by the encounter with her aunt. Still thinking about Jack's repeated exhortations for her to die.

Despite the thoughts that occupied her mind, she couldn't forget the weight of the gun at her side and the tension of the holster that held it, even when her elbow wasn't bumping against it. The few times they passed a police officer or cop car, she looked around and picked up her pace, expecting to be stopped. But either the gun had stayed hidden or no one cared. Luckily it had turned out to be a quiet night, no signs of frightening creatures – of either the imposing gray kind or the seductive blonde variety. Mina breathed deeply.

"What?" Jack asked.

"What?" Mina looked at him, head cocked. "Nothing."

"If you say so."

They approached the entrance to the subway, abandoned at this time of night, since the shoppers had gone home and the clubbers wouldn't be forced to go home for a few hours yet. Jack stopped, his hand on her arm.

"Do you hear that?" he said.

"What?" All she heard was the white noise of the city: the whispering rain, the soft thrum of the subway, and a distant drumbeat. She focused on opening her senses, remembering

Jack's concern about her filtering before, but there was still nothing out of place. "I don't hear anything."

"The buzzing." Jack closed his eyes. "Like electrical wires on a rainy day?"

Mina tilted her head, straining to hear whatever Jack did. She looked up at the electrical lines, but still didn't hear the buzzing. She tried filtering instead of hearing every extraneous sound. She blocked out the rainfall, the PA announcements, the sirens, leaving only the slow tempo of deep drums. "Nope, no buzzing," she said. "Just music."

"This way." Jack headed down the stairs into the station. At the bottom, he jumped the turnstile, in full view of the attendant, if the attendant's head hadn't been buried in a book. Mina looked over her shoulder then followed his lead. The platform was nearly empty. A homeless man lay on a bench under the flickering fluorescent lights, his face covered by a newspaper. Water dripped onto the tracks from above. Garbage cans overflowed onto dingy tiles. The low, slow percussion got louder.

Once in the station, Mina felt, rather than heard, the buzzing: a swarm of bees spreading from her gut through her body. She walked down the platform on tiptoes to keep her boot heels from click-clacking on the tile. Mina peered down at the tracks to her right as a handful of rats scurried along the wall, heading away from her. As she neared the end of the platform, she heard a commotion on the far side of a pillar. A figure bolted from behind it, screaming, blood gushing from a gash on his shoulder.

Mina pulled out her gun as the buzzing pulsed through her veins, her blood throbbing in time with the dirge that filled her ears. Luckily the safety was still on, giving her time to realize that the figure was human. She breathed deeply, trying to force her hands to stop shaking.

Jack mimed something that he obviously thought she should understand. Working through his gestures, Mina caught the gist: she should go left while he went right. What she was supposed to do after that, she had no idea.

She thumbed the gun's safety off as quietly as she could, then slid along the left side of the pillar. She stepped out from behind that minimal protection, willing herself to not make a sound.

A gray creature crouched in the sickly green light. Tattered remnants of dirty clothes hung over wiry muscles strung under taut skin. At first, it didn't realize that they were there, as it hunkered down over a bloodied, torn corpse and gnawed away at a limp thigh. The tinny classical music piped through crackling speakers did nothing to cover the slurping and sucking, and she couldn't block it out. Mina forced her rebellious stomach to order, and cocked her gun.

The creature looked up at the sound, blood dripping out of its mouth from pointed teeth, its lips pulled back as it sniffed the air. Its black eyes shone like obsidian as it looked at her, a low growl rising from deep in its chest. It snarled. It shifted.

Jack shot the creature in the back, the sound ricocheting through the empty station. It turned to him and howled, a long keening sound. Jack shot it three more times as it advanced on him, its black blood mixing with the red of its victim. After the fourth shot, it spun around and ran on all fours, like a gorilla, towards the tunnel. Towards Mina. She barely had time to bring her gun up and get into the stance Jack had taught her before it was on her. She squeezed the trigger just before she was bowled over by the creature. Twisting to right herself, she threw her empty hand out to slow her fall and stop her head from making contact with the platform. The creature skidded to a stop in front of her, its talons skittering on the tiles. It turned, sniffing the air, and stepped towards her, its lips curled. Mina rolled over onto her back, to meet death face on. She brought her arms up and fired again, hitting the creature in the shoulder. It bared its teeth at her. She responded in kind.

Jack appeared at her shoulder and fired. The creature growled before fleeing into the dark tunnel.

Mina breathed hard, the gun held out in front of her in stiff, shaking hands. Jack put one hand on her shoulder, the other on the hands holding the gun.

"You can relax now," he said as he gently pushed her hands down and slid the safety on.

"No, I don't think I can," she said, forcing herself to breathe deeply to counteract the shaking. "Is it always like this?"

Jack didn't answer. Instead he looked down the track to where the creature had disappeared into the dark tunnel.

"What is this thing?" Mina asked.

Jack shook his head. "I don't know. I've never seen anything like them before."

"Them?"

"That wasn't Quinn."

"How do you know?"

"Wrong clothes, or what's left of them. No scars from gunshot wounds."

"Yeah, I noticed that. Could they be some kind of vampire? Maybe he just healed."

"No," he said, though his voice rose in question. "I'm sure the Hierarchy is as it has always been. Besides, it feels different than a vampire. In the blood, you know?"

Mina nodded. She had felt the difference, more of an itch than a hum. And she'd heard the difference. This thing's blood sang to her too, but it sounded nothing like any of the vampires. There were no woodwinds or strings, no metallic percussion. Just a low, slow drumbeat that sounded like death. "But it definitely likes blood. And flesh." Mina forced herself to look at the body it had left behind. A woman, smeared with blood, her leg mangled.

Just then, the hand twitched. Mina jumped back as it grabbed at Jack's leg. It was slow, so when it lunged out with teeth bared, Jack had time to pull away and plunge a silver-streaked blade into its temple.

"We should take it to the Sanctuary," he said. "It might help us figure out what these things are."

"We should cut off its head," she said. Jack turned to look at her. "It might not be dead," she added.

A shuffle and squeak drew their attention down the platform. A city worker in orange overalls and a pushcart stood there, frozen. The confused look on the man's face slowly resolved into a scream. Shrill, loud and constant, it echoed along the station, enveloping them. Heavy footsteps thudded down the far stairs.

"Change of plans," he said. "Live to fight another day." He ran towards the other end of the platform, in the trail of the creature's bloody footprints. Mina followed his lead, a cold breeze raising goosebumps on her neck as she jumped off the platform and entered the dark tunnel.

A SCARLET FEVER

SLEET SLANTED DOWN from the granite night sky, forming icy rivulets across the uneven asphalt. Shards of light from car headlights ricocheted off the wet pavement. The man in the fedora had the collar of his overcoat turned up, as if to protect himself from the cold, though it also effectively hid his odd appearance. He slowed his pace, imperceptible except to the shadow that stalked him, sensing perhaps the presence of his pursuer, unwelcome but not threatening, at least not tonight.

"Trying to sneak up on me, old man?" Matteo said as he stopped and turned around.

"Just letting you know I was here, didn't want you to think I was here to kill you," Dar said, emerging from the dark into the shadows. "But the day will come."

"In some ways, it will be a shame to kill you," Matteo said

"The feeling is not mutual. And why do you presume you'll beat me? I've killed your kind before."

"Huh, not my kind." Matteo focused in on Dar, his hollowed eyes hooded in shadow. "Should I just bite you now? So you can finally see how useless it is to fight the beast within? So you can get a taste of what you've been missing? You could be my second in command."

"And what of Luca?"

"Luca," Matteo said, looking over Dar's shoulder. "Luca poses a problem. But not one that can't be solved."

"Even if I thought the offer were sincere, I'd still pass." Dar watched a cab disgorge its load of half-drunk, half-clothed revelers. "We have more pressing concerns than crossing swords."

"And what would that be?" Matteo asked.

Dar didn't say anything. He'd long ago learned patience and the power of silence.

"We need to figure out what's attacking us, without respect for the order of things," Matteo finally continued, his body fidgeting.

"Something's attacking the Necrophagos?"

"Don't play coy, Darius," Matteo said. "It doesn't suit. You know your enemy as well as I know mine. You know one of ours has been attacked. And I know your Quinn is dead."

"Really? Your information is a little out of date. Quinn isn't dead."

Matteo's lips approximated a smile. "No, not dead then. Turned into something different, some other kind of undead."

"Yeah, something."

"Something maybe even worse than me?" Matteo said. Dar didn't answer, so Matteo prodded. "So are you going to start talking?"

"Are you?" Dar's pierced eyebrow arched.

Matteo breathed deeply and rubbed his temples with spindly fingers.

"You have no idea, do you?" Dar said. "So let's stop playing cat and mouse. You don't know. I don't know."

"What don't we know?"

Dar's lips started to form a snarl. He stopped himself. "What this thing is or where it came from." Dar watched a black van drive slowly past then looked at his nemesis full-on. "Or how to kill it."

"Okay, you don't know and I don't know," Matteo said, nodding in concession. "Does anyone?"

Dar shook his head, his mohawk limp in the rain. "Not Pietro."

"And your pet Librarian? You've been to see him."

Dar inclined his head at the statement. "I'll tell you what he knows if you leave him alone."

"A little over protective."

Dar snarled.

"Alright," Matteo said, holding up his gloved hands.

"Swear?"

"That will make you trust my words more?" Matteo rolled his eyes. "I swear."

Dar's eyes narrowed, and it took him a moment to speak. "So far, nothing. He's looking into it."

"That's all you have?"

"And you have something more?" Dar said, then looked at the police car that pulled up across the way, lights flashing but sirens silent.

"I know there's more than one, and they seem willing to work together, or at least don't tear each other apart as soon as they get close. Unlike us."

"That's it?"

"That's as much as you have."

"How do you know this?" Dar asked, watching an officer get out of the police car before shifting his attention back to Matteo. He saw the tightening of Matteo's lips, as the man glanced across the street then back at Dar.

"I have my sources."

"Really, that's all I get?" Dar said.

"That's all you've earned." Matteo's eyes narrowed, as Dar's fingers twitched. After a minute's stalemate of baleful looks, Matteo continued. "I'll leave your pet be, if you tell me what you learn. I want you on my doorstep as fast as your dracul limbs can carry you. Otherwise, who know what will happen to him if I need to darken his doorstep."

"If you harm him –" Dar started.

"I said nothing about hurting him. He's an old man, he might have a heart attack." Matteo pulled up his collar, adjusted his fedora and melted into the night.

Dar watched him go, an insidious worm of doubt gnawing at his stomach.

CHAPTER TWENTY-FIVE

DAR DREW HIS FINGER along the fogged window of the coffee shop. Most people nowadays would think it a random squiggle. Only a very few would recognize the ancient word in an archaic script: a ward of protection against evil.

The cafe was quiet, despite it being the kind of night that drove people inside to warm drinks and comforting companions. In the blurry street, only a few intermittent souls dodged the frigid puddles. Maybe the cold and drizzling dark were keeping holiday shoppers at home. The thickness of the raindrops that flung themselves at the glass boded snow. It had taken him a lifetime living in this city to learn to read the rain. Even though his undying body was less susceptible to the vagaries of weather, the cold damp still made his desert blood shiver.

It had been a drier cold in the land of his birth, though he could still feel the bitter bite of those surprisingly common winter nights of his childhood when snow had fallen like an unwelcome mantle over the hillsides. Nights when, as the third son in a poor family, more delicate than the others, he'd had to fight for every scrap of warmth, huddled with his brothers under threadbare blankets, hoping to stave off frostbite and hypothermia until the wan sun rose the next day. Those had been long nights. Nights that had ended sometime in his teens (he couldn't say exactly, age being a reckoned thing in the village), when he'd been plucked off the street to become the pampered pet of a privileged noble, all because of a lopsided smile and a hurried touch. After that, his nights were kept warm by fire, alcohol and fervid bodies.

But the snow of his childhood had been different from the snow here. Here it was soggy, sticky, seeping. He thought sometimes about moving somewhere warmer, someplace drier. But if he was honest, Dar liked the city and his comfortable position in it. It was vibrant and alive and one of the centres of the after-dark world. He was in the midst of that, a leader, and it was easy to hide amongst the other freaks and fringe cases that were drawn here, no matter how freakish he became.

Turning away from the window, his dark mohawk fell over his kohl-lined eyes. The rings in his nose, lips, ears and eyebrows, glinted in the low, holiday-themed light. Acrid steam rose from the cup he occasionally reached for and turned before setting it back down. Rhys, the Librarian, his friend, sat across from him, sipping the tea he clasped tightly in his knobbly hands, never putting it down. He saw that Rhys studied him, rather than the sidewalk or the other patrons.

"Anything you care to share, old friend?" Rhys asked, blowing on his tea. The scent of cinnamon, cloves and oranges wafted towards Dar, stirring up more sleeping memories.

"No, nothing in particular. Holidays just put one in mind of home and hearth."

"Hmph." Rhys took a sip of tea and looked out the window. Or rather looked at the symbol Dar had drawn.

Dar could guess at the reasons for his friend's taciturn response, and gave him a lopsided smile: home and hearth had never been very warm for Rhys. Through the wrinkles and the gray, Dar still saw the young man he'd first met years ago at Oxford.

"So," Dar said, bringing both their minds back to the present, "have you figured out what we're dealing with?"

Rhys didn't answer right away. Instead he looked around the coffee shop, then out the window, at the till, before peering into the depths of his tea. Then he took a long sip and a deep breath before finally looking into Dar's brown eyes. "I need to see the creature."

Dar's eyes narrowed. "Do you know what it is or not?"

"I need to see it." Rhys fidgeted with his mug. "I need to be certain before I unleash this knowledge on the world."

"Too bad, you'll have to live with uncertainty."

Rhys stayed silent, so Dar continued. "We can't kill it. How are we supposed to get it to you so you can see it?"

"You're not," Rhys said, swallowing. "You're supposed to get me to it. I need to go out on one of your patrols and find the creature."

Dar stopped turning the mug in his hand. "No."

"Why not?"

"Why not?!" Dar looked at Rhys, who glanced away for a second before straightening up and facing Dar. Dar went on, his voice hushed. "Because you're, well, old. You can't move like we can. And I don't want to be responsible for your death, old friend."

"You'd be surprised at how fast I can move. I was quite the athlete in my day."

"I know. I remember, but how long ago was that?" Dar shook his head. "And even when you were young, you couldn't move like I can. You're human. "

"Take me to one of these creatures, old man, and I'll tell you what it is," Rhys said, his jaw tight.

"Why won't you tell me now?"

Rhys opened his mouth, closed it again and looked out the window. "Because I can't be certain until I see it. And I need to be certain about this. Second-hand descriptions are not good enough."

Dar looked him over. "I call bullshit."

Rhys turned back to him from the window. He took his time in responding, sipping his tea. "I could ask Matteo to take me."

"You wouldn't." Dar's jaw tightened, knowing how stubborn Rhys could be. "You know better. You can't trust him."

"And I don't," Rhys said, looking into Dar's eyes. "I've spent years helping you, reading for you, knowing things no man should know, doing things no man should do. Now I'm old, you put me out to pasture?" Rhys gripped his tea mug with one hand, the other flat on the table. "No, I think you can do what I ask this once. I can take responsibility for my own self."

Dar started to reach out to take Rhys' hand but then drew his hand back. "What you're asking could be your death."

"I know. But, unlike you, my death is inevitable."

"It didn't have to be," Dar said quietly, to his cold coffee, despite knowing that that ground had been trodden so many times into the quagmire of history. When Rhys didn't rise to the bait, Dar sighed heavily. "Fine, since it's not just me, I have to agree to what you ask. We need to know what this thing is and how to kill it. So fine."

"That second part, how to kill it, could be more difficult than the first," Rhys said, as he picked up his mug in shaking hands.

"So you do know what it is?"

"I have a suspicion. One I'd rather not have."

"You take your life in your own hands."

"I know," Rhys said, looking into the dregs of his tea, as if to read a hazy future in its leaves. He swallowed hard before putting the cup down on the table. "Better my life than everyone else's?"

Dar stayed silent.

CHAPTER TWENTY-SIX

BARE-FOOTED ON THE warmed concrete floor, Luca stood at the wall of glass, looking out at the city, its lights blinking in and out. He could sense the life out there, washing over him in heady waves. He could sense the death he'd wrought. And he could sense something else – a waking power looking for a conduit.

He pulled on his leather pants, then went to grab his shirt from where it was wedged under the woman's body. He ran a hand along her dark leg. Still warm. Still human. He'd learned his lesson; he didn't need his father or anyone else sniffing around any more than they already were, upsetting a precarious balance. He yanked his shirt out from under her. A sigh escaped from her open lips, but her mascara-smeared eyelids remained closed. He had left her alive, left her human. Barely. He leaned over and licked her thigh. Her leg twitched. The wound was healing quickly; by the time she woke up, it would seem little more than an itch to scratch. He pulled his shirt on over his toned torso, the inky spider on his back moving as his muscles tensed and flexed, and grabbed his leather jacket from the floor. Well-fed and kitted up, he was ready to hunt again. But this time he was after different prey.

As Luca left the high-rise of gleaming steel and glass, the security guard watched him with a practiced disinterest. Luca's blood was on fire, lit up with adrenalin as he stepped out into the cold, slushy night, and zipped his jacket up further.

He raised his hand to hail a cab. It wasn't that far to St. Francis' Cathedral, but it was a miserable night, and he didn't want to get his shoes wet. The cab driver tried to chat on the ride over. Thankfully the trip was short and Luca could put him off with a stony silence and a deathly stillness. By the end of the ride, the driver was fidgeting and drove off as soon as Luca had thrown him some cash. Luca headed across the square, almost devoid of life, except for the hardcore homeless huddled under cardboard or second-hand sleeping bags, if they were lucky. A few stragglers took the shortcut through the square from the clubs and restaurants on the one side to the subway station on the other. He followed them and entered the station.

The station: the nexus from whence the demon emerged, the shadows whispered, and to which it fled again, taking its harvest of souls. Luca knew the truth: the base of an army of iron death. His army, so the voice promised.

The platform wasn't any busier than the street had been. The bright lights gave even the halest people a ghoulish cast. Luca took stock of the security cameras, and noted that there were no transit police patrolling at present. He walked quickly to the end of the platform, glanced over his shoulder, then headed into the twilight of the tunnel, lit by flickering yellow lights spaced far apart at irregular intervals, given that half of them were burned out.

Luca sniffed the air, his teeth bared, his eyes gleaning any light they could. A fetid breeze came from somewhere to his left. From the general miasma, he teased out a faint hint of something tangy and sour, and the slightest scent of death and decay. Delving into the darkness, his ears picked up furtive shuffles but he couldn't tell whether they belonged to rodents, men who lurked in the dark afraid of what else lurked in the dark, or to something else infinitely more foul. The etchings on his skin had started to itch and the shadows whispered in his ears, but they gave no direction.

So he followed his nose. As he descended further into the twisting tunnels, the smell got stronger. It told him two things: something didn't know how to take care of its kills, and he was getting close to the object of his desire.

He heard a muffled gurgle around the corner, and saw shadows play on the slimy wall. A wet, slurping sound replaced the gurgle. Luca moved closer. And the sound stopped. His sensitive ears, those of a predator, could just pick out the faint ebb and flow of a hunter's calm breath. It knew he was there. At least he wouldn't surprise it. He tried to match his breathing to its as he rounded the corner.

Luca finally came face to face, for the first time, with the creature he'd helped create. One soldier in a terrible army. His army, the one Luca had been promised when he helped raise the creature from the mire of legend. It bared its teeth, and swayed slightly as it rocked from one foot to the other, but it didn't attack. Not yet, anyway. Its muscles rippled under ashen skin. He took another step forward. Its nose and upper lip twitched. Luca took a deep breath and tried to follow the instructions he'd received: show no fear. He stepped even closer. A vein throbbed in its neck, and its talons clenched. It gnashed its teeth, serrated like a shark's, but didn't bite. Perhaps the rusty whorls, imbued with lead, that now covered most of his torso were doing what they were intended to, a return on the pain it had cost him to get them. Luca raised a hand towards its face, until it flinched and pulled away from the dull metal object Luca held: an equilateral cross, worn smooth from hundreds of hands, the arms whittled to soft points by a thousand worries.

The shadows had told him the leaden branding protected and the cross controlled, but he hadn't been sure until this moment that it would work. He lifted his other hand towards it, then stopped and waited for it to sniff at his fingers before continuing. When he finally touched it, its skin felt like leather, thick and strong. It flinched and mewed as he ran a hand down its torso before stepping back.

"You're beautiful."

The creature huffed.

"An unnatural-born killer."

The creature stepped back a little into the shadows. Luca heard a sound behind him and froze. He turned around, forcing himself to move slowly despite the adrenalin that spiked his blood.

"Or should I say killers." Luca smiled, showing his fangs. "'What I have done, let no man undo'. And to think, all I had to offer in exchange was my father."

A breath of noise pierced the darkness. They all turned towards it. For the first time, Luca noticed what he had missed in his singular focus to find the creature: a faint humming in his blood.

One of his own kind. He moved towards the tunnel, intent on killing whatever vampire dared follow him.

In a fraction of a heartbeat, between the diastole and the systole, the creatures attacked. Luca snarled at his attackers. Remembering the cross, he tried to drive the sharpened point into the creature that raked his other arm with its talons. It howled and backed away. The other one followed its lead. The injured arm burned, hanging heavy at his side. He touched it with the hand that held the crucifix; hand and cross came away dark and wet.

The voice had said that the creatures wouldn't harm him. The voice had lied.

MATTEO SEETHED IN AN alley of the subterranean tunnel, gripped in a battle between fury and contempt. The hum of distant trains barely penetrating his subconscious. Hearing Luca's betrayal, Matteo had turned to the soothing darkness, enveloping himself in its calming cloak as he worked through the best way to repay his son for his treachery.

Shock and anger at what he had witnessed warred for dominance, the dripping water beating out a staccato to underscore that internal battle.

Anger won out. A cold, white fury blazed in his gut. He had waited too long to take Luca in hand, and now his son had to pay the ultimate price for his insubordination.

Matteo had built an empire in this new place, agonizingly slowly, not upsetting the precarious balance, not drawing too much attention, not until the time was right.

Too cautious, he realized. If he had shown more of his nature, more of what had allowed him to rise to power in the sunless world, his son might have paid him the proper respect, or at least shown the proper fear.

As he breathed into his belly, he considered what to do about his treacherous son. In and out he breathed. There was only one answer. He must do what he would to any of his conclave who defied his authority. A calmness descended, as one of the sputtering lights from the nearby mainline pulsed to life.

"Luca must die," he whispered to the shadows. The shadows whispered back.

His breath caught in his throat. Something else lurked in the darkness. Not Luca, and not one of his creatures. A metallic tang interwove with the normal mustiness of the tunnel air, and he tuned his senses to the space between light and dark. An itch crawled over his skin, starting from his toes and fingers until it reached his throat. A remembered sensation, and not a welcome one. A single word came unbidden to his lips.

"Angelos." It explained a lot. Like how Luca dared to dance with demons. "Show yourself," Matteo continued. There was no movement in the tunnel, the sounds of the subway had faded. "I know you're there."

A howl roared through the catacomb. The sensation dissipated into the shadows. Matteo paused for a second, hoping the creature didn't take care of his son before he could.

Then he faded away into the darkness himself.

CHAPTER TWENTY-SEVEN

RHYS STOOD LIKE A STATUE on the deserted subway platform, suddenly in the path of an arrow of sinew and bared teeth that shot out of the black abyss. Mina didn't understand why Dar had let this old man tag along, Librarian or not. Nonetheless instinct kicked in: she ran towards Rhys, sprang up and grabbed one of the pipes running overhead, with a speed and agility that went beyond preternatural into primal, somehow pulling off a gymnastic leap over the charging creature. She managed to clear its long talons but her hands slid on the slick pipe, and she had to tuck and roll to evade the second creature that followed fast on the heels of the first.

The first creature slid to a stop in front of Rhys, who held up a large, matte gray crucifix in a surprisingly steady hand. The creature snarled.

"I've never seen the likes of you before," he said, his voice small in the cavernous station. "But I know what you are now."

The creature opened its jaw wide, as if to swallow Rhys' head whole. Even off to the side as she was, Mina could smell its breath, like stale vomit.

The creature snapped its jaw at Rhys, who flinched but stood his ground, his hand clutching the crucifix tighter, pressing it towards the creature. It opened its jaw again, its sharp teeth gnashing as if to rend hand from limb. Instead, its muscles tensed and a deep howl rumbled from its gut and up its gullet, before it turned on its heels and fled back into the tunnels.

A vampire emerging from the tunnel jumped out of the way to avoid being knocked down. Without hesitation, two guns were trained on the new arrival. Jack pulled the trigger in a heartbeat. Mina paused a second before firing, some pull of a thread in her mind causing a hitch in her movements. Her bullet hit just wide, shattering the tile over the intruder's shoulder as he leapt to the side. Jack's bullet tore through the vampire's leather jacket, grazing the man's arm. Lucky for him, it didn't hit anything vital but he still cursed – the sting of silver setting in.

"Luca," Jack whispered.

Luca drew his own gun to return fire. He took aim at Jack, perhaps deeming him the greater threat, and let off a shot. But Jack was a step ahead, and lunged out of the way, behind one of the concrete support pillars.

Mina wasn't as quick thinking and stayed exposed to take aim at Luca. He looked at her, his amber eyes burning into her, and again she felt that twinge, something beyond the normal hum of vampiric warning: a twang in her ears, a twitch in her gut. But it was jumbled in the chaos around her.

That moment's hesitation nearly ended her life. But some sixth sense, natural or not, forced her to break eye contact and turn just as a third person...vampire...thing entered the station, like a white specter. It lunged towards them from the tunnel, its limbs moving disjointedly like an albino, leaping spider. She had never seen anything move so fast, and barely got a shot off before it was on them, taking Luca down.

Another shot echoed in the station. The ghostly form snarled and leapt towards Jack, away from her and Luca. Jack kept shooting. The specter dodged all the bullets, clambering along the ceiling and pushing off the walls. Jack continued to squeeze the trigger on his semi-automatic. The specter coiled its muscles, ready to lunge.

Jack's gun stopped firing. The specter sprang but Mina had recovered from the shock and lunged in front of Jack, aiming at the flash of white against black.

After letting the shots off, she fell back, taking Jack with her. The specter fled, and the other vampire had disappeared as well. It was all over in seconds, though the tempo of her heartbeat in her ears seemed to disagree as waves of adrenaline coursed through her veins.

"What was that?" she asked, as Jack helped her up. "Or is it something else you don't know?"

"No. That I know. A nosferat. In this case, Matteo, ruler of the local Necrophagos. If you're alive and unbitten after meeting him, you're lucky."

Jack reached up and took her face gently in his warm hands. He turned her head to one side, examining her bloody cheek. He let go. "You are unbitten, right?"

Mina's stomach twitched, her hand reaching up to her face before she forced it down. "Yeah, I think so. Just concrete scraping flesh."

"It'll heal." His unfathomable eyes looked into hers before he turned and headed down the platform to where Dar knelt beside Rhys. Mina followed.

"I'm all right, thanks to this one," Rhys said as they approached, nodding at Mina. He pushed against Dar as he stood. "I'm not as feeble as I look. I managed to keep my tea and biscuits down as that creature lunged at me. And when the shooting started, I ducked out of the way. Unfortunately, it seems I've lost some padding over the years." He rubbed his backside.

"I just asked if you were all right," Dar said. "Jack, Mina, you okay?" Dar eyed the blood on Mina's cheek.

"Just a few scrapes," Mina said, though she was drowned out by shouts arising at the far end of the station.

"Time to leave," Dar said, leading them into the dark tunnels, in the opposite direction from which the creature had fled.

THE GROUP OF THEM WALKED back to the Sanctuary, their haste only moderated by Rhys' human pace. Dar and Rhys led the way, heads together in conversation, Dar's hand on his old friend's back. Occasionally they glanced back. At Mina.

Jack followed behind, between her and the other two, as close to them as he could get without being obvious.

He would suck as a spy. It was clear to her that he was trying to eavesdrop, even though they seemed to be talking about inconsequential things, despite what they'd just been through: history, the weather, her.

Mina brought up the rear, hands stuffed into her pockets, more to hide the shaking than to protect against the cold rain. Her skin vibrated and her stomach churned as the unfamiliar mix of excitement and fear swirled in her blood. In one night, she'd come face to face with multifarious harbingers of death.

She'd faced the creature and had her first encounter with what, until recently, had been the biggest, baddest bogeyman in the vampire world: a nosferat. It was much closer to the creatures in the old, late-night movies than the slick image that had come to predominate in recent years: more spidery specter than suave, blood-sucking gentleman. It was an ashen, angular, long-limbed creature of fang and famine. She understood now why people, and vampires, feared them. Her adrenalin-soaked impression was of an arachnoid wraith, all pointy bits and odd angles, faster than anything she'd encountered before. She didn't understand how that thing could exist without people knowing about it; she could still feel the cold pit of fear in her abdomen.

For some reason the nosferat, with the malevolent intelligence in its eyes, scared her more than the other creature. And that was saying something. Although she'd seen the other creature before, in the fetid basement abattoir, slick with gore and blood, it seemed more menacing now: its gray form free to slink back into the shadows of the underground; its longer teeth and sharper nails able to rend flesh from bone; its shining skin able to blend with the slimy walls. More able to become one with the darkness.

"The night comes," a voice said from her periphery. A hand grabbed her arm. Lost in thought, she instinctively grabbed the man's wrist in her own unyielding grasp, ready to twist and throw him against the wall, but a meow from her feet cleared her adrenaline-choked brain enough to process who had grabbed her.

"Mike," she said, taking a deep breath. "Now is not a good time." She squeezed a little harder, trying to force him to let go without hurting him. His sharp eyes flicked from her face to over her shoulder, to where Jack had stopped, maybe 10 yards ahead. Mina followed his gaze. Mike let go, but he wasn't done.

"Death stalks you," he said, leaning close. As his stale sweat permeated the air around them, Mina realized that she'd never smelled alcohol on him during any of their interactions. She didn't smell it now either, and his eyes were clear. "But the Night still comes. Look." His eyes traveled a wide arc across the sky. "It falls like a rain of burning pitch on a world that has lost its belief. The Herald speaks: when Night comes, the rivers run red, the streets fill with the dead, and even the sun dare not rise."

Mina felt a pressure on her leg, and looked down to see his cat rubbing against her, perhaps seeking solace from his rantings.

"Okay Mike," Mina said as she inched away, towards where the others watched her. "Got it. I'll be on the lookout."

He continued, as if he'd never been speaking to her, but to some invisible host of people. "The Night comes, the way paved by its messenger. But you will wish for Death when the Night comes."

"Who the hell is that?" Jack asked when she caught up with them.

"No one," Mina said, looking at Mike. "A local street person. I used to give him change, buy him coffee." Mina watched as Mike settled down over his grate, talking and waving his arms, even though there was no one to listen. He quieted a little as his cat curled up in his lap and started to groom itself.

"He seemed harmless," Mina said. "But he's gotten way off-kilter lately. I wonder if I should call someone."

"Who?" Rhys said, looking at Mike. "There's not much that can be done unless he's a danger to himself or others." Rhys turned his gaze to her. "Is he?" he asked, his eyebrows raising in a question.

Mina shook her head. "I don't know anymore."

They walked the rest of the way in silence, Rhys beside her, puffing on an empty pipe, looking at her out of the corner of his eye, though he was trying to hide it.

"Do I need to be invited?" he asked as they arrived at the gate.

"Not unless you have something to tell me," Dar said, but still he made an elaborate sweeping gesture. "Please do come in. Age before beauty and all that." Dar's lips quirked in a stifled smile as Rhys peered at him.

"Do you realize that I've never seen the inside of your new home?" Rhys said as he entered the Sanctuary. "It reminds me of the grand halls at school. You know, where we used to...." Rhys trailed off. Dar led them to an alcove, where Rhys settled back into a comfy chair, Dar perched on its arm, while Mina sat on the floor.

Jack stayed standing, arms crossed, and was the first to speak. "So now that you've seen it, can you tell us what it is?"

"Right to business then?" Rhys said. "No pleasantries?"

"Sorry," Dar said. "He's forgotten how to interact with humans. Would you like something to drink? Coffee? Tea?"

"I wouldn't say no to something stronger if you've got it. Scotch? The peatier the better."

Dar motioned with his hand and a familiar floated out of the darkness and headed downstairs.

"So do you know what it is?"

"Hmmm? Oh yes. It's a gargoyle."

"Gargoyle?" Mina asked, not sure she'd heard him correctly.

"Yes. Gar-goyle."

"Like the statues on churches?" she asked.

"I'm pretty sure those things weren't stone, Rhys," Jack said.

"Are you sure?" Dar asked, his normally copper-tinged skin suddenly ashen.

"Yes," Rhys replied solemnly.

Jack looked from Rhys to Dar. "What? This makes sense to you?"

"Yes, and no," Dar said. "I had heard stories that they were once alive, when I wandered through forgotten villages in shadowed vales in the Caucuses and old Europe. Tales from the old, senile ones, that they'd heard whispered furtively by the First Ones, passed down from lore to legend. That in the days of darkness, there ravaged the world an insatiable hunger and its name was Gar Guile. But they were just ravings of addled minds, without detail. I didn't think they were true, and certainly had no idea what they would look like if they were."

"Gargoyles," Rhys said. "From the Latin, the gullet, the throat, the swallower of man and beast. One of the first order of daemons, spawned by the underworld, created in the archangel Gabriel's revolt against heaven."

"Gabriel?" Mina said. "Really? Those are just fairy tales."

Rhys looked at her, his eyes narrowed. "Guess what, my dear – you're a fairy story." Mina didn't respond, so he continued. "Did that look unreal to you? Gabriel was so angry at being cast out of paradise – her anger wasn't entirely unjustified, if you ask me – that she seethed with it."

"She? I thought..." Mina started until Rhys shushed her with a wave of his hand.

"He, she, do you really think it makes a difference with archangels?" he continued. "The form she chooses to wear most of the time more closely resembles the feminine of our species. I feel it wise to respect that. Anyway, when she failed to bring down heaven, she set about corrupting God's creations. One of those corruptions was the gargoyle. Another was the first vampire."

The familiar returned with Rhys' Scotch, then faded into the shadows again.

"So do the fairy tales say how we can kill this thing?" Jack asked.

Rhys took a deep sniff and small sip of his scotch, his eyes closed, before answering. "Good question, but just as important is how do you stop them from spreading – they can be autochthonous."

"Huh?"

"They self-procreate," Mina said. They all looked at her. "What, I know stuff. I was a good student. I even thought about being a doctor. Once upon a time."

"What your Mina says is correct. Full of surprises, she is," Rhys said. "They can reproduce themselves, if needed and provided with a catalyst, and they will. All of which means that they're like cockroaches: if you see one, there's more. And, as you've found out, they can also spread like vampires – if they don't completely destroy their prey, the prey becomes them."

"What if we kill their maker?" Jack asked. "Like vampires?"

"What do you mean?" Mina asked.

"Apparently Jack believes the old-world legends of the vampire hunters," Rhys said. "That if you kill the sire, you kill the spawn." He looked from Mina to Jack to Dar. "But we know that's not true. Vampires have survived the death of their sires. Otherwise we wouldn't be here."

Jack glanced from Dar to Rhys, as Mina tried to follow the thread of an undercurrent she had no context for.

"Maybe there's some trick to it," Jack said. "Maybe it has to be the spawn that kills the sire."

"Ensuring its own death?" Rhys took a sip of Scotch before shaking his head and continuing. "No, I don't think so."

Jack opened his mouth to respond, but Dar forestalled him. "How do we kill them then?"

"Of that, I am not exactly certain," Rhys said. "The texts are cryptic. However, it is possible, I know that. The first gargoyles were not born stone; they were turned into it. But the secret seems to have been lost to the ages. You need to go back to the oldest vampires, the First Ones, they might know, if you can find one." Rhys tilted his glass then set it upright again, his eyes peering into its depths as if to find an answer. Mina watched as the caramel liquid slowly drizzled down the inside of the glass.

"There's someone who might know." Dar looked at Jack before continuing. "The closest we have in these parts."

Jack's face slowly resolved into a mask of resistance. "No," he said, shaking his head. "No way."

"Do you have another idea?" Dar asked.

"Yeah, go and hunt this thing with whatever weapons we have."

"That approach will likely kill you," Rhys said.

"That might be better than what he has in mind." Jack's jaw pulsed as he clenched his teeth. His arms flexed, crossed over his chest, and his dark eyes bored into Dar. Dar looked back calmly.

Rhys looked from Jack to Dar. Then back again. His eyebrows raised and his mouth opened. "Oh."

"No," Dar said, looking at Rhys, who casually played with his bowtie.

"I haven't said anything," the old man said.

"After all these years, I can hear the gears turning in your head."

"Would someone enlighten me?" Mina asked, but she was ignored.

"I just want to go with you. I promise to keep my distance."

"No," Dar and Jack said in unison.

In the short time she'd known him, Mina had never seen Dar this riled, though she might not have caught the subtle signals without her newly heightened senses: the slight reddening of his face, the tension around his eyes, the carefully controlled breathing.

"I survived this trip," Rhys said. "Besides, you need me. I know the questions to ask. I'll understand the answers."

"You don't want to go on this trip," Dar said.

"Surely I do. Why wouldn't I want to meet Jack's maker?"

Mina's eyes flashed to Jack. He was staring at a gilt painting on the wall over Dar's head as if to escape into the image.

"Better you than me," Jack mumbled, turning up his collar, sinking further into his jacket. He looked at each of them in turn, before finally settling his gaze on the floor. "Fine. If we're going to do this, we'd better get some sleep. It's already sunrise, and we'll need to leave well before sunset to get it done tonight."

CHAPTER TWENTY-EIGHT

MINA RUBBED HER EYES against the darkness of the forest, trying to force herself awake. She was still tired despite having slept like the dead after they'd returned to the Sanctuary early that morning; sleep had embraced her in defiance of her vertiginous mind and feverish blood. But now the endorphin high had been replaced by a hangover. And she got the sense that this was an occasion when alertness was called for.

A trickle of icy water had found its way under her collar and now snaked a path down her back. Her nose ran and her feet were cold. The fact that they weren't as cold as they would have been a couple of weeks, in her previous life, did little to ameliorate her mood.

"I hate the woods," she said to no one in particular. No one answered. The only time she'd liked nature were the family hikes, before her father passed. But she remembered those outings as dry and sunny. "I still don't get it. Why are we here?"

"We're looking for someone," Dar said as he scanned the forest, where even the trees shivered as if to shake off the rain. "Or more accurately, stomping around until she finds us."

"Right. Jack's maker." Mina wasn't surprised that his maker was a woman. "But why are we looking for her again?"

"When you're looking for information about something from time immemorial, you ask something from that time. She's the most ancient vampire haunting these parts. Not one of the First

Ones, but close enough that she might have heard the stories of gargoyles when the oral history was fresh."

"So why are we out here? Where it's cold and wet. If this 'she' is so wise, why isn't she inside somewhere warm?"

"I didn't say she was wise," Dar said. "I said she was old. She's wild, a revenant. And this is her territory."

"Um, okay."

Jack looked at her, his dark eyes shining. "A revenant, a vampire gone mad." He turned his attention back to the dark woods, one hand resting on the blade at his side while the other loosened the gun in its holster.

"You've heard the stories about these woods, that there's a serial killer, or a monster?" Rhys said.

"Not really."

"That people who come here alone disappear, and animals are found dead, drained of blood?" he added.

"I tend to avoid the wood," Mina said. "Bugs, cold, trees."

"Well, that's the revenant," Dar said without looking at her, his hand fidgeting with the hilt of a dagger in his belt.

"Okay, then why will she come out at all? She can't feed off of us. Well, except Rhys." Mina looked at him, and shrugged. "Sorry."

"Oh, I'm not the bait." Rhys looked at her before turning his gaze to Jack's back. "He is."

"Why...?" Mina stopped talking, the question fleeing from her mind as the twitter in her stomach turned to somersaults.

"She's here," Jack said, saying what they all knew. Without a signal, the group moved to keep their backs to each other. Mina peered into the dark woods surrounding them, barely lit by the flashlight Rhys carried.

Mina's ears twitched, as a faint caterwauling like misplayed bagpipes crept towards her from the woods. "Damn it, I'm going to have to learn to block that out," she mumbled.

"What?" Dar asked, glancing over his shoulder.

"Nothing, just the cold talking." Mina turned her attention to the woods around them. Solitary drops of rain fell from the trees to disturb the detritus of the forest floor. Concentrating, she shuffled through the sounds, tossing out the irrelevant and teasing out a snuffling, like a dog searching for a bone.

A whooping howl, like a coyote, rose from the woods. It echoed and reverberated, seemingly coming from all around.

"Lin, if you don't stop that, I'll leave," Jack said. Abruptly the sound stopped, shrouding the forest in a ghostly silence that had an empty echo all its own.

"Chagadai, my heart," a lilting voice said from the darkness at Mina's right. "My blood, my soul. Why disturb my lonely peace?"

"You have no peace, Lin."

A ghastly woman emerged from the trees into the tenuous circle of light provided by the timid moon and weak flashlight, desiccated pine needles barely shifting under her bare feet. "True words flow easy from false lips. Why then do you disturb my madness?"

Her long hair, a dull black, was matted and knotted with bits of twig and moss. Ragged nails, fingers and toes, were embedded with dirt and God knows what else. A layer of grime streaked the exposed patches of her once pale skin. She was clad in an odd assortment of clothes, some too big, some too small. A pair of worn jeans were belted snug around a small waist, one leg torn, the other rolled up to expose a bony calf. An over-sized quilted plaid shirt that had lost its buttons was layered over a too-tight tank top. Her mottled lips were cracked and stained where her long fangs flashed as she sneered and sniffed at them. Her eyes were bloodshot.

Underneath it all, Mina could see that she had once been beautiful, the fine bone structure and still smooth skin visible under the grime. Delicate limbs demonstrated a muscle memory of cultured grace not yet entirely forgotten.

"You brought guests, maybe," she said, as she came up to them, with the same spider-like movements of the nosferat Mina had encountered in the subway, and sniffed around. She stopped at Rhys, and Mina inched closer to him. "A gift? Is this one for me?" Lin asked, her voice pitched a little higher. "It does look tasty." Her red-rimmed eyes stared at Rhys as her lips lifted like a smelling cat's.

A gurgling escaped from her as Jack's hand went to her throat, while Mina and Dar closed ranks around Rhys.

"Hands off," Jack said. Slowly she turned her head towards him, betraying no discomfort at the awkward angle.

"Why use my fair hands?" she said with a smile that was worse than her sneer. "When I have teeth for tearing, why break a talon?"

Regardless, she eased a step backwards and Jack released her throat. Her sneer returned as she massaged her throat.

"Why are you here then?" she asked. "Without a gift in exchange, you expect some boon?"

"Just information."

Lin made a huffing sound and slunk a step towards the shadows. "Knowledge is priceless, hoarded as the gems of dragons, shed like lost love's tears."

Jack sighed. "Please Lin," he said through a tight jaw.

"I know not a thing. The world abandoned me. So I abandon it." She ran a hand over her shoulder, as if wiping away dandruff.

"Bull shit," Dar said. "You were driven out. You couldn't even live by the rules of the Necrophagos. You wouldn't even rein in your hunger, check your thirst to stay hidden from the human world. So they kicked you out. And this is what's become of you."

Before Mina even had a chance to blink, Lin was up against Dar, almost as tall as he was, a low hiss escaping her lips.

"Dar, that's not helpful," Jack said, his voice careful, even, but Mina heard in his voice the undercurrents of tension that coursed down the muscles of his neck.

"I do not like this one," Lin mewed. "Stinks of cinnamon and spice. And too uppity."

"Just not susceptible to your faded charms," Dar said. "All that's fair and foul wrapped up in a pretty package."

"Both of you, that's enough." Jack looked at Dar before turning to his maker. "Lin, for old times' sake, will you please answer my questions?"

"No." She crossed her arms and took another measured step back.

Mina looked at Dar and Jack, then back at Lin. She shifted a sliver and moved her hand to the gun under her jacket.

"Mina, don't move." Jack didn't look at her, but his arm went out in front of her. The revenant's gaze swiveled her way before returning to Jack.

He looked steadfastly at Lin but said nothing more. After an eternal silence, she uncrossed her arms. "I won't say a word until you send them away." She smiled at Rhys. "Except for the food."

"You know I can't do that, Lin." She stepped back into the darkness. "But you and I can talk alone, away from them."

"Jack, that's not a good idea," Dar said.

"No, it's not." Jack looked at him. "But you brought us out here," he said quietly, then looked at the spot where Lin had been and spoke more loudly to the shadows. "But within sight of them."

Lin slunk back out from among the trees, and sidled up to Jack. She sniffed him before running a blackened tongue along his jaw. Jack's neck muscles twitched but otherwise he showed no response.

"Chagadai, my pain." She looked at the group over Jack's shoulder, her eyes flicking from one to the next before resting for a second on Mina, then returning to Jack. "Eternal thorn in my heart, how can I refuse?"

She stepped over the uneven ground to a cluster of rocks behind them, her quick, quiet, disjointed movements bringing to Mina's mind the ghosts of the Asian horror films her brother used to watch. Jack followed with the lean grace of a hunting wolf.

The rest of them were left to stand sentinel in the cold. Never a paragon of patience, Mina soon grew tired of watching and her gaze wandered over the woods. She could feel that the plump gibbous moon waned somewhere beyond the circle of dark trees; she couldn't see it in the small overcast patch of sky above the clearing, but she could feel the tug in the pit of her stomach.

"Does it get stronger, the pull of the moon?" she asked Dar.

He looked where she did, at the source of the tugging beyond the trees. "Yes, though not as strong for us as for others, like the Werekind."

"Werekind," Mina said, her voice flat, trying not to betray the endless font of questions.

"The Werekind," Rhys said, shifting towards her. "Humans who change into wolves, bears, cats...well, they change into creatures reminiscent of animals. They're weaker or stronger, more human or less, depending on the dictates of the moon."

Mina felt an aura of warmth coming off of Rhys. She didn't even mind that his woolen jacket, damp from the tramp through the sodden forest, smelled like wet dog. Rhys continued with relish. "Saturn, Jupiter and Mars come into play as well, though I could never figure out how. And apparently the longer they stay Were, the more they resemble the animal cloak they wear."

"The Werekind. Not just werewolves then?"

"Hah. And not at all like what they show in the movies," Rhys continued, his voice switching to teacher mode. "The Were: the felines keep to themselves, unlikely to attack, but they're unpredictable and enjoy a good hunt a little too much; the canines are a suspicious lot, loyal to their own, but don't back them into a corner; the ursa just want to be left alone, don't disturb them and they won't disturb you, well, unless they're really hungry."

"So keep to the city and I should be fine?"

"Pah! The cats keep to the city, the wolves to the peopled woods, the bears to the lonesome wilds. And that's just the main Were tribes. Most of the things that go bump in the night like to be where the people are."

"How many things don't I know?"

"Countless," Dar said.

"Thanks," Mina said.

"I'm still learning," he said. "This gargoyle is new even to me, and I'm over a thousand years old."

Mina coughed. "Thousand...?" She did the math in her head.

They all hushed at movement on the rocks. Jack strode towards them trailed by his maker, her eyes shining and her lips wet. Fresh blood stained Jack's hand.

"You didn't," Dar said, more fact than question.

"How else did you expect me to pay her price?" Jack's hand grasped Lin's throat as she moved towards his wrist. "I didn't let her actually bite me, just fed her a few drops. But all she's given me is riddles."

"More, please, I need more," Lin mewed. "Long months have gone by without human warmth." Her voice became shrill as she fought against Jack's grasp. "Forest sustenance. Deer crow vermin bat. It drives a woman insane." Lin's tongue flicked at the hand that held her, but couldn't quite reach the blood.

"Rhys, your excuse for coming was to decipher her riddles," Jack said. Rhys stepped forward. Lin's head turned around, further than it should be able to. She looked at him with shiny eyes, licking her lips.

"Not for you, I told you before," Jack said, his lips close to her ear. "Tell him what you told me, or I'll take back the blood I gave you."

"Soft and changeable," Lin said, breaking from his grasp with a twist of her torso. "The heavy scythe of Saturn cuts down the Gargoyle."

"See, nonsense," Jack said, looking at Dar.

"Sorry," Dar said, sighing. "I thought...."

"Was there more?" Rhys asked, his face lit up with a smile.

"Seeketh false silver, hardened with antimony or burning blue light."

"Oh ho," Rhys said, his hands clasped, giddy as a child on Halloween.

"This makes sense to you?" Jack asked.

"Of course, my boy," Rhys said. "Saturn's heavy scythe...tricky, tricky woman." He looked at Lin. She smiled at him; Mina almost thought it was genuine. Rhys turned to Jack to explain. "Plumbum. Lead. It's lead. I guess hardened into bullets or buckshot with the use of antimony, melted into a silvery liquid or lead flame, though that might be as toxic to the people around as to the gargoyles."

Lin growled. "Now riddle me this, code breaker, what enigma is there in your blood?"

When she didn't get a rise out of Rhys, her eyes slid over the others, coming to rest on Mina.

"You," Lin said. In the pulse of a heartbeat, Mina found the woman's cheek beside hers, as her lips whispered over Mina's ear. "Tell to me true, what do you hear, my dear, when you stand by Jack?" A small catch of breath escaped Lin's throat as Jack's hand went around her neck again, but she kept her fathomless eyes trained on Mina. Mina stared back through narrowed eyes, until Lin's eyes rolled up and over to look at Jack.

"Enough Lin," Jack said. "Rhys, do you have a crucifix?"

"Of course. I also have a Star of David and a hamsa." Rhys patted his jacket.

"Crucifix will do fine. Hand it over, will you?"

Lin's eyes went wild at that, and she started to struggle. Mina went to help Jack, flinching from the wrath in the wraith's eyes, as he tied his maker up, binding the knot with the crucifix.

"Not fair, Chagadai."

"I need to make sure you won't stalk us out of the woods."

"You know me too well, my love," she said with an edge to her voice as keen as a Japanese sword, holding little love.

"Yes, I do. And I know you'll free yourself soon enough, but this should give us enough time to get away."

"I will make you pay," she said, her voice soft.

"I know. You always do." Jack placed a hand on her cheek. "Until next time."

JACK BREATHED DEEPLY. The warming scents of cinnamon, cloves and cardamom that wafted from Rhys' mug, perched precariously on one pile of books as Rhys shuffled through another, took off some of the chill he felt. Jack let the smells rake over memories that were better left buried.

He and Dar were crowded into Rhys' crammed apartment, the others left to stand watch on the street. Jack was tense, trying to avoid knocking over the unstable piles of books and papers as Rhys' cat wove through his legs. Sheets of dust rose and fell as Rhys searched through tome after book after scroll, searching for plumbum, sisa, rasas, qian: lead.

"I know I've seen it, just recently," Rhys said, muttering, pushing his glasses up his nose. "I just didn't understand what it meant." His gnarled fingers surprisingly nimble, Rhys pulled a small book with a grimy cover from the bottom of a pile, while rescuing his tea from the top.

Looking at the book, a sickened pit gnawed at Jack's gut, as he sensed what the cover was made from.

Rhys flipped through the brittle pages, disturbing an acrid, bitter smell that crept across the room.

"Ah yes!" Rhys stabbed a page. Twisted letters spilled across the parchment, in a language Jack had never even seen. "See here,"

Rhys continued. "'Lead halts the winged monster, turning the beast more to stone'. I just assumed they meant the dragons."

"Dragons?" Jack said.

"Mmm, yes. It says liquid is best but solid is easier – ha, technology's come a long way – gaseous is too dangerous to friend as well as foe. But it takes a ton of lead." Rhys looked at them, his eyes large behind his glasses. He took a sip of tea, disturbing the spiced memories again. "Well, not literally a ton. But a lot."

"But that doesn't make sense," Jack said, his overloaded mind catching up with Rhys'. "These things, these gargoyles, don't have wings."

"No, *these* gargoyles don't," Rhys said, staring at his tea.

"But how many gargoyle statues have you seen without them," Dar said, looking sideways at Rhys.

"Hmm...more than you think, more without wings than horns," Rhys said between sips of tea. "And I didn't see any horns on these things. Likely our little outbreak hasn't completed the transformation. Whether it's time dependent or requires some unknown trigger...." Rhys shrugged and took another long sip of tea, his eyes closed. "Mmm, cardamom, licorice and Oolong."

"Seriously?" Jack said. "You're absorbed in a cup of tea at a time like this?"

"What better time is there?"

MINA SHUFFLED FROM one foot to the other, as a mist that bordered on frost settled on her face. She felt the cold less acutely now, but eventually it still seeped into her bones, a dull ache rather than a biting chill.

She scanned the early morning street-scape, cast in cold blue as it waited for the sun to rise. The townhouses across the way were mostly dark, except for random slivers of light around heavy curtains giving away the early risers and the smattering of outside lights left on. A few hardy plants still struggled to survive the descending winter, a testament to the stubbornness of life nestled amongst the brown of their less tenacious companions. A collection of garbage cans and recycling bins told her it was pickup day today.

She scanned the rooftops and saw where Simon had positioned himself down the road, on top of a diner that seemed out of place in this gentrifying neighbourhood. Then again, so did Rhys' place. She glanced down the street towards where Bee stood watch outside Rhys' front door. Mina saw that she was performing a similar scan, the muscles of her neck tense, one hand hidden under her jacket, where Mina knew it rested on the grip of a gun. Her own hands were under her jacket: it was warmer there.

A noise brought her attention down the street, towards the main intersection. A weak streetlight cast an anemic halo around a garbage bin, where a cat perched precariously on the edge, inspecting the contents. Apparently, it didn't like what it saw. It jumped down and sauntered in her direction. A clatter arose as a cart turned onto the side street. The man pushing it bent over the first recycling bin, picked out the bottles and cans and gently placed them in his burgeoning cart before straightening and trundling to the next.

Mike. He was enough of a fixture in her neighbourhood that Mina could recognize him at this distance. She'd never seen him outside of a radius of a few blocks, and certainly never collecting cans. She sighed. She'd always given him the time of day, as well as whatever change she could spare. In amongst his innocent ramblings, she'd been able to discern a tale of an interesting life, a time before the streets. But lately his rambles had turned to nonsensical ravings.

A movement at her feet drew her attention away from Mike's continued progress in her direction. The cat. His cat; she recognized it now, the missing notch in one ear. It looked at her. She looked at it. It mewed. She scanned the street quickly before kneeling down to scritch it between the ears.

"You're surprisingly clean and hale for a stray," she whispered. The cat answered with a sharp nip. "Ow! And you obviously still have a good set of teeth." She frowned at it as she stood up and looked at her finger. It hadn't broken skin. "Fine, if you're going to be like that."

The cat swished its tail at her before heading back down the street towards Mike, who was almost on her. She saw that both Simon and Bee had noted the intruder's advance, their scans returning frequently to Mike. She gave a brief shake of her head. Hopefully they would know it meant that he wasn't a threat. At least, she hoped he wasn't.

Mike stopped short, finally seeming to notice their presence. He looked past Mina to Bee, then looked over his shoulder. Whether or not he saw Simon, Mina didn't know. The cat jumped onto the cart to stand sentinel.

"Hi Mike."

"How do you know my name, shade walker?" Mike said. "Who told you? Well, it's not my true name, so there. Ha!"

"Mike, it's me, Mina. We've talked before"

"Mina?" He looked at her again. Took a step closer. "The shadows have descended, and Night follows at their heels," he said, his quiet voice carrying down the empty street. "The blade of Night cuts into the daylight hours." He took another step closer and pointed a finger at her. "But the line between the good and the wicked flows through each of us, shifting and shiftable." He pressed the finger into her shoulder. Bee stepped towards her. Mina and Mike both noticed the movement, and Mike took a step back. Mina shook her head again.

Mike absentmindedly stroked the cat that rubbed against his arm. "Even the end is not destined, it's decided," he said before turning his cart and crossing to the far side of the street. He continued to mutter as he pushed the cart back along the other side. Mina turned to the presence at her shoulder.

"What was that?" Jack asked, stepping up beside her.

"Just an old acquaintance. He's harmless." She saw Dar at Rhys' door, warm light spilling into the street. "You done then?"

"Yeah."

"What did you find out?"

"We need to visit the Smith. Wanna come?"

"The Smith? This person gets a 'the'?"

"Yes. And its their vocation, not their name. Like a blacksmith."

"What century do you live in?"

"Where else would we get bullets with liquid silver, or, this case, lead?" he said as if it was the most normal thing in the world. "And stakes of lead and antimony."

CHAPTER TWENTY-NINE

"TOMORROW, I SAID." Dar's voice rose a few decibels too loud for the sleepy street. Something skittered down the way, knocking over something metallic. He breathed deeply. "The Smiths will wait until tomorrow; they'd prefer if we waited until tomorrow."

"What should we do while you go off on your mysterious errand?" Jack asked.

"Take her back to the sanctuary." Dar nodded towards Mina, then turned to Bee. "Put her through some more training."

"But –" Mina started. She'd been through enough for one night.

"Where are you going?" Jack said.

Dar looked down the street to the horizon point, where the sky was a lighter shade of inky blue. "Tomorrow," he said.

TOMORROW CAME TOO QUICKLY. Although Dar had barely slept, he hadn't left his room, imagining Jack lurking outside to challenge him. In the end, after he'd put off the errand as long as he dared, he'd opened the door to an empty hallway.

He hadn't even needed to sneak out.

He sighed as he pulled out his phone and dialed a number he hated calling. Tomorrow had come too quickly indeed, though the sun was still above the horizon, beyond the blanket of clouds. The person on the other end was none too happy about being woken up.

"If you want to meet, we meet now," Dar said. "The cemetery in 15," he added before hanging up, not waiting for a response. Although he was only 10 minutes from the cemetery, he wanted to get the lay of the land before the meeting.

As it turned out, Matteo was waiting for him when he arrived, a ghost among the gravestones. Matteo was cloaked in a long wool jacket, fedora pulled down, scarf pulled up. The sun was just slipping below the horizon when Dar walked up to him.

Matteo pulled the scarf down, and Dar could see the tension in the tic of the nosferat's jaw.

"Why have you dragged me from my warm, dark bed on this miserable afternoon?" Matteo asked without preamble.

"You ordered me to report to you as soon as Rhys had found anything," Dar said, making no effort to keep the vinegar out of his voice.

"You didn't have to," Matteo said, teasing a waspish smile out of his thin lips. "I could have gotten it from him myself."

Dar glared at Matteo, his jaw aching. "You promise you'll leave him alone, if I tell you?"

"I promise I won't harm a hair on his head."

Dar sighed, scanning the gravestones around him. Perhaps the cemetery hadn't been the best place to meet; certainly some creature was listening to their conversation. "Plumbum," he said.

"What?"

"Lead, you need lead to kill the creatures." Dar related everything he knew about the gargoyles, everything Rhys had learned. Except where the information had come from.

After he was done, Matteo had stood silently, perhaps also contemplating the creatures that lurked amongst the dead. He looked as if he had another question, but when he spoke it was not a question Dar had anticipated.

"How's my grandchild doing?" Matteo asked, more of a statement than a question.

Dar had been looking at a headstone: *Sara Atwell 1963 - 1973 'Let the wild rumpus start'*. His gaze flashed back to Matteo, his mind racing along threads of possible meanings. There was only one conclusion at the end of all the threads.

"Mina,"

"Yes." Matteo pulled his lips into a smile, baring his fangs. "Your new recruit."

"Great," Dar said, forcing a full smile onto his face. "Fights like a demon."

Matteo's smile fell like a blind being drawn over his waxy countenance. Dar tensed as he stepped closer. "For your sake, I hope not," Matteo hissed, then stepped back. As he pulled up his scarf and tipped down his fedora, he added, "And you'd better have told me everything. I'd hate to have to ferret out more for myself."

Then he disappeared into the mist-shrouded night, leaving Dar tense and testy, alone amongst the dead.

MINA WALKED THROUGH the doors of the Sanctuary and breathed a deep sigh. She'd had to go back to Whittaker, Whittaker and Lee to sign more papers, and the lawyer's office was not a place she ever wanted to be. Whatever Mr. Whittaker was, he was more than your average lawyer; she could still feel it in her blood, in the niggle at the base of her throat. And seeing Dale, knowing she would have to 'die' soon, it took out of her whatever life she had left. Now she just wanted to crawl into bed and stay there for a solid day.

"Hey," a voice from the shadows called.

It took a second for Mina's eyes to adjust to the soft light inside after the neon-streaked night outside. "Simon."

"Want to 'train' with us before Bee gets her hands on you?"

Mina glanced into the alcove to see what they were doing. She shook her head. "I don't know how."

"To play video games?" he asked.

She shrugged. "Too busy studying, drawing, smoking behind the gym."

"Come on, I'll show you."

She hesitated for a moment, then followed him into the arcade. She flopped down into a bean bag chair beside Sha. Simon dropped down beside her, handed her his controller, and showed her the basics.

"Ready yet?" Sha asked, starting another round whether Mina was ready or not. It didn't take long for Mina to get the gist of the premise: they were rival vampire hunters, stalking and staking creatures of the night, and beating the snot out of each other while they were at it.

It took Mina a couple of rounds, where her character was soundly and bloodily beaten, to get the hang of it.

"One more round?" Sha asked, her eyebrow cocked. "Best three out of three," she added, obviously as aware as Mina that she'd won the last two with ease.

"Sure." Mina regarded Sha with a shrug and a smile. Simon shifted beside her. "Unless you want to play." She offered him the controller.

"Nah, I'm enjoying this. Payback for trying to mace me." His eyes glinted with amusement.

Mina turned back to the screen as Sha started the next round, which followed the same trajectory as the others: Mina's character was on his knees, Sha's getting ready for the coup de grâce.

Mina jostled her controller, bashing the buttons.

"No, no! Arg, the other button," Simon said. His hand reached for the controller. "Please just die so I can take over."

Mina jerked the controller away. "I got this."

"You two love birds done?" Sha said, shifting her controller.

Mina arched an eyebrow. "Let's do this."

Sha's character lifted its arms, preparing to bring them both down and knock Mina's off his feet in a spray of blood. Then Mina taught Sha a lesson in playing weak when you're strong. In a handful of moves, she had Sha's character on her knees and positioned for a roundhouse kick to the head.

"Arg," Sha said, venting her frustration.

Then the door banged open, letting in a blast of cold air and Dar's wraith-like form. His face was tense, his lips thin. His eyes latched onto Mina and didn't let go. He strode towards her, his coat leaving a trail of water across the floor.

"When were you going to tell us?"

Mina stood up, grabbing her jacket to hold in front of her. She took a step back, glancing at the others, who looked from her to Dar. "Tell you what?"

"Your maker."

Mina paused, trying once again to bring an image from that night into focus. "I told you, I don't remember."

"Matteo suggested otherwise." Dar took a step closer. The others took a step back.

"Matteo's not my maker."

Dar pulled up, inches from her face, to tower over her. "I thought you didn't remember."

"I..." Mina started. She looked around at the others. "I don't. But it's not him. He doesn't, I dunno, *feel* right."

"How can you know that, unless you do remember something?" he asked, though his tone sounded rhetorical to Mina.

She stood taller, matching Dar's posture. "I didn't choose to be a vampire." She spat the words out, in a torrent of frustration, anger and loss. She cast her mind back to the night again, the night when she went from being a lost human to a confused vampire, but all she came up with were amber eyes and a discordant twang. "I didn't ask for this."

With that, she pushed past him and stalked out the door.

JACK CLOSED THE OUTER doors to the Sanctuary, shutting out the icy rain. He shook his head, sending slush onto the wood. But he couldn't unsee what he had seen: Dar talking to Matteo as if they were old friends.

He stepped into the nave and came face to face with a tense conclave of vampires.

"Why didn't you stop her?" Dar said, striding towards him.

"Stop who?" Jack asked, pausing in his traverse across the space.

"Mina," Simon said, his voice quiet.

"She just stomped out of here," Dar said. "Upset at being called out."

"Upset that you implied she was a liar," Simon said. Dar's gaze swiveled towards him, and Simon went silent.

"What are you talking about?" Jack asked, shifting uncomfortably in his wet jeans.

"Her maker is one of Matteo's," Sha said.

Jack looked from her to Dar, staying silent.

Dar's eyes narrowed as they focused on him. "Leave us," he said over his shoulder, his eyes not leaving Jack. The others hesitated.

"Now," Dar said, waiting until the others had cleared the space before speaking again. "You knew?"

"I didn't know," Jack said, running a hand through his hair, dislodging more water. He sighed. "I suspected. A couple of weeks ago I was watching Luca when he picked a woman up at a dance club. The next night, we found her."

"And you didn't stop him?"

"I had been given specific instructions to watch, not interfere. By you, if you recall." Jack watched Dar. "And he, I assume, had been given instructions to not sire a new vampire."

"Why didn't you tell me what you suspected?"

"What's there to tell? She was a new vampire in need of guidance. Haven't you always said we turn no one away?" Dar was silent, so Jack went on. "You accepted me after all."

Dar looked up at him from the floor. "That was different."

"How so?" Jack asked, his eyebrow cocked.

"We weren't at peace."

"We're not at peace now," Jack said. "At best it was a ceasefire. And someone broke it by making her."

Dar sighed. "I had hoped...." He stopped, his shoulders sagging.

"Where's she gone?" Jack asked.

"I don't know, she just left."

Jack turned towards the door.

"Where are you going?" Dar asked.

Jack paused, his hand on the wood. "To find her."

"You're allowing yourself to be blinded," Dar said, his quiet voice barely carrying over the distance between them.

Jack cocked his head, but didn't turn back. "And you're changing. We all have our own crosses to bear."

THE MUSIC WASHED OVER Mina as she crouched in the alley behind the club, taking with it the anger, the pain, the self-loathing. But nothing could take away the coppery tang of blood-tinged vomit. She leaned a hand against the wall, her fingers finding a piece of metal to make a fist around, and heaved again. Nothing came up, the pit in her stomach still leaden, but she stayed bent over and let her eyes slid sideways to the man slumped on the ground beside her. She forced herself to become motionless and listen, closing her eyes. A whisper of breath and a weak heartbeat: he was still alive.

Mina let out a long, slow sigh and stood up, pulling herself up hand over hand along the length of metal. Her stomach felt empty except for the stone of contempt. She had just wanted to get away, release some tension. Instead she'd almost killed a man.

Just a nibble, a quick bite, a little sip. Before she could stop herself, his heart was slowing.

The hunger had screamed at her: more. A quiet voice, almost drowned out, replied: no. She'd dragged herself away, the skin of his wrist clinging to her fangs as she yanked it away from her. She'd released her other hand from around his neck, and the man had slumped to the ground. She'd dropped his wrist as if it burned. Despite Jack's exhortation to not throw it up, she had turned away and done just that.

She looked at the man's ashen skin and took deep, shuddering breaths. "He's still alive," she told herself. Though the hunger still pulsed through her veins, throbbed in the pit of her now empty stomach, demanding to be feed.

"Well, if it isn't our wayward vampire."

Mina froze for a fraction of a second at the voice, then turned to face the source. A wraith in gray wool and a black fedora moved towards her. She stepped back, reaching her hand behind her back, before remembering that she'd left the Sanctuary in a huff. Unarmed.

"What do you want?" she asked the specter, while casting her eyes around the empty, narrow alley. *Dead-end alley*, she corrected herself.

"I want you of course." The man stopped and lifted his head so Mina could see the ghostly face under the fedora. The nose was a little too angular, the lips a little too thin, the eyes almost as pale as his face.

"Get in line," she said.

The wraith stepped closer, and Mina went into a fighter's stance, lowering her centre of gravity, putting one foot behind the other.

"Now, now, why not come the easy way? One way or the other, you will come. And if you come willingly, there's so much I could offer you." The creature spread its arms wide, down to the end of its spidery fingers. "If not, all I can promise is pain."

Mina huffed. "What can you possibly offer me that I'd want?"

"That is a question." He clasped his hands in front of his hips and looked down. "Somehow I don't think you'll be swayed by riches or power like some of them." He glanced up at her. "Freedom then."

"Freedom?" she said, an eyebrow arching. "How can you offer me freedom?"

His eyes slid sideways to the man whose breathing and heartbeat were returning to normal. "Freedom from guilt when you do what you were born to do," he said his voice soft.

Mina looked at the man then slid sideways, placing herself between him and the specter, as she shook her head.

The wraith's lips went even thinner, and his eyes burned into hers. "Freedom from the pain then. The sorrow." He placed the palm of one hand on his chest, and reached towards her with the other. "I can feel the ache."

Mina shivered from the force of the sadness and loss she'd repressed. Looking at him, she felt the knot in her chest ease, and had no doubt he could fulfill that promise: lift the ache of her parents' deaths, of losing her family and friends, of being an outsider in the world. She breathed in deeply, in fits and starts, then let it all out.

"No."

"Who do you think you are?" the wraith snarled and lunged at her. She ducked and twisted, reaching back for the piece of metal she'd used earlier to pull herself up, realizing now that it was loose. Continuing her twist, she swung her makeshift weapon at the creature's legs as hard as possible. He dodged, but she was prepared for that, whirling the bar in a figure eight and driving the sharp, rusty end into the vampire's torso. It wasn't silver or ash, but she hoped it was enough.

A roar filled the small alley. She yanked the bar out, and blood seeped from the wound. The vampire took an unsteady step towards her. Just then a shadow filled the far end of the alley, between them and the street.

"What are you?" the wraith growled, clutching the wound, then ran at the new arrival, vaulting into him and knocking him to the side. The man turned to track the wraith's path.

In profile, haloed by the streetlights, Mina could see features she knew.

"Jack."

"Matteo," Jack said, before turning towards her. "What was he doing here?" His eyes fell on the man's body then flew back to her face.

He knew. She could see in his eyes that he knew. He knew she'd lost control. He knew she'd almost killed someone. And he knew she'd been tempted - for a second - by Matteo's offer.

She crouched down beside the man, taking the wrist she'd fed from to check his pulse. She leaned in towards his, listening to his breath. Both still slow but steady and even. Jack dropped down beside her.

"I know," she said, before he could say anything.

"What?"

"I know, okay? I know I broke the rules, I know I messed up. I know I almost killed him because I was selfish and lost control." She nodded towards the man, then turned to look Jack in the eyes. "I know I don't want to be one of Matteo's brood. Offering freedom but giving death."

"I know," he said, holding her gaze for a second, before looking down at the man.

She followed his gaze. "Let's get him home, okay?"

Jack nodded. "Let's get you home."

CHAPTER THIRTY

MINA WAS UNDERGROUND again, though she didn't understand why she'd been asked to come along, other than that Rhys said she should. Something about furthering her education.

I'll have to think of some appropriate way to express my gratitude, she thought as another drop of water fell from above to land on the tip of her nose. She sighed some of the tension out of her shoulders. *At least down here the drops are warm.*

And what else were they going to do with me, leave me alone? So she was trudging through an underground passageway, steadfastly avoiding looking too closely at the slime-coated ceiling and trying not to think about its impending promise of an eternity spent buried under a thousand tons of rubble.

"Can vampires die of hunger?" she asked Jack. Her hand was on his back. So she wouldn't lose him in the dark, she told herself, even though her heightened senses could see him well enough in the ambient light provided by random incandescents strung out along the tunnel.

"What?"

"Can we die of hunger, or thirst, or whatever?" He stopped. She ran into him before catching herself. "Just wondering."

"You know, I don't know," he said, half looking at her over his shoulder. "There are some who try to capture us, and other creatures of the netherworld, to experiment on us, trying to define and control us. If you're really curious, you could ask them." He started walking again, quickly catching up with Dar.

Mina's hand dropped. "Oh. Wait, who?" There was no one to hear her now, and the rattle and bang tumbling down the tunnel from the patch of light up ahead drowned out any questions she might have asked. She hurried to catch up, deftly avoiding the bits and bobs of detritus scattered along the tunnel.

The glow grew stronger and heat pulsed languidly down the corridor. Strands of hair clung to her face. Dar and Jack seemed impervious to the heat. Dar looked his normal coiffed self, his mohawk strident despite the damp. The only hint of heat on Jack was a slight flush to his usually stony face.

Mina stepped through the square of light to join her companions on a small, creaking landing, followed shortly by Bee. She glanced around the cavern, a reverence to rock and metal. A narrow set of stairs led up, disappearing into a dark ceiling populated by what looked like black lava stalactites. A wider set of stairs led down into a pit which held huge ovens from whence the red light emanated, wafting heat through the space.

A rhythmic clang clattered through the cavern from the far corner. A titan of a man swung a hammer with precision and grace. Mina watched him as they descended to stand a few metres away, waiting for acknowledgment. He was covered in tattoos of whorled red ocher. As he moved, his muscles flexed, causing the whorls to dance like flames.

Mina was mesmerized. The only space below his neck that was free of tattoos was a space below his collar bone, over his heart. Her gaze was drawn to the emptiness, only to realize that it wasn't empty: an anvil had been seared into his flesh. She was so caught up in the designs on his skin, glistening with sweat, that it took her a moment to realize it was suddenly quiet.

"It's the symbol of my guild," he said, his voice a surprisingly soft brogue for such broad shoulders. He had been looking at the project in front of him. Now he turned to her. "The Smiths: strong, unbent, unbiased...as long as you're fighting for the right side. We get branded when we choose to follow in our forbearers' footsteps." He laid the hammer gently beside the anvil and picked up what he had been working on: a sword. He ran a hand along the flat. Mina glanced from the sword to his face, then back. He noticed her looking and lay the sword down.

"Finn, we have guests," he said over his shoulder. His voice wasn't loud but it carried through the space. Shortly, a young woman with hair of burnished copper appeared from one of the side caves. She wore goggles, and long leather gloves covered her muscled arms. She was statuesque, partially covered with the same whorls as the man, but the flesh above her left breast was empty, no tattoo and no brand. She lifted the goggles off her face onto her head. Mina could see that she was beautiful, despite the tracks left by the goggles.

"Jack," she said. Mina looked at Jack with an arched eyebrow as the woman assessed the rest of the group.

"Dar. Bee." She nodded at each of them in turn. Then turned her frank eyes to Mina. "You I don't know," she said, taking off the gloves. "Finn, Keagan's daughter." She held out a hand to Mina.

"Mina, I'm new," she said taking the proffered hand with its strong grip and smooth callouses. "Who's Keagan?"

"That'd be me," the man said. "The one you were admiring so frankly a few seconds ago. I can assure you that I taste like wet wool."

Mina's eyes narrowed, a slight curl caught at the edge of her lips. "I was admiring the art, not the canvas."

Keagan stopped for a split second, like a deer in headlights. Then his laugh rolled out, cascading over the hiss, clang and crackle of the smithy.

"So you're the blacksmith?" Mina said, glancing around the shop.

His face went dark as quickly as it had turned sunny. "Bah! I'm not a blacksmith. I am a Smith."

"O-kay." Mina looked at the others.

"You couldn't ask an ordinary blacksmith to do what he does," Dar said. "He does more than make things out of metal, he works magic into it."

"Which leads us to business," Finn said. "What magic do you want us to work?"

"We need lead," Dar said. "Plumbum."

"Lead?" Keagan asked. "That's a new one."

"Mmm. Something new stalks the night."

"I'd heard rumours. You've figured out what it is then?"

"Yes, well, Rhys did," Dar said. "At least we think he did." Dar paused, shifting, not looking at Jack, whose jaw tensed. "With Lin's help, so we're not sure it's totally reliable."

"Oh," Finn said, looking from Dar to Jack.

"Is there no one who doesn't know my business?" Jack said, then stalked over to one of the ovens.

"I don't," Mina mouthed, but no one listened.

"Brought up memories best left buried, then?" Finn asked.

"Opened old wounds with a rusty nail, more like," Dar said.

"Enough of the soap opera," Keagan said, fidgeting. "What is it then?"

"What?" Dar said. "Oh, a gargoyle."

"Gargoyle? You know I don't do stone, right?"

"I thought you did everything," Mina said. "Surely there's wonders made of stone."

Keagan looked at her, his eyes a stormy blue. He looked at Dar and smiled. "Her I like. You should keep her."

"Oh god, not this again," Mina said.

Dar rolled his eyes. "She doesn't like to be kept."

"Really?" Keagan said. "I'd love for someone to keep me."

"Gargoyles...lead...a kept man," Finn said. "And I'm the soap opera?"

"Liquid lead bullets to be exact," Bee said. "Spikes and blades of lead, hardened with antimony apparently."

"Apparently?" Keagan said.

"So Rhys said." Bee shrugged a shoulder and glanced at Dar.

Keagan nodded. "Just so happens I know where to get some lead." He walked over to a glass enclosed office and came back with a tablet, its silver case and blue screen incongruous in the arcane space.

"What if some of Matteo's lot comes looking for lead?" Finn asked.

"Give it to them," Dar said, looking from her to Keagan. "As long as you leave enough for us. We may be accidental allies in this."

"When do you need it for?"

"Now," Dar said. "But as soon as possible will have to do."

"Come back in a couple of hours," Keagan said. "I can have a few clips of lead bullets for you. The rest you'll have to wait for."

After leaving the searing heat of the smithy, Mina breathed in deeply, relishing the crisp night air. She arched her back and looked at the patch of sky above. The roads shone with iridescent pools, but above, through gaps in the fleeing clouds, a hazy moon was visible. A sliver shy of full, waning gibbous.

"What now?" she asked as the others piled out of the abyss.

"We go to church," Dar said.

Mina looked at him sidelong. "What? Why?"

"To pray for our immortal souls, of course," he said then pulled his charcoal hood over his mohawk.

MINA GLOWERED AT FATHER Pietro through narrowed eyes as he touched a taper to a series of votives.

"Would you rather have been taken by the Necrophagos?" he said, without looking at her. His quiet voice carried in the empty vastness of the cathedral.

Mina looked at the candles he had lit, their flames lazily licking into life.

"You all keep telling of their nefarious ways," she said, pulling her shoulders back. "But so far I haven't seen that they're so bad."

The priest lit the last candle, carefully blew out the taper and looked at her. "We've all been a little preoccupied. Perhaps we've been remiss in your education."

A creak squawked from the back of the cathedral. Five heads swiveled to find its source. A wide-eyed young priest stood there, his robes ill-fitting on his lanky frame.

"My new assistant priest," Father Pietro said, leaning in and lowering his voice. "I don't think I like him, though I know that is un-Christian of me."

The young priest started towards them. "Anything I can help you with, Father?"

Pitching his voice louder, the elder priest responded. "No Mark, I'm fine. Just providing a prayer and some guidance for some of our more errant parishioners."

Mina refocused on the candles, and forced her hand to make a long-forgotten sign of the cross. "Thank you, Father," she said.

The young priest's eyes traveled over her, then across the other three vampires, before he finally left the sanctuary.

"'He is too lean, and thinks too much', or whatever Caesar said. And always watching. Luckily, he doesn't yet know this old building, the tender points, the creaking joints." The priest brought his gaze back from the door the young man had left through to the four of them. "So what 'prayers' can I offer to you errant folk?"

"How's the work on the outside of the cathedral progressing?" Dar asked.

Pietro looked at him, an unspoken question written on his face. "Slowly. Funding comes and goes. Meanwhile the old stonework wears away. I wonder sometimes if that's why we're so quiet, people don't realize we're open for business." His gaze traveled over the darkened interior, his brown eyes flecked with gold in the candlelight. "Then I remember: we live in a godless world."

"But not one without demons."

"No, we still have our demons." The priest fingered the plain cross that hung around his neck. "And I at least still have my God. So what can I do for you, other than discussing masonry."

"Would you like some new statues for your church?" Dar asked. "They'd be free."

"Huh, why do I doubt that there wouldn't be a cost?" His face hardened for a second before finding its serenity again. "Explain."

"We think we know what new creature stalks the night," Jack said. The priest arched an eyebrow. Jack continued. "Gargoyles."

"Gargoyles?" A small smile curled his lips. "Stuff of legend."

"Like us?" Dar said, arms crossed, his dark eyes peering at the priest from behind a flopped over fringe of mohawk.

Pietro looked at him, his eyes fiery in the muted light. He tipped his head ever so slightly. "Point taken. Where did you discover this bit of information? It's certainly not in any of my references."

Jack scratched his wrist and looked away.

"From Lin," Dar said.

Pietro looked at Jack, his eyes flaring to life. "You allowed that?"

"It was the only way, Father," Jack said. "With her riddles, Rhys was able to dig up the details. New weaponry is on order. We think it will turn them to stone."

"You think?"

"As you say, stuff of legend," Dar said. "But we need some way to dispose of them. We can't have stone statues suddenly appearing around the city."

Pietro sighed. "So you want to decorate my church with them?"

Jack shrugged a shoulder.

"I wonder what my new priest will think of that."

CHAPTER THIRTY-ONE

THE SANCTUARY WAS QUIET as the grave. Mina turned over in her cold bed, to look at the shadows on the dark wall.

When the sun set, they would go out en masse to hunt creatures that would have been beyond belief a few short weeks ago. But she was now an unbelievable creature, and she had seen the gargoyle with her own eyes, a nightmare made flesh. She'd seen its wiry strength, its hungry eyes and its sharp talons and teeth meant for tearing flesh from limb. She'd seen the carnage they wrought.

She turned over again, and closed her eyes, but that just made it worse. She sighed and opened them again, swinging her bare legs out of bed. The floor was cold on her feet, though the rest of her flirted with hot and cold.

She opened her door, onto an empty hallway where motes of dust drifted lazily in the half-light.

Golden slivers poked out from under a few doors. Including the one at the end of the hall. She tiptoed quietly towards it and, leaning into it, sensed the breathing on the other side. She tapped lightly on the dark wood. It was an eternity before it opened, letting out a pool of warm light. Jack stood there, his chest bare, still wearing his black pants. His skin was infused with red, backlit by candlelight.

"Would you mind some company?" she asked, her arms hugging her waist, suddenly aware of her half-dressed state, and his.

He stood there for a minute, not saying anything. Mina was just about ready to turn tail and run when he stepped back and opened the door wider.

MINA SENSED THE WINTER sun setting outside, too early, even though the twilight in Jack's room didn't change. He still slept like the dead, whereas she felt like she'd hardly slept at all. Her head rested in the crook of his arm, and from her vantage she saw hidden copper streaks in his hair sparked by the few tenacious candle flames. Her hand rested on his chest, which she watched rise and fall. She shifted her head to the smooth skin of his chest and listened to the slow trip-hop beat of his heart. He would wake soon.

She extricated herself with care out of his arms, and out of his bed. Possibly out of his life after tonight, if the hunt for the gargoyles went pear-shaped. She was even more aware of her half-naked state now, even though not a single piece of clothing had been dislodged, from either of them. They'd talked. Just talked. She'd asked him about the vampire world, not yet daring to ask about his life pre-turning. He'd asked her about her art, her tattoos, her family. Though she could still feel his fingers as they traced a path over her tattoos.

Now, she looked around his room, with its austere bare walls. In her short time at the Sanctuary, she had more decoration than he did. It could have been a monk's cell, except for the shelf piled high with irreligious books, and the desk covered with notebooks and a scattering of paper. She tried to peek at what things

Jack would write about, but it was all written in a script she'd never seen.

His breathing changed. She glanced over her shoulder before opening the door, millimetre by millimetre, and tiptoeing back to her own room. In her room, there were no books except the mystery she'd picked up from the communal shelf upstairs, thinking it would take her mind off things, but her desk was already strewn with pencils, markers, and paper. A half-finished piece lay on the desk: *Hibiscus syricus*, a single rose of sharon, vibrant white against a dark background, its centre a red heart. But the colours were wrong, too dark, and it would soon join the other crumpled papers in the waste basket. It wasn't right, not quite like the flowers in the half-finished tattoo on her back. She glanced at the family photo on her bedside table. It had been her mother's favourite flower. It had been a little too early in the year to have them at her funeral.

A sound outside her door brought her back. A knock. She placed a hand on the wood. A smile crept to her lips. Brett. She opened the door, the smile turning to a half grin.

"I have to work tonight," he said. "But I thought we could have a bite first."

She looked him up and down, pleasantly surprised that he filled out a suit as well as he did a pair of jeans.

"You clean up well."

CHAPTER THIRTY-TWO

MATTEO OPENED HIS EYES, wide awake in an instant. The waning moon had set. The heavy, velvet curtains that surrounded his bed blocked out any stray light and muffled any errant sounds.

But there was a buzzing in his ears, a prickling in his blood that he couldn't quite identify. It reminded him of some shadow of a memory, some reminiscence stubbornly just out of reach. He closed his eyes again and focused his attention on it, trying to ferret it out. Whatever it was, it receded, ebbing like the moon.

Frustrated in his attempts to nail it down, Matteo opened his eyes again. He was hungry, not for blood but for the hunt. A yearning he'd experienced with an unnerving frequency recently, causing him to abandon plans and schemes and common sense. He accepted that he was a hunter, he enjoyed it, quenching a burning beyond thirst. But he'd always been able to control his baser instincts to serve a greater purpose: the pursuit of power. Something had awoken that long-buried thirst and a desire to toy with his food.

He threw the bed curtains aside and, placing cold feet on an icy floor, strode to the window and commanded the blinds to rise.

The lights from the city bathed his ghostly form, a form that hadn't changed so much from his human life. With each step deeper into vampirism, each century passed, it had elongated, tautened, become paler and more angular. But the sinewy muscles gained in street fights and bloody battles still flexed under that ashen skin. And the scars that criss-crossed his back, laid down when he was a young man, had grown paler with the rest of him, their faint tracing still visible, if anyone got close enough. But if anyone did get close enough, he called on glamour, a slight warping of the light, a subtle shift in the eye of the beholder, to hide his true form, past or present.

Matteo placed his hand on the window and cocked his head. He judged that it was about four hours until midnight, time for a bite to eat before he went on a different kind of hunt.

"Fuck it," he said to the empty room. "What's the point of being a predator if you can't play with your food now and then."

He cloaked himself in his most human attire and headed out for the hunt.

RHYS COUGHED INTO THE back of his gloved hand, and tightened the scarf around his neck. He was heading home after a day spent in the stacks at the university library. He loved the musty smell and the trill in his stomach when surrounded by so many words from so many souls, all binding and twining together millennia of human experience. But trips to the library raised a tickle in his throat nowadays. He blamed the dust.

He was late, and knowing Grey would be caterwauling to be fed as soon as he crossed the threshold, he walked with purpose down the rain-slicked street. He carried an ornate cane, carved ashwood, with swirls of inlaid metal. He didn't carry an umbrella, having realized long ago it did little good in weather like this, where the rain fell at a slant, causing any brollie to be tossed about by the eddies that tumbled and flowed around the buildings. The best he could do were some good, weatherproof shoes, a mac and a snug hat with a broad brim. And the warm wool scarf wrapped tightly around his neck. The bookbag slung over his shoulder was also weatherproof, and held his old laptop and a notebook full of scribbles and doodles.

A niggle of a cough crept up on him again. He tried to suppress it, tamp it down, but it had a will of its own, and escaped with an unexpected force, causing him to stop and hunch over. The sound of the rain changed as he brought his head up. He slowed his steps and gripped the cane more tightly: he didn't need to be a vampire to know he was being stalked.

Rhys stopped at the lamplit street corner and turned to face his pursuer.

Matteo.

The Necrophagos almost blended into the crowd, his fedora down and collar up, hiding the monster that lurked within. If Rhys didn't know better, Matteo might almost look like one of the other workaday souls, the life sucked out of them by their 9-to-5, flowing like a school of fish into the subway.

But Rhys did know better. "Why do you haunt me?" he asked, heedless of the crowd.

"Why do you judge me so harshly?" Matteo asked in return.

"I've read your biography." Rhys coughed into the handle of his cane.

"Unofficial. Full of errors." Matteo smiled. "Maybe I'm here to protect you. There's some creature going around killing people."

Rhys stayed silent.

"Not just people," Matteo continued, his thin lips getting thinner. "Vampires as well. My people." He cocked his head back and forth as if trying to crack his neck. "I want to know what it is." His tone brooked no refusal.

"I'm sure you've heard what it is through the rumour mill," Rhys said, his breath catching in his raspy throat. "Vampires are horrible gossips, I'm told."

"I want to hear from you. You're apparently the one who puzzled it out."

Rhys looked down at his cane, pondering, then he looked back at Matteo, a decision made. "Gargoyle."

Matteo snorted, derisive, before his face became still. "So it's true. You're sure?"

"As sure as I can be about a creature from the annals of pre-history."

"How did it come to be?" Matteo cast a sideways glance at the crowd before returning to Rhys.

Another tickle threatened to turn into a cough, but this time, Rhys suppressed it with a shrug of his shoulders. "They. How did *they* come to be – that I don't know."

"Semantics. How can we control them?"

"Logistics," Rhys said, his eyes narrowed. He fought the cough trying to work its way up his throat. "We don't control them, we kill them. If the rumour mill told you what, I'm guessing it told you how. Lead, plumbum...I don't suppose you have some extra lying around?"

Matteo didn't answer, asking another question instead. "What about Ms. Sun?"

Rhys hacked into his hand, the cough winning the fight this time. "What about her?" he replied, a question for a question.

He looked over Matteo's shoulder, watching the stream of people that parted to flow around Matteo then knit themselves together again, though Rhys received no such consideration, a shoulder jostling into him, despite his apparently more advanced years. "What's your interest?"

"Curiosity," Matteo said, an eyebrow arching. He tipped his head as a skater punk brushed his shoulder. His dark eyes watched the perpetrator for a few seconds, until the kid tumbled off his board a few feet away, then they returned to peer at Rhys. "Do you know her maker?"

"No." Rhys looked into Matteo's eyes. "It's not you." His voice raised in question despite reading the answer in Matteo's face.

Matteo moved his chin. Rhys took this to mean his assumption was correct. His eyes narrowed as he looked into Matteo's.

"But you know," Rhys said, again cloaking an answer in a question.

Matteo made no response.

"Who can it be then?" Rhys said, not expecting an answer, his mind already working through the short list of candidates. He coughed again, a rattling phlegm-filled body-raking thing.

"You should get that checked out," Matteo said, his fathomless bleached eyes staring at Rhys. Then he melted back into the crowd, leaving Rhys alone in the halo of streetlights.

JACK STOPPED SHORT in the underground twilight, his right hand raised to signal Bee and Mina to stop. His ear twitched at a sound down the tunnel to his left but his nose told him that it was one of the everyday outcasts who made these tunnels their home, and only the familiar murmur of the two other vampires pulsed in his blood.

"Onwards and downwards?" Bee asked over his shoulder, no doubt sensing what he did.

Jack gave a curt nod, then continued on following the faint scent of death they'd picked up a few turns back. Its fetid pungency was hard to tease out of the metallic, mildewed underground miasma. But Jack was too familiar with the smell of violent death to mistake it for anything else: the shit and the sweat and the incipient rot. It might not be their creature causing the death. He imagined there were any number of corpses buried down here, with the warren of tunnels that twisted under the old city. But one thing was for sure – this death was new.

He stopped again at the next intersection – another tunnel led off to his left.

"This way," he said, leading them down the new branch. The smell grew stronger. He unholstered his gun and loosened his daggers in their sheaths. His gun felt strange, the weight of the lead bullets noticeable in his trained hand. They had picked up a small supply of ammo from the Smith on their way out for the hunt. He wished he'd had a chance for some target practice with it.

"Make your shots count," he whispered, turning his head to see that Bee and Mina had similarly armed themselves. "These are all we've got."

He crept forward, his blood prickling with a thick and heavy drone – a sensation he identified as not vampire.

His ears picked out a snuffling ahead. A gurgle. A gargoyle. He closed his eyes. Something else was intertwined with the hum of the gargoyle – not human, not Were. Vampire.

An intake of breath behind him caused him to swing his head around and glare at Mina, her eyes were narrow and lips wide. She looked away, at the ground, and he inched forward, refocusing on what was ahead.

Stillness.

Shit.

The sudden silence was broken by a shriek. A streak of mottled gray muscle shot past him, grazing Bee, who dodged a split second too late. She was thrown with a bone-crunching thud into the tunnel wall. Jack reached down to help his friend up as Mina gave chase.

Bee limped after her, but Jack paused a split second. The murmurs he'd heard earlier were no longer interwoven; they'd separated into two distinct threads of sound – one had disappeared down the tunnel with the gargoyle, the other had not. He glanced over his shoulder, squinting into the darkness, before turning to follow his comrades in their pursuit of the gargoyle.

It wasn't hard to follow. The blood that spattered the gargoyle's skin was like a rank perfume to the beast inside Jack. It was, however, hard to keep up with, as it twisted and slued along the paths of its home, its long limbs covering the ground rapidly. But its height also meant it had more difficulty navigating some of the narrow spaces and unexpected overhangs. A howl up ahead led Jack to suspect that it had gotten clipped by something.

He rounded the corner shortly after Bee, and his eyes adjusted quickly to the green light spilling into the tunnel from a station up ahead. St. Frank's Station, his internal map informed him.

He watched the creature clamber into some sort of shaft over its head, pulling itself up with talons and wiry muscles. Before he could stop her, Mina followed its lead, with a lithe leap that he couldn't mimic.

"Fuck me," Bee said, looking up as she reached the shaft. The grate lay askew over the opening at the top, revealing a patch of dark sky. No sign of Mina or the gargoyle. Wayward drops of rain fell on their faces.

"Boost me," Jack said, tucking his gun away, before launching himself up the shaft, using Bee's shoulder as a step.

Hauling himself up the shaft and emerging into an alley, he unholstered his gun again and took stock. One way led to a small street that opened onto St. Frank's Square. In the other direction, the creature crouched, trapped in a dead end. Mina ran towards it, gun drawn.

"Mina!" Jack ran towards them. But he was too late. The creature launched itself at her, low like a charging lion. Mina leapt to the side, her arm and leg pushing off the wall. Twisting as she moved through the air, she came down behind the creature, one knee on the ground, holding the gun as if she'd known it for a lifetime rather than days.

"Fuck me." Jack froze, his eyes on Mina, but reacted as the creature flung itself towards him. He went into a crouch, bracing for impact, ready to send all his pent-up tension through his shoulder into the creature.

A pop echoed along the brick walls, a silenced shot. The creature let out a sound like a broken bagpipe before falling heavily on the rain-slicked, uneven asphalt.

It thrashed, a death throe. The thrashing slowed to twitching. It tried to drag itself up but it could only manage a crouch, its limbs no longer responding to its fury. It opened its mouth for a final howl. No sound came.

Jack looked from it to Mina, who walked towards him, checking her gun before holstering it. Bending down, she rapped the creature lightly with her knuckle.

"They really do turn to stone," she said. "And quickly."

Jack was silent as he looked at her.

"What?" she said. "I was careful."

"Holy shit," Bee said as she came up behind Jack, finally having climbed up the shaft.

CHAPTER THIRTY-THREE

LUCA SLAMMED AGAINST the wall, a crunching sound indicating that something had broken. But he forced himself not to flinch as he looked into Matteo's white face, remembering that they were being watched. That he was being judged.

"Did you really think you were strong enough to play with powers like this and win?" Matteo asked, clearly not expecting an answer. "To use gargoyles as pawns and come out unscathed?"

Luca stood up carefully and walked back to his father. "Guess what?" he said, spitting blood, flecks landing on his father's pale face. "I have been." He wiped his lips, then pulled his shirt open with his right hand, his left trapped in the rigour of rapid healing, and exposed Matteo to the demonic etchings that traversed his torso.

His father didn't cringe, didn't cry out, didn't cower. Instead he calmly unbuttoned his shirt.

"I understand the seductive allure of the voices that lurk in the shadows." The brand on his left pectoral was clearly visible now that Luca realized what it was, dusky rose rather that the rust red of Luca's own branding, but nonetheless the same: a wound that never completely healed.

Luca's right hand fell to his side, as useless as his left. He tried to glance over his shoulder without turning his head, then he looked back at the simple, solitary whorl on his father's torso. He thought of the epistle that had been written into his own flesh, the nights of searing pain. He fixed his eyes on his father's, raising an eyebrow and curling his lips into a sneer. Matteo had no idea.

"Not this voice," Luca said. "You would be the one with an army of gargoyles if you had heard this voice, and heeded it."

"Ha." Matteo let out a short, sharp laugh. "It's always the same story," he said, buttoning his shirt. "If not the same voice. I thought I'd taught you better than that: when you play with the devil, the devil always wins."

Luca used every fibre of his physical and mental sinew to stand tall and not move as his father strode towards him. Matteo grasped his head, gently at first. Then he dug his sharp fingernails into Luca's scalp, drawing blood, applying a steady downward pressure, until Luca caved and fell to his knees. Luca's cheeks flushed.

"And I'm the devil in this family," his father said.

"But I control these creatures," Luca said, his hot anger over-ruling his better judgment. His left hand recovering its movement, it grazed his leather jacket, where it fell upon the lead crucifix.

"Really? So you ordered them to attack the Necrophagos? Your own people?"

Luca wanted to say that they weren't his people, that they were cowards who cowered in Matteo's shadow. But he stayed silent, marshaling his power, biding his time.

Matteo went on. "If they do anything you do not expressly command them to do, then you are not in control. You are being controlled." He ran his fingers through Luca's hair, slick with blood even though the wounds from his father's fingernails were already healing. "Do you even know by what?"

Luca's jaw clenched as a little worm of doubt started to eat away in his stomach. *But in for a penny....* His hand shifted in his pocket, twisting the crucifix in his hand so the sharpened point was between his index and middle finger.

"You should know you cannot trust the things that go bump in the night. A lesson I didn't need to be reminded of by my own son." His father beckoned to the shadows that lurked in the dark. A number of Necrophagos peeled themselves off the walls to do his bidding. Matteo let go of Luca, pulling out a white handkerchief to clean his son's blood off his hand. "Take him back to the manor. Confine him while I figure out how to fix the mess he's brought down on us. And the best way to deal with him."

Luca drove the sharpened end of the lead cross into Matteo's leg then launched himself up and away. The echo of his father's snarl pursued him along the passageway. He ran without looking back; a wound from a blessed crucifix or a silver one might sting, even fester a bit, but this one was not silver and certainly was not blessed. Lead might constrain a gargoyle but it did little to a vampire. Except piss it off.

MATTEO SAT IN HIS CHAIR of bones, still as a statue, his skin an incandescent pallor of variegated marble. His half-open eyes stared at a spot in front of him. For interminable minutes, he said nothing, did nothing.

The conclave of vampires gathered in the room tried to stay just as still; nobody wanted to be the one to disturb his brooding repose. They stared at the same spot on the floor, or at him, or at the mica flickering in the marble floor. Anywhere but at the empty space at Matteo's side, normally occupied by Luca.

No fire had been lit. The room was cold, even for a vampire, and the only illumination came from infrequent bronze sconces that cast weak balls of light that seemed to shrink from the silent room.

A scuff from the right side of the room was followed by a silent sigh of relief from all the other vampires that it hadn't been them, as Matteo's eyes changed the focal point of their penetrating stare. The offending vampire, Ryan, studied the floor in great detail.

Matteo run his hand over his thigh, which had started throbbing, indicating that the healing had begun, hastened by his most recent meal.

As if on cue, a whimper rose from the corner. "Someone deal with that," he said. Ivan moved to do his bidding.

"Not you," Matteo continued, beckoning Emily and Ivan closer.

Ivan noticed Em's shoulders sagged slightly at being called out, and his own back stiffened. The others took a step back.

"Sir?" Em said, her leathers creaking as she straightened.

"You may know the habits of my ersatz son best."

"We watched him as ordered, when he went out trawling," Ivan said, when Em didn't respond, a quiet voice from his broad chest. Em's eyes flicked his way before flicking back to Matteo. Matteo let the unspoken rebuke hang in the air: apparently you didn't watch him closely enough.

Matteo's eyes shone as they bored into Ivan, who shifted from one foot to the other. "I want you to lead the hunt for him," Matteo finally continued. "You know his habits, his haunts, his hungers." Another silent sigh of relief rippled through the vampires who weren't Em and Ivan. No one doubted the price of failure. "Find him but try not to kill him, if you can." Matteo's gaze returned to the spot on the floor, which had yet to melt under his scrutiny. "Killing him is my prerogative."

CHAPTER THIRTY-FOUR

LUCA STALKED ALONG the dark tunnel. These creatures were his. His army, so the voice had said. Only his army was playing hard to get. They'd moved their nest. Now he had to put his hunter's skills to the test, while evading his father. His nostrils flared. His skin itched and his blood was on fire. His father's words rattled in his skull. These irritations fueled his single-minded pursuit: he had paid the price, he deserved the reward.

He caught a faint whiff of a scent, noxious decay tinged with coppery bitterness. One of the creatures had passed this way. But the trace of its passing dissipated almost as soon as he sensed it. This trail wasn't fresh. But the hunter in him knew that one trail often led to another.

His eyes picked up shades of light, a flicker of red from a broken light or a sterno fire. And then the weight of the shadow pressed down on him, constricting his chest and tightening around his throat. He gasped for air. Reason told him that he could survive a lot longer with a lot less oxygen than when he was human, but instinct still prevailed.

I am disappointed. The voice was flat.

Luca's mouth opened as he strained against the smothering darkness. The noose around his throat eased, and he fell forward onto his knees.

My master is angry. The voice was cold.

"I...." Luca sucked in great gulps of air.

You were supposed to sacrifice your father. But you couldn't.

"I can...." He tracked the pinpricks of light that speckled his vision.

You were supposed to kill the girl. You didn't.

"I didn't know," he said, placing his hands up the wall behind him, coming to standing.

You didn't know? You didn't know that feeding her your blood would turn her? The voice was hungry.

"I didn't think she'd bite me." Luca tried to focus on the crepuscular coagulation in front of him.

No, you didn't think. So you were told: fix it. Kill her or claim her. Pain shot through Luca's brain, but he stayed silent, his face hot under the scrutiny of the Cimmerian shade.

You were told to bring her to me. Is she here? The voice was flat again.

A worm of fear snaked through Luca's gut. He inclined his head a few degrees downward.

"I can bring you my father," Luca said, looking at the grimy cement floor.

You have one last chance. The voice whispered. *Your father, the girl, yourself. I no longer care.*

Luca breathed deep, taking in the mustiness mixed with a metallic tang. He quieted his mind, slowed his pulse, with a steely force of will.

"Then I can –?"

The coalescence flared, and Luca felt like he would be flayed by a laceration of tenebrous talons but he stood silent and still.

Then you can have your army. The shadows sighed. *You know what to do?*

He looked up without moving his head. "Perform the sacrifice. Say the words you taught me."

Say the words. Perform the sacrifice. A whisper of decomposing leaves, warm and dry. Then the voice was gone.

Luca leaned against the wall, closed his eyes, then let a smile form on his face. "I'll show my father who controls the gargoyles."

Breathing in slowly through his nose, he stood up and opened his eyes then continued along the tunnel, not realizing that the hunter had become the hunted.

ICICLES OF RAIN SLANTED down from the mercurial sky. He rubbed his back against the grimy concrete. Try as he might, he couldn't quite find the right place to scratch that would release the itch. He huffed through closed teeth.

He lurked at the edge of the darkness, not yet daring the light. His hunger gnawed at his belly. He ran blackened fingernails over it. He hadn't eaten for a day, but it might as well have been a thousand. He felt his belly would consume him from the inside if he didn't eat soon.

But out beyond the shadows was death. No, not death. A fate worse than death: an eternity bound by stone. Where there was no way to slake the hunger or quell the thirst.

Still he would have to venture out soon. The creatures that ventured into the shadows had become fewer and fewer.

His companion stood off to the side, slightly behind him. It churred, its hunger was no doubt as keen as his. Still he snapped back, willing it to silence. He lifted his head and sniffed, his chin passing through the barrier between light and dark.

Then he heard it.

A clink. A clatter. Something was coming along the main alley. He took a small step forward, holding back his fellow, a gnarled hand on its chest. The noise came closer. He inched a bit closer to the lighter dark and sniffed again. It smelled like the underground, mildew layered with sweat. But there was something else, an itch on the inside of his ear.

The noise grew louder. Just a few more steps would bring its source to their hiding place.

Then he heard it.

The hiss followed by a long low growl.

"What is it, Pan?" a voice came from around the corner. A mournful meow responded.

He stepped as close to the edge as he dared.

"This is the quickest way to the station," the voice continued. "Ow."

He stood on tiptoes waiting for the owner of the voice to take another step, just one more would bring the man close enough to be grabbed.

"Fine, if you're going to be like that, we'll take the long way. Moody cat, sometimes I don't know why I put up with you." After that the voice was drowned out by the sound of metal clanging against metal and grinding on asphalt.

He dared to peek around the corner. He watched as a man in an over-large coat disappeared the way he'd come, pushing a cart away down the small side street towards the main road. The cat perched on the man's shoulder looked back at him. He almost howled his frustration.

Then he heard a breath behind him. Felt it whisper over his skin.

He went still, willing his tingling muscles not to move, his ears not to twitch. Then inch by inch, he turned towards the shadows.

He and his companions were no longer alone.

CHAPTER THIRTY-FIVE

MINA STOOD IN THE DARKNESS, eyes closed, listening to the sounds of the underground maze and to the trilling in her gut. She breathed deeply, trying to calm her quarrelsome nerves.

Her success earlier that evening had demonstrated the power of lead. That gargoyle now squatted in the rubble of the eternal construction zone that was St. Frank's Cathedral, waiting to be hefted aloft to decorate the church in perpetuity. After dropping their trophy at the church, they'd met up with the others, where it was decided that they would hunt until dawn, to try to eradicate the remaining gargoyles to stop the further spread of the infection.

Things hadn't gone to plan.

They'd found the nest alright, and split up. Mina, Jack and Bee came in from one direction while Dar, Simon and Sha came from the other. It had seemed like a good idea at the time, confront them on two sides, cut off their means of escape.

Corner them. They'd forgotten the raw fury of cornered animals. And there were more of the creatures than they'd realized. One had come up from behind, and their group had been scattered. She'd gotten separated from the rest, and now she didn't know where they were, if they were still alive. She couldn't feel them, couldn't hear them in amongst the dirge of the gargoyles and the hum of the trains.

But they'd all find her soon enough if they came looking, friend and foe. The gash in her arm, the result of a casual slice from a fleeing gargoyle's talons, would draw them like sharks. Even though it was her own blood, it still filled her nostrils, blocking out other smells, making her dizzy and nauseous in equal measure. She refused to think about what else it might draw, but she didn't dare waste movement on bandaging it. It would heal soon enough, the wound edges already transitioning from burning to itching.

Mina opened her eyes. The darkness was slightly less inky, lit by the weak lights of a train pulling out of the station up ahead. She hugged the cold wall of the nook she was harboured in as the train passed her, and felt her hair lash her cheek in the whirlwind that followed it.

The last car passed and the twilight of the tunnel settled around her again. She heard a sound down the way, the screech of brakes. Maybe. She didn't want to find out for sure, so she ran down the tracks towards the station.

The platform was empty, no sign that the others had passed through. She pulled out her phone and thought of calling Jack but if he was in a similar fix, the ring might draw a creature to him. She put her phone on mute and slid it back in her pocket.

"Sanctuary," she whispered. *The only way to regroup is to head back to safety.* Decision made, Mina flew up the stairs, taking them two at a time. When she crested the top of the long staircase, she tilted her face to the sky and drew in a deep breath of cool air, and savoured the icy rain that fell on her face.

The street was quiet, the last of the revelers home in their beds. Mina turned to get her bearings, then started the walk homeward. A sound in the side street to her right made her pause. A pricking in her blood told her she shouldn't go down that overshadowed laneway, though she saw nothing but a pile of crumpled newspapers partway along. She sighed and turned into the lane, shuffling forward foot by foot.

An itch in the pit of her stomach told her to draw her gun, and one lesson she'd learned these past couple of weeks was to listen to it. But before she could even get her finger on the trigger, she was tackled from behind. Her gun went skittering across the dingy asphalt, while she tucked and rolled up into a crouch.

The creature that had run her over stood in front of her, its back to her, sniffing the air.

But this was no gargoyle.

She shifted towards her gun.

The man turned.

She froze.

They stared at each other for a long second. Mina ignored the niggle at the base of her skull, some memory trying to get her attention.

She dove for her gun. But not fast enough, not far enough. Her finger tips touched metal before she was dragged away.

She twisted and turned, trying to unsheathe the dagger on her hip. It might not kill a vampire but it could hurt one. Slow him down, loosen his grip on her ankle.

Her fingers were on the barrel when her arm was pulled away, her wrist in a crushing grip. The hand let go of her ankle, and she used the moment to yank hard on her captured arm, trying to throw her attacker off balance.

Her action succeeded in pulling him forward and down: a knee drove into her stomach, slamming her back onto the cold pavement, knocking the wind out of her.

Her wrist was still imprisoned and he was now on top of her. The hand that had been on her ankle grabbed her hair, forcing her head back. She bucked and tried to get her feet under her but it was like trying to shift a bag of sand.

Still she fought as teeth sank into her neck. Warm liquid oozed over her neck, into her hair, as hot tears traversed her temples. She tried to scream, but she didn't hear it if she did. She felt the fight seeping out of her through the punctures in her neck.

There was a tug as the fangs came out, but no pain.

"Do you remember this?" A man's face swam in her watery vision. She saw her blood on his lips as he spoke. "Do you remember me?"

She tried to shake her head, her voice lost. But she did remember, as she looked into the amber eyes, glowing red in the night.

She was meeting her maker.

"Payback's a bitch, bitch." Droplets of her blood spattered across her cheek as he spoke. Then his head swung around at some faint sound, like a rustle of dry leaves. He had pulled a knife from somewhere; she saw the glinting blade out the corner of her eye. He looked back at her, his brow furrowed. Despite her pins and needles vision, she focused on his face. He was the man from the club, the one who'd bit her – the one she'd bitten in her struggle to save herself. And now he was going to destroy her. Mina let out her last breath.

He opened his mouth to speak, then his face disappeared and she was alone in the dark, lying in the filthy side street. She kicked at the empty air. She heard the rustle of leaves again, calling to mind crisp autumn walks with her father in the park. Maybe Death flew in on desiccated, papery wings.

She didn't want to die – again – to transition into whatever was next in this unending death. She had finally started to accept her new life, her new home, her new family. A family that would now look at her with even more suspicion.

If she survived the night.

She cried for help, pleading with the universe, but it came out as a whisper. She tried to bring her hand to her neck, to feel the damage the fangs had done, to staunch the blood, to undo the bite, but her arm was leaden.

Finally, the rustling leaves arrived at her side. A face appeared over her. A face she knew.

Mike, her lips mouthed. Crazy Mike.

"See, what'd I tell you?" Mike said. "Night comes."

Then he too disappeared and the world faded to black.

CHAPTER THIRTY-SIX

A WHISPER VIBRATED in her stomach, in that space between belly button and sternum. Far away she heard a man's soft voice call her name.

Opa. Father? She searched for the source, for signs that she was dead for real, though she didn't think death would hurt this much. But everything was darkness except for random quicksilver flashes in her vision that kept time with a nearby tapping.

She took a deep breath, trying to fight the leaden lethargy in her limbs and the fog in her brain.

She opened her ears, trying to latch on to the man's voice. But it had been replaced by a pernicious drone. The thought to swat at the buzz poked at her brain but her heavy limbs wouldn't cooperate. An icy sensation spread from her shoulders through her body, numbing the pain.

The quicksilver streaks resolved into flashing points of light as the tapping increased its tempo.

Rain. Falling on asphalt. She ran the tip of a frozen finger over the oily surface, its grime barely registering. Underneath the tapping of the rain, a low, heavy tune started to creep towards her.

So this is not death then. It wouldn't be so cold and damp, unless she had her own personal hell.

Just as she came to that realization, the tune got louder and the endless buzzing resolved into a siren of alarm as another face floated into her mind's eye, composed of pinpoints of light, glow-worms on the inside of her eyelids. Strong brow, pointed ears, a mouth full of sharp fangs.

Gargoyle.

She kept her eyes closed tight, hoping it was a nightmare. But her other senses belied that hope, and the image of the creature imprinted itself on her mind's eye in pinpricks of silver.

As the outlined face opened its maw wider, unhinging its jaw, she was overwhelmed by the smell of decay, like rotten cantaloupe. She tasted sour bile as it rose in her throat. She blocked her nose as it sniffed at her, its snuffle barely heard over the drumbeat in her ears. Even though it crouched over Mina without touching her, she felt its weight bearing down, making it hard to breathe.

Mina considered playing dead, but knew its senses were even more highly tuned than hers. She forced her icy fingers around the hilt of the leaded blade at her side. The stony face tilted to the side, as if listening. She held her breath, straining to hear what it did.

In a shower of light that stabbed the inside of her eyelids, it returned its attention to her, opened its cavernous mouth again and prepared to feast on her flesh.

Mina's eyes flew open as she stabbed upwards, through the soft skin under its jaw and up into the cranium. For a second it froze, then Mina shut her eyes as the blood rained down on her. A cascade of quicksilver, like a hail of needles, fell across her tightly shut eyelids. Finally, the warm drops stopped.

That's when she realized that she was stuck under a creature rapidly turning to stone.

She tried once more to find her wayward voice.

"Help." It came out more as a gulp than a shout.

A shiver passed through Mina. *Get up*, a whisper told her, her own voice or someone else's, she couldn't tell. She rolled over onto her side, pushing through the scrapes and bruises, wriggling out from under the gargoyle. She saw that she still lay on the rough, cold asphalt.

Get up.

She tried to obey but then an invisible fist slammed into her stomach, curling her up like a frightened armadillo. She dropped back down, scraping her cheek. A tremor travelled through her, top to toe.

She heard a sound behind her and tried to turn around, to face her fate full on, but convulsions seized control of her body. A shadow loomed over her and she tried to focus, without success. So instead she turned inward to other senses: warm earth and fire, brass and wooden percussion.

Jack. Jack knelt beside her.

"Has she been attacked by the creature?" a voice she knew said from over his shoulder, but she still couldn't focus on the figure.

She tried to answer but her body was racked again, her back arched and she struggled to breathe.

Softly, Jack wiped her neck with the edge of his white T-shirt. Her eyes rolled at the blaze of red that appeared when he drew it away.

"No." Jack's head shook and left trails in her vision. "Vampire."

With a final tremor, all the tension left her muscles, but her body was no more hers to control than when it had been locked in rigour.

"We need to get out of here," the voice said. Sifting through threads of memory, she put a name to it: Dar. "Tonight's events won't have gone unnoticed."

Jack nodded.

As if on cue, footsteps ricocheted down a nearby alley, accompanied by shouting. He threaded an arm under her head. The other he drew around her knees. He pulled her to him, then shifted her across his shoulders, into a fireman's carry.

"We won't make it to Sanctuary," Dar said. Mina felt Jack's head shake against her side. By some unspoken decision, they started running.

Mina tried to watch for the source of the shouting but it hurt her head to crane her neck, and she already felt like she was going to vomit. Jack was unlikely to appreciate her throwing up on him for any reason. So she closed her eyes and lay her hot check against the cool leather of his jacket, clasping her hands under his arm.

She managed to hold off vomiting until they reached the church, where she promptly disgorged her watery stomach contents all over Father Pietro's shoes.

JACK LAID HER DOWN, bruised, battered, bloody and bitten, on a wooden pew. The priest knelt beside her, brushing sweaty strands from her face and looked at her with warmth, despite her assault on his shoes, while Jack disappeared out of her line of sight.

"I thought I'd see you again," the priest said, his voice soft. "Though I didn't think it would be so soon, and I hoped it would be under different circumstances." Jack returned, bare-chested, with a damp T-shirt in his hand. He knelt beside her, dislodging the priest.

Father Pietro looked over his shoulder then back at Jack. "That's holy water."

Mina watched the horse tattooed on Jack's left pectoral gallop as he used his shirt to dab more blood from her face.

"It wasn't being used for anything else at the moment."

The priest looked at Jack, a frown wrinkling his forehead. "I thought I told you to take care of her. And now here she is, already dracul."

"These are difficult times, Father. It's hard to take care of anyone." Jack turned his head sideways, glancing at the priest before returning to look sidelong at Mina. "Let alone a headstrong dhamphir who thinks she knows everything."

Despite his harsh words, his voice was soft in the cavernous cathedral. Mina opened her mouth to retort but her eyes flitted shut and she slipped into unconsciousness.

WHEN SHE AWOKE, GROGGY and disoriented, Jack, Dar and the priest had been joined by Bee, Simon and Rhys. She could hear them whispering about the creatures, a ceasefire broken, a thickening of shadows. And her.

She opened her eyes a crack, the dim light of the cathedral piercing after the darkness of unconsciousness. She slid her eyes towards the others without moving her head. They kept their heads together in heated discussion, Rhys gesticulating her way, Dar shaking his head, Jack staying still and silent.

She let their whispers wash over her as she scanned her body, from toes to crown. She ached and throbbed but she felt the itch of lacerations zipping up and strained tendons knitting back together. She was a vampire, she'd heal.

Which led her to imagine a world where Dale or his kids had to face a gargoyle, where Cam met Mina's maker on her walk home from the hospital. Mina swallowed hard. Jack was right: she had to die. She knew she had to die. She just didn't know how. She stared into the recesses of the vaulted cathedral ceiling, studying the painting above her. Despite her intermittent Sunday school attendance, she couldn't name the scene. A man, swathed in white and red knelt on the ground, his torso bent over a rock, his head in his hands. A tree arched over him, its branches infused with a light he didn't see. She tried to name the colours the painter had used: alizarin crimson maybe, phthalo blue, but it was no use. The luminosity was skewed by shadows; the hues shifted in her new nighttime vision. Her family, her friends, even her art, lost to the night. A tear slid out the corner of her eye, down her temple, into the hair above her ear.

The others continued to converse earnestly at the front of the church a few metres away. Mina returned her focus to them, listening beyond the words they were speaking.

"How do we kill these things?" Jack said, his voice pitched low and resonant.

"We know how to kill them," Dar replied, an edge in his tone. "Lead."

"Lots of lead," Rhys added, his breath catching in his throat.

Mina altered the tuning of her hearing. She heard Father Pietro's heartbeat, heard his pulse catch every once in a while. She heard the phlegm in Rhys' chest as he breathed in, out, in a steady effort. She tuned into the vampires' blood song: Bee's hollow drumming, Dar's twang, Simon's pipes. Then there was Jack, a quiet percussive whirlwind of wood, leather and brass.

"But the lead only works if we can find them, and they seem to be multiplying faster than we can ferret them out," Jack said.

I can find them, Mina thought, hearing a dirge creep up from the base of her skull.

"Maybe you're approaching it from the wrong perspective," Father Pietro said. Mina twisted the words around her head.

"What perspective would you suggest, Father?" Bee said, her deep voice quiet. "We could ask Mina, what it's like to look at things a different way when you're peering into a jaw of serrated teeth, pinned down by a mass of muscle." Mina felt Bee glance her way, felt the woman's muscles tense.

Mina breathed deeply and let go, then tried to tune into the song in her own blood. She thought she caught strains of woodwinds before they fluttered away, chased away by tendrils of throaty cellos and nasal harpsichords. She tracked the sound; she recognized it, had heard it somewhere before. If only she could hold the threads, she could figure out where.

"The creatures are elusive, yes?" the priest said. "Hard to kill, especially without drawing unwanted attention." He paused. "But there is the idea that if you cut off the evil root, slay the progenitor, the offspring die with it."

"Like the myth about killing a vampire's maker," Rhys said.

"None of us are sure about that one," Father Pietro said. "Though myths tend to have a kernel of truth."

"How do you know it won't be like cutting the head off a hydra?" Dar said.

"I don't."

Mina could hear the shrug in the priest's voice.

"Is the alternative any better?" Rhys said. "Hurling your people against them, an unstoppable force against an unmovable object. A clash of titans that ends in carnage, for you and yours. Assuming you can find them all."

Silence. Mina traced the threads of the cellos' song through the weft of memory. Thrump, thrump, thrump, the cellos sounded. Her breath stopped.

The gargoyle. She'd heard the same song, a sensation more than a sound, as it loomed over her in the station; she hadn't recognized then that the creature and the sound were related. But that wasn't what niggled at the corner of her mind.

"Um, I'd like to point out that we have no idea who the progenitor is," Jack said. "Who raised these things from legend to reality."

Trill, thrump, thump, the cellos sounded, underscoring his words.

Mina's eyes flew open. She'd felt this song before.

Luca. A faint trace of the song had clung to him, cloaked by the harpsichord music in his own veins, when he'd bitten her – when she'd bitten him. Her maker. But not just her maker. The progenitor of the gargoyles.

If I kill him, he takes the creatures with him. She ignored the tidbit about vampires dying when one takes out their maker. Instead, she inched towards the end of the pew, sliding along her back, quiet as possible, willing herself silent. A heaviness descended around her. There was no catch, no hiccup in the conversation of the others.

She heard the stop-start of a band warming up in the square as she shifted further towards the wall. She imagined herself as a shadow, a ghost, and breathed deeply, dampening her pulse, slowing it so she could focus on any sound of disturbance in the conversation. Inch by inch, she sidled off the pew and into the small aisle by the wall. She shuffled and slunk and slipped out the side door.

The door Jack took me out of the night we met.

Mina walked back to her old apartment, hoping Cam wasn't there. She'd wash off the blood so she didn't frighten people, looking like a zombie. She'd put on some clean clothes so she felt more human. Then she'd find Luca and kill him, and destroy the animating force behind the gargoyles.

Even if it killed her.

CHAPTER THIRTY-SEVEN

IVAN CREPT DOWN THE grimy stairs to the culvert, filled with an icy river of muck and mire. To the bowels of the park, surrounded by cantankerous old trees, where he and Em had followed Luca's trail. They'd called Matteo, and now they were leading him to his son, the slaughterer to the lamb. Except this lamb could fight back.

Ivan didn't want to be anywhere near the coming confrontation. And he didn't really know how he had ended up here, on these stairs, in this park, with these people. How he'd ended up one of the Necrophagos.

Unlike Em. He knew more of her story than he cared to. She'd been a Necrophagos, even before she knew they existed. They were the strongest, she said, the fittest. The wickedest, he'd added silently. They should rule, she said, just like she'd ruled over the weak men and wicked women in her hometown. But that town had not been enough, and she'd run away. A lone woman at a time when that was not done, she'd fled into the arms of a dark stranger. When that didn't work out, she'd found Matteo. He had no idea what happened to her maker.

The care and concern of the Athanatos made them weak, she said. Sacrifice meant you were dead, and with no sure guarantee of anything gained.

He'd never questioned her philosophizing to her face; he didn't know when he'd stopped questioning it in his mind.

Maybe when he'd stopped thinking about his slaughtered family and friends, the pain turning to numbness. But all that now faded into the distant recesses of his brain, drowned out by the dripping rain and the thrumming in his blood. He breathed in through his mouth, his fangs on edge, forcing himself to be still, like an archer before releasing the bowstring.

This confrontation was a long time coming, he should have been more prepared. Em had said Luca was due for a reckoning, her voice singsong with relish at the thought.

But still Ivan wasn't prepared for what awaited them at the end of the tunnel. He didn't know if any of them were.

A creature, skin ashen and bloody, scabs on its back, was crouched over a heap of bones. It had stopped gnawing on whatever it held in its hand. Another two stood hunched over it, perhaps waiting their turn to tear into their prey. The three of them stood still as stone in the flickering light.

Ivan drew his gun and saw Em do the same out of the corner of his eye. Matteo stepped in front of them, holding out his hand. Don't move, not yet, the sign said.

The figures rose up to their full inhuman height and turned to them, parting to reveal a figure behind them.

Luca.

"Luca," Matteo said. "My wayward son."

Luca spread his lips in a self-satisfied smile.

"Father," he said, holding his hands out at his sides, palms forward, in a gesture mimicking welcome. "Have you come to kneel before me?"

Matteo stood silent for a moment, head bowed, hands clasped in front of him, long fingers intertwined. He looked up. "Why would I do that?"

"You will bow before my army or be trampled by it."

"Your army? You really think you control it?" Matteo said, his lips pulled back over his fangs.

"I'm here, aren't I? Safe in the midst of monsters."

Ivan scanned the scene. Luca staring at his father, eyes shining, cheeks flushed. Creature on the left rubbed its back slowly against the edge of the culvert, a soft rasping as its skin moved over metal. Creature on the right flashed its fangs as it picked at its teeth with a bloody talon. Creature in the middle sunk into a crouch again, one foot in front of the other, hand on the ground, facing away from the corpse, facing them. It huffed. Ivan slid his glance sideways to Matteo, as he felt the nosferat's muscles tense.

"We've been over this," Matteo said. "They may be monsters but they're not yours."

"I've had enough of your weasel words. It's time for action. Have you come to bow before me or die?"

"Neither." Matteo's breath stopped and he stilled. "I've come to kill you."

Luca's muscles tensed ever so slightly. His arms came down to his sides. His shoulders rose and fell, his head sunk. "Before you do, I'd like to say one thing."

Matteo cocked his head. "Speak."

Luca lifted his head, a smile on his lips, and let out a torrent of words Ivan didn't understand. But from the look on Matteo's face, he did. And that look sent a painful shard of ice through his gut. He didn't think it was possible for the nosferat to go a lighter shade of pale.

Matteo was silent for a moment, eyes wide. His mouth moved but words didn't come.

"Where did you learn that phrase?" he finally spit out.

"From a messenger."

"A messenger? That's all the name you have for the thing that gave you this benediction?" Matteo drew his lips back over his long fangs and drew his shoulders back. "The same voice that made promises from the shadows? Do you know what you've done?"

"Absolutely. Something you never dared to do."

"No, something I was wise enough not to do. You cannot rule if something rules you."

Luca rocked back and forth, deaf to his father's words. His eyes were glassy when he looked at them. "I've been wanting to do it for months now, but the search started long before that. The messenger stayed my hand, waiting for the right moment, the right sacrifice. Waiting while I learned the proper timbre listening to the low music of these creatures."

A frown lengthened Matteo's pale face. "You know the fact, but you don't realize the truth."

Luca stopped moving, and his nostrils flared as his father's words finally seemed to penetrate the fevered pitch of his brain. "Your truth?" he said, his lips curling around the words.

"No, the irrevocable truth: you've called down the herald of Night, woken the harbinger of Death. The insidious messenger who's whispered worms into your ear."

Luca paled, then he pulled up, making himself larger. "That shows how little you know. I've woken Night, will have soon enough." He looked at his father. "All that's needed now is a sacrifice. Then I will reign over you...oh, wait, you'll be dead." Luca nodded towards Em and Ivan. "I reign over them. Over everyone."

"Is that what this Angelos told you," Matteo spat, the venom of his words dripping from his fangs. "How can you reign on earth when you're surrounded by the army of Night? When you've cracked the cage of the Abyss, the prison where she's slept, scheming, regenerating, for centuries?" Matteo shook his head. "This isn't your army, it's hers. Idiot!"

Luca snarled and launched himself at Matteo, too quickly for Ivan to get a shot off. Father and son tumbled along the grimy concrete. He caught a flash of metal; Matteo had pulled a blade. It slid across Luca's chest; Luca howled but the cut was too shallow to still the vent of his fury. He tore at Matteo with his fingernails, tried to tear at Matteo's throat with his fangs.

Finally, they parted enough for Ivan to get a shot, but then remembered that his gun was loaded for gargoyles, not a vampire. Luca turned his fiery eyes on Ivan, the anger in them palpable. Luckily Ivan's shot was quickly followed by one from Em – even though the bullets wouldn't poison Luca, they still injured, leaving him weakened.

Likely realizing this himself, Luca howled and took off down the tunnel. Emily started to run after him.

"Stop," Matteo said, his voice reverberating off the concrete walls. "Although I want to take care of Luca myself, we have more pressing concerns. Night is not picky: Blood is blood. Luca will be dealt with soon enough. Now that Night is coming."

LUCA BRISTLED, HIS nerves on end. His father was still alive, unbowed, unsacrificed. And the woman, *his* progeny, had gotten the better of him again. She was supposed to be dead, again, but the whispers told him a different story: she lived. Despite leaving her bloody and alone in the dark, she had survived and was out there somewhere, stronger than before. He could feel her, underneath the adrenalin, and hear her, over the hum of vampires and thrum of gargoyles. Both of which hunted him now.

He snarled at the cold sky. "I should be leading an army, my father crushed under my heel, gargoyles bowed down before me. And the bitch should be dead."

He shivered as an icy drop of rain, on the edge of becoming sleet, dripped from his hair and weaseled its way under his collar, down his clammy chest.

Luca had made other vampires before, ones who lived feverishly and flared out quickly. Then his father had become old and worried. Worried that the humans would find out about them. Worried that they'd be hunted more assiduously than ever by the Hunters. Worried that he'd lose money on the battle. That's when Matteo had made a truce with the local Athanatos.

And that's when Luca realized that his father had become weak. That's when he knew his father needed to be taken down. That's when he'd chanced across the Shade in the shadows, little more than a puddle of darkness.

He could still hear the voice as it sounded that night, as he walked from club to club, prey to prey, when it snaked from the gray edge the existed between the dark and the light, under the trees in the park.

Luca, son of my father's son. Its words had been a raspy whisper, like a breeze through desiccated leaves.

Sated and satisfied, Luca had almost passed by, not hearing his name in the rustle.

Matteo needs to be removed. The breath paused.

Luca stopped and slid his gaze over his right shoulder. Despite his cat-like night vision, he could barely make out anything, just an extra heaviness in the shadows. And eyes that flashed red in the moonless night.

Luca had turned to face the voice. "Who are you?" he asked. "What are you?"

I am an emissary. You can call me Angelos.

Luca arched an eyebrow. "'Messenger'? From who?"

I have a message for you. That rustle of dry leaves again. *A gift really.*

"I asked from who?"

The shadow sighed. *Someone with the power to give you Matteo's power. To make you king of your conclave...and beyond. Someone willing to give you an army.*

Luca's eyes had strained to make out a shape from the shadows, without moving closer. "I'd like to know who I'm dealing with."

A relation. The words were drawn out with tension. A deep breath came from the dark. *Are you really going to look a gift horse in the mouth?*

Luca's barked laugh was too loud in the hushed park. "The Trojans should have."

A fable told to Greek children to explain how they won a war they should have lost. History is told by the victors. You could be one of them. The shadow paused. *The sun comes. I lose patience. Do you want the gift or not? I can take my message elsewhere. There are others in the conclave with ambition.*

Luca's nostrils flared. He took a step forward. "What is this gift?"

It doesn't come without a cost. It requires a sacrifice.
"Matteo?"
That will do. The answer had come on a whisper of desiccated leaves and searing pain, burning into his brain and flesh.

Returning to the present, Luca breathed deeply, still feeling the tightness of the shadow's burning brand on his chest, the first symbol in an arcane series. As he inhaled, he could still smell the scent of rotten eggs and sickly sweetness before the wind and rain whipped the shadows away and the odor was replaced by urine and overripe garbage.

"The Shade wants a sacrifice," Luca said, striding out of the shadows and into the harsh neon. "I'll bathe the night in her blood."

MATTEO HAD FELT THE gargoyles following him for a while now, a heaviness between his shoulder blades. Why they had left Luca, why they were following him, he didn't care. He was done being careful, cautious, safe. His body vibrated. It had been too long since his last meal, and even longer since he'd hunted, and he was starting to feel it. He needed to feed. But he was having a hard time focusing with the creatures pursuing him. He turned down a darkened laneway.

"Let the hunters descend," he whispered to the darkness then turned and faced the creatures and whatever fate had in store for him. The creatures had joined him in the alley. The smaller one took a step forward, its weight balanced between both feet.

Preparing for fight or flight? Matteo wondered, as he drew himself up. But he didn't draw any weapon. Not just yet.

"Why do you follow me?" he asked the stony shape. "Did my son send you?" The runt chuffed, turning its head sideways but keeping its eyes on him as it rocked back and forth on its bare feet. Matteo noticed that the talons on its hands were matched by a set on its feet: short, black, built for finding crevices to grasp and cracks between muscle and tendon to tear into. Bony spikes protruded from elbows and legs, making him wonder about the strength it took to survive such an agonizing transition.

Maybe one that was still going on, he thought as one of the other creatures scratched its arm and whimpered.

"You really are a phenomenal creature." The creature chirred, and cocked its head. "It's too bad I'll have to kill you if you attack me," Matteo continued. "I'd much rather be your ally, take care of you. Together we could claim dominion."

The creature stopped its rocking, the larger one sniffed at the smaller one's ear, then snapped its jaw. The smaller one snapped back, without taking its beady eyes off of Matteo. For his part, Matteo moved his hand to his side but still did not draw blade or gun.

Then the small one sank down onto one knee. It took Matteo a second to realize what was happening, when the runt chuffed at the larger one, and it too went down on one knee.

They're kneeling before me. As easy as that, Luca's army had become his...for the time being. Though it wasn't much of an army yet. And he was sure if he was truly its general or its captive. Matteo held his breath. He wasn't one to trust a gift horse, and wondered at what this army would cost him. Still he took a tentative step forward, followed by another – nothing great came without risk.

He lay his hand on the creature's bare scalp, ran his fingers down its rough jaw, under its prominent chin.

"Rise, my child."

CHAPTER THIRTY-EIGHT

MATTEO STOOD IN THE shadow of the trees, watching the woman approach. He'd stood here before, at the edge of the park, near the path that bisected it, serving as a shortcut from downtown to the B-Line. He stood silent and relaxed as people walked by into the park. As the woman did now.

She looked like she was coming from the hospital, scrubs showing under a wool jacket, sensible shoes on her feet. A doctor? She looked too young, but how could he judge, being near to ancient. A nurse maybe. At some point, she'd pulled her tumultuous curls back off her face into a haphazard chignon. When she passed under the street lights, he saw her olive skin was flushed red by the cold air. She looked at her wrist, then glanced over her shoulder, looking in his direction without seeing him.

He breathed deeply, releasing it in a hiss through his teeth, willing his pulse to a slower tempo. After being hand-fed for so long, having his meals brought to him, he had to reawaken the hunter inside. His body rebelled at first, but finally he imposed his will, forcing his blood to beat steadily, as he watched the woman get closer. What phenomenal prey for breaking a fast. He stood stone still in anticipation.

With a last glance over her shoulder, the woman turned into the park. After she'd passed, Matteo slid from his shadow and followed. She clutched her bag closer and hastened her pace. Matteo's breathing stopped for a fraction of a second, as he wondered if he'd lost his touch. But no, he realized that she was afraid of a more ordinary bogeyman.

He closed the distance between them, silent despite the stop-motion movement of his ancient joints. There were times he missed being a dracul, being able to pass as human without effort. But there were benefits to being a nosferat. Like being able to see, before she did it, that she was going to reach into her bag to pulled out her phone. She put it to her ear, but hadn't dialed a number, a detail his inhuman ears picked up on.

Matteo got closer still. Despite his excitement at this first true hunt in a long time, his pulse was now regular and slow.

"Hey, it's Cam," the woman said to the phone. "Yeah, just heading home from my shift at the hospital." The woman continued talking to herself, unmolested by run of the mill monsters. Perhaps it was too wet, too cold for them. Perhaps there were fewer of them than the newspapers said. Perhaps they sensed that a greater monster was after this particular prey.

Matteo inched even closer. If he had been breathing, she could have felt it on the back of her neck.

At that moment the woman's phone rang, snapping the tension between them.

"Merda!" the woman said as she dropped her phone in the wet leaves that littered the path.

Matteo slithered around in front of her as she crouched to pick it up. The flickering light from the street lamp ahead of them cast him in a silhouette, and he knew from years of living with an absence of light that it made him a featureless shadow. A shadow he finally let her see.

She stopped digging in the leaves, and turned to look at him. Her breath caught in her throat, her mouth open. Surprisingly she didn't scream. Instead her fingers spidered out, surreptitiously seeking her phone. Matteo took a step towards her, out of the masking light. Her fingers grabbed her phone and she took off down the path. Though he couldn't see them under those loose pants, Matteo sensed that she had the lithe limbs of a runner, a gazelle.

Poor gazelle. No match for this lion. He was sure she could already sense the futility of flight, they usually did. But still she ran. Matteo let her have her lead, savouring her adrenalin as it seeped out her pores into the cold night air.

But seeing the end of the path ahead, he knew this chase had to come to an end. He sighed as he descended on her like a blanket, taking her into his arms like a lover, except his grip was serpentine, constricting, preventing her from taking a deep breath, stifling her ability to scream.

"It's okay, cara mia, it will all be over soon," Matteo said, his lips whispering over hers.

Her eyes sparked, fighting the inevitable. "I don't want it to be over," she said, her voice barely audible over the sound of rain on leaves.

"That doesn't change the fact," he said.

"My name's Camellia," she said in gasps, using precious breaths. "I have a mother who will be heartbroken, and a father who, who..." Her lungs finally failed her. Matteo let his grasp loosen slightly, and one hand brushed wet curls off her face.

"We all had families once," he said, his fangs sliding down her neck, her pulse beating rapidly below the surface. "I have a son who stabbed me in the heart."

She let out a light gasp as his teeth finally pierced her skin. Matteo drank deeply, in ravenous gulps. It had been so long since he'd truly hunted for his supper. He'd forgotten the difference it made, the adrenalin giving the blood a Marsala sweetness. He was like a drug addict finally getting a hit. Still, he forced himself to pull away. Despite the fact that the balance was now irrevocably tipped, he couldn't let himself lose control. Not if he was to come out on top.

He heard a branch snap in the trees beside him. He stood up and glanced at the slate shadows that lurked there, on tenterhooks. Gargoyles: three of them. He looked down at the woman, the fire quietly fading from her wide, brown eyes. He could let them have her, rend her limb from limb. Or he could let them make a fourth gargoyle.

Or....

Her chocolate hair framed her paling face, pulled out of its loose chignon during their struggle, and her ashen lips were parted in a final silent plea. Her thick eyelashes fluttered. She stirred something deep inside him, tugged at a thread buried deep in the abyss of memory.

Matteo ran his tongue along his teeth, then brought his wrist to his mouth, feeling the sting as he bit. He let the drops of blood fall onto her lips before placing his wrist firmly against her mouth, cradling her head with his other arm.

"Drink, cara Camellia. You say you want to live. Then drink."

For a long second, they were frozen in this tableau. Then her throat moved, her tongue against his tender wrist, as a tear slid down her cheek.

The silent shadows slunk back into the woods, reluctantly going in search of some other meal.

CHAPTER THIRTY-NINE

I'M A VAMPIRE.

Mina repeated these words to herself like a mantra, as she stood in the shadowed doorway across the street from the club. The words tasted bitter but rang true. She let them settle over her like a cape.

She had finally accepted that she would have to die. But first she had to even the balance in the battle with the gargoyles: she had to take down their maker. And hers.

The club was the same one where she'd met Luca a couple of weeks ago. Slushy snow settled on her eyelashes, dripping down her face. She shut out the music that pulsed from the club, focusing her attention on a single thread of harpsichord harmony. She took a deep breath and refocused. The strain quickened, grew louder. The door of the club opened and her quarry slinked out, looked left, right, then turned up his collar against the damp snow and headed towards the park. She followed, staying well away. He was nervous, looking over his shoulder, scanning the road in front of him. Mina willed herself to be silent, dampening the sound of her blood.

A block and a half from the club, he turned down an alleyway.

Mina paused in her pursuit, debating whether she should follow him on her own or call backup. But this was what she was here for, why she'd left the comfort of the church, the safety of her new family. She glanced over her shoulder. Across the road a taxi was pulled over, its light off, the driver holding some animated conversation on his cell. If she focused, she could catch the gist – he swore he wasn't cheating, but his glances up to the building on his left and the speed of his heartbeat told her that he was a lying, cheating dog.

Other than that, the street was mostly empty. There was no sign that she had been followed when she left the church, or if she had, then they hadn't caught up with her. She glanced the other way. A block up a homeless man in a parka, hood up against the snow, pushed a shopping cart towards her. He was talking to himself but she couldn't quite make out what fascinating subject warranted the litany.

She refocused on the object of her hunt, and the music in his blood, slowed now that he was away from the club. She crossed the street and entered the alleyway.

Mina was ready to meet her maker on her own terms.

She stopped, letting her eyes adjust to the soft darkness that enveloped her. She shut out the noises from the street, the drone of the overhead wires wet with snow. She shut out all extraneous sounds, including her own heartbeat. He was near.

She loosened her blades, and took a cautious step forward, placing the soft sole of her boot down as quietly as possible, one foot then the other, like a cat after a mouse. Now that it had started to snow in earnest, she realized her choice of footwear was perhaps unwise, the smooth soles that padded softly along the asphalt provided little grip. Peering down the alleyway, she couldn't see her prey. His melody was muddled, dampened by the buildings and the falling snow.

She came to an intersection. An even smaller passage led off to her left. She closed her eyes and listened to her gut, but something gnawed at her intestines, an incessant low growl, as if it were hunger. She ignored it, and sent her senses creeping out in search of the tendrils of vampiric song.

Mina's eyes flew open and she drew her knives, one for each hand. The tendrils of sound came back full force, twined with a vicious energy. She was body-slammed into the wall at her right, sending pins and needles reverberating down her arm. Her right hand spasmed, causing her to drop the knife it held. She slumped against the brick and slid to the wet asphalt. Unyielding hands clasped her throat and other wrist.

She looked up into amber eyes and snarled. The hand on her throat tightened and lifted her, sliding her up the wall until she was on her tiptoes, level with the face in front of her.

"Sweet child of mine," Luca whispered in her ear, leaning in, before breathing deeply into his nostrils. "I can smell myself in you, did you know that? I can hear you in my head."

Mina bucked her hips and managed to bring her knee up into his crotch, but without the necessary power behind it. Her wrist was slammed into the wall behind her.

"Ah!" She let the sound escape despite her best efforts.

"Drop the knife," he said, his voice even as he drove her wrist into the brick again. This time, she stayed quiet.

"Why do you haunt me?" he said.

Mina tightened her lips. She felt his breath against her skin. "You created the gargoyles."

He pulled his head back and tipped his chin towards her. "Why do you think that?"

Instead of answering his question, she asked one of her own. "If you die, does the infestation die with you?"

"You think you can stop this by killing me?" His eyes sparkled with amusement. "You have no idea. You can't stop Night from coming. Anymore than you can stop death."

"What is this thing people have about night. I'm not afraid of the dark." She tried to kick him again, but couldn't get her leg up between them. "I'm a fucking ray of sunshine."

"Look at you, wriggling like a worm. And you thought you could kill me?"

He stepped back and drove a knee into her gut, letting go of her throat. She slumped to the wet asphalt and gasped to catch her breath. She was twisted at an awkward angle, the hand with the knife above her, the wrist still held by his relentless grip.

"My father wants you alive," Luca said. "If I bring you to him, I could buy my way back into his good graces." He bent his knees, bringing his lips close to her cheek. "But the herald wants a sacrifice. And I want you dead."

Her hand hit the wall again; this time she couldn't resist the force and the knife clattered to the asphalt.

"Good girl."

Mina bared her teeth at him and hissed, her hands clenching and unclenching. Her free hand scratched at the asphalt.

His tongue traced along her jawline. "Maybe not so good after all," he said into her left ear. "Do you remember this?" he asked as he squeezed her left hand and raked his fangs over her flesh.

Mina turned her head into his. "I have my own fangs now," she said, as her right hand finally came to rest on the hilt of the knife she'd dropped when he'd first slammed her into the wall.

He cocked his head and looked at her. The knife, held backhanded, sliced his cheek as it arced across, a red line welling up almost ear to mouth.

His hand went to his cheek as he reared back, letting go of her arm. Mina jumped up, red droplets from the knife falling to the ground.

Looking up from bloody fingertips, he growled then slammed a right cross into her jaw. Unprepared for the force, Mina was driven back, her body following the path of his fist, her torso torqueing around. She caught herself as she slammed into the wall, skinning the knuckles that held the knife and scraping the palm of her free hand. Her head hit the wall last as it followed the path of her body.

"You ungrateful bitch," he snarled. "I gave you a gift and this is how you repay me?"

Mina shook her head, trying to stop the ringing. She spoke from the wall, without looking at him. "Your *gift*? All I wanted was a drink, a turn on the dance floor, and some stress relief." She clenched the hilt of the dagger.

"You certainly seemed to want it that night," he said, stepping towards her.

"I wanted sex. I consented to sex. Not to a life as one of the undead." Mina heard the whisper of metal, a dagger being drawn. Coiling her energy, she launched herself away from the wall, slamming into him. Twisting in the air like a vaulting cat, she landed in a fighter's stance behind him, ready to strike again. Luca's eyes flashed fire when he turned to face her.

"You chose this life when you bit me."

"You attacked, I defended. There's no way I could have known."

He took a step forward, and Mina glanced at his knife. Matte whorls of poisonous silver flowed along its length, embedded in the shining steel blade. She spun around, aiming a roundhouse kick to his head. Luca dodged that easily enough. But his dodge gave her the split second she needed to steady and rebalance. And send an axe-kick at his hand, driving her knee up and the top of her foot over his hand. He smiled for a split second, surely thinking she'd overshot, until the bottom of her foot came down onto the back of his hand. His blade clattered to the ground. Luca growled and made to pick it up but instead drove his left shoulder into her gut. She staggered back, winded.

Luca grabbed her hair and spun her around, snaking his arm around her throat in a choke hold.

"You can make this easy or hard," he said. "Your choice."

She slammed the back of her head into his face.

"Hard it is." He tightened his hold on her throat and grabbed her crotch, lifting her off the ground. Mina kicked her feet out, thrashing to get away. When that didn't work, she tried a different tactic. She relaxed and took a deep breath, sagging against him, becoming dead weight.

He picked her up and shoved her forward, sending her sprawling. Mina saw the ground coming towards her as if in slow motion. She reached out her left hand to stop her fall, and pick up the knife she'd dropped, then used her right foot to propel herself up and over. She spun around in her impromptu roundoff and popped up to face him. In a heartbeat, she threw the blade, lodging it in his left shoulder, at the same time drawing the foot-long, hardened ashwood stake from behind her back.

He stared at her, his eyes blazing wide. "How...?"

Mina followed the path of the dagger she'd thrown, and launched herself at Luca before he had a chance to ask his question, driving the stake into his chest.

"What are you?" he asked, eyebrows coming together, as she leaned her weight into him. The sharpened end of the stake slid past bone and sinew.

"You should know, you made me," she said, her lips moving against his as she drove her ash stiletto deeper, into his heart, feeling his pulse slow as the fire in his eyes receded. She twisted the wood, driving the stake deeper still, then stepped back.

"I'm a vampire."

CHAPTER FORTY

WITH LIAM AND MAGGIE already tucked into their beds, Dale hung the last string of red garland on the tree then turned for Hana's approval. She was nestled on the couch, reading, a cat curled on her feet, which were tucked under the blanket her mom had brought from Korea. Enjoying an evening off for once, a rare break from her night shifts at the morgue.

Hana looked up from her book and smiled. Dale disappeared for a minute then returned with two glasses of red wine, placing one on the coffee table in front of his wife before sitting down at the other end of the couch. The book in her lap open but forgotten, Hana dislodged the cat, reaching out with a toe to prod Dale. Being a smart man, he took the foot in his hands and started massaging. Hana sunk down, leaning back into the pillows, and sipped her wine.

Outside, the slush had turned definitively to snow. Large fluffy flakes floated down from a slate gray sky, and settled on Mina's eyelashes before melting and dripping down her damp face. She was cold and wet and covered in blood. But that was okay. They were warm and happy and safe.

Mina stood there and watched for a while longer, until Dale stood and took Hana's hand, leading her up the stairs to bed.

"I'm a vampire," she whispered, even though they couldn't hear her. "And I need to die."

MORE ABOUT BLOODBORNE PATHOGENS

DID YOU ENJOY *A Scarlet Fever*? Please consider leaving a review – they really help me get the word out.

Want to find out what happens next? The next book in my series will be released in 2018. Sign up to my mailing list to be the first to know when it is out: http://creneastle.com/contact/

About the Author

Author of the Bloodborne Pathogens dark fantasy series, C. Rene Astle gained a love of fiction, fantasy in particular, and a voracious appetite for story literally at her mother's knee, being read The Hobbit and Chronicles of Narnia as bedtime stories - because those are the types of stories her mom wanted to read.

From her father, she got an enduring curiosity about the universe, earned shivering in the dark beside a telescope on cold, Canadian winter nights waiting to witness some celestial event.

Now she fits in writing between her day job, gardening and getting out to enjoy supernatural British Columbia.

Read more at www.creneastle.com.

Made in the USA
Lexington, KY
30 April 2018